The Price of Innocence

The Price of Innocence

The Legacy Series – Book One

Vicki Hopkins

To order additional copies of this book contact:

Holland Legacy Publishing
www.hollandlegacypub.com

TABLE OF CONTENTS

DEDICATION

To God, my faithful mentors, supportive friends, loving family, and departed English grandfather, whose name and lineage inspired me to leave a Holland legacy.

PROLOGUE

Paris, France – 1878

Suzette nervously watched Madame Laurent take one last assessment of her appearance before leading her up the grand staircase of the opulent Chabanais. Her hand brushed a stray curl from Suzette's cheek and then arranged a few other strands strategically on her plump breasts spilling over her bodice. Unfortunately, it was too late to do anything about the red blotches creeping up her porcelain neck.

"As I stated earlier, I've procured Lord Holland for this evening. You shall not be disappointed. He's one of the more satisfying and kind patrons we have." Madame Laurent grasped Suzette's cold hands in firm reassurance, before announcing her final instructions.

"I know you're apprehensive, Suzette, but this is your job. I have done my best to provide for you. Do your best to satisfy him, in spite of your obvious fright. After all, this is a business. If my customers are not gratified, I will not be happy." Madame Laurent released her hands and turned to ascend the stairs ahead of her employee. "Come along now. He's waiting."

Suzette sighed, reluctant to follow the austere brothel mistress. She was dressed as a French queen and heading for the Louis XV Chambre to lose her virginity. Her legs could barely climb the red-carpeted path to hell. Her deflowering had arrived, and Suzette was terrified.

As she laboriously placed one foot in front of the other, her mind drifted to the events that had cruelly driven her to this moment. Tears filled her eyes as Suzette painfully recalled the last day with her loving father. Everything had changed in her innocent life—everything.

CHAPTER 1

"Papa, can I get you anything else?"

Edgar saw his daughter glance warily across the table at his tired, wrinkled face. He lifted the last piece of bread to his mouth, chewed it slowly, and then swallowed. No doubt he looked pale and exhausted, and he noted the concern in her eyes.

"Did you have a hard day?"

"No more than usual, angel."

He dabbed his mouth with his napkin, and then smiled at his daughter. "Thank you for dinner. Very good, as usual. You never disappoint, Suzette."

"You're welcome, Papa."

Suzette gloated over his kind approval. Each night, without fail, he thanked her for dinner. Edgar knew that she enjoyed doting over him whenever possible.

Satisfied and full, he watched his daughter stand to her feet. Suzette removed the empty plates and dirty utensils. As she passed by his chair on the way to the kitchen, she bent down and gave him an affectionate peck on his cheek.

"I'm glad you liked it. You should go and rest now. You look exhausted."

Edgar Rousseau exhaled a long, drawn-out sigh. His daughter had correctly sensed his weary state of mind and body. He felt drained after spending the entire day lecturing. His feet pounded, and his backed ached with every move.

He had a solid vocation as a professor at the University of Paris, and for the most part, he enjoyed his job. However, his day had been filled with arguing students debating the New Republic. Traditions, family roots, and passionate views were deeply inbred in the student body, most of whom came from aristocratic and bourgeoisie families.

Confrontation went against the grain of his good, mild-mannered nature. He had discovered that as he grew older, it had become harder to handle the daily stress of work. Unfortunately, retiring was impossible to consider. He had a daughter to marry off, and financial matters that needed to be settled.

Suzette headed for the kitchen, and Edgar rose from the table, silently cursing his aching joints. He felt old and decrepit. His hair had turned noticeably gray over the past year, and he had gained a considerable amount of weight around his belly.

He meandered over to his favorite overstuffed chair, flopped into the seat, and embarked on his usual after-dinner routine of reading the newspaper. The words blurred before his tired eyes, and his disordered mind refused to concentrate on the articles. He squinted at the paper for some time, and then lifted his gaze toward the kitchen.

Edgar peered over the rims of his reading glasses to watch his petite, auburn-haired daughter performing her chores. A pang of nostalgia stabbed his heart. She had grown into the beautiful likeness of her mother. The resemblance was uncanny, and each time he considered their similarities, sadness swept over his soul. He couldn't help but think of his dear, departed wife, Marie. When he did, grief clutched his heart. It had been twelve years since his wife's death, yet the wounds were as fresh as the day she died.

After the passing of his wife, Edgar had naturally become extremely close to his daughter. Though he had brought on a governess to care for Suzette during her young, tender years, he had dismissed the woman upon his daughter's sixteenth birthday. Suzette insisted that she was more than happy to assume the responsibilities of running a household. Edgar's modest salary forced him to agree.

Suzette had done well in taking over the management of their residence. He had no doubt that she would make a splendid wife, mother, and caretaker one day. Although he believed his daughter deserved better, Edgar allowed her to cook and clean, because Suzette assured him that she enjoyed such tasks. He hoped that when she married, she would live comfortably enough to assign such menial jobs to the household staff instead.

The newspaper no longer held his attention. He set it down and stood from his chair. His wobbly feet shuffled over to his daughter's side. An odd sense of discomfort pressed heavily upon his chest. He needed rest.

"I think I'll retire early tonight, Suzette. Would you mind?" He placed his hand gently upon her shoulder.

Suzette encouraged his decision. "No, Papa, of course not. Go and rest. I'll be fine."

Edgar smiled at his daughter, and with a tender kiss on her cheek, he bid her goodnight. As he slowly lumbered toward the fireplace, he briefly stopped to look at a picture of his wife on top of the mantel. Silently, he prayed that she would visit him in his dreams. He needed her comfort for his weary and lonely heart.

A moment later, he retreated down the hall to his bedchamber. Edgar entered and then closed the door behind him, hoping to find respite and solace after a long day.

* * *

Suzette watched with concerned interest as her father retreat down the hallway to his bedchamber. After hearing the door close, she returned her attention to the pile of dirty dishes. She smiled thinking about his pause at the fireplace to look at her mother's picture. His nightly ritual touched her heart.

For years, Suzette hoped that his mourning would subside, and he would remarry. It was another unanswered prayer to add to her list. When her own grief subsided over the death of her mother, she fervently prayed for someone to fill the void. Eventually, as God's silence grew harder to bear, she stopped asking and refused to hold onto silly hopes.

Obviously, her father did not want to remarry, even though Suzette longed for a mother's tender embrace and female wisdom. Now, at the age of eighteen, she ached for female companionship even more. She had no confidant to ask the many questions about womanhood that beset her mind.

After finishing her chores, she removed her stained apron and hung it up on the back of the kitchen door. The quiet apartment gave her a chill. She walked past her father's door, stopped, and heard the sound of snoring coming from the other side. Thankful that he had quickly fallen asleep, she smiled with relief and made her way to her room.

She closed the door and walked to the window, parted the heavy curtains, and looked at the street below. Snow flurries danced about like white butterflies. The view sent goosebumps up her spine. It had been a long winter, and she was tired of the cold. She hoped this would be the last trickle of snow, because springtime was just around the corner. It wouldn't be long before new life bloomed from the barren earth. It was by far her favorite time of the year.

Suzette pulled the curtains tightly shut to keep out the cold draft, and then walked over to her chest of drawers. A small wooden jewelry box, with a variety of compartments, sat upon a white-laced doily. She pulled out a little drawer at the bottom of the case and retrieved a folded piece of paper. A smile brightened her face. It was time for her nightly ritual.

Suzette walked over to her bed, sat down, and then carefully unfolded the precious document. Lovingly, she lifted the ragged corners of the white parchment and read the words. Her fingers traced along each stroke of the quill until they reached the end of the message. When finished, she brought the note to her lips and kissed it reverently. Her eyes sparkled.

Suzette folded the parchment carefully into the same creases, stood up, and walked back to her dresser. She returned the paper to its hiding place. Tomorrow night, she would resurrect it once again, read it, and kiss it goodnight, just as she had done for months on end since its arrival.

Cold and tired, she yawned, and then undressed to slip into a beige, cotton nightgown. She turned out the oil lamp and climbed between the cool, crisp sheets. The cold made her shiver, and she pulled her wool blanket up to her chin.

After closing her eyes, she faithfully mumbled her nightly prayers, blessing her father and those she loved. Within a few minutes, Suzette fell asleep and traveled to a world of troublesome dreams, where she found herself lost and filled with fear.

The cold night passed, giving way to a rude morning awakening. A small sparrow chirped as it sat on Suzette's windowsill. She rolled over, pulled the pillow over her head, and moaned as she tried to decide whether to shoo the bird away or get out of bed. Unable to fall back asleep, she sat up and swung her pillow to the side heaving a sigh of frustration.

For a few moments, her dark and convoluted dreams haunted her, but she shrugged them off. She raised her arms above her head and stretched. The ice-cold wooden floor greeted her toes as she climbed out of bed.

"Burr," she moaned. Suzette grabbed her white robe off a nearby chair. She slipped it on, tied the sash, and then headed out her door down the hallway. She stood by the bath chamber and noticed an eerie silence permeate the air. Usually at this time of the morning, her father would be in the kitchen boiling water for his tea.

Suzette glanced around. The only sound her ears detected came from the chirping bird perched on her windowsill. She walked down the dark hallway toward her father's door and leaned her ear against the wooden barrier, expecting to hear his snore. The silence persisted.

Suzette stepped back and with a light tap of her knuckles, knocked softly.

"Papa? Papa?"

When no answer came, she thought perchance her father had left early for work. She walked to the sitting room to see if his jacket had been removed. It remained exactly where he placed it the evening before, hanging on the coat rack by the front door.

A sense of dread clutched her heart. She turned quickly around and ran across the wood floor toward her father's room. Her bare feet slapped against the floorboards.

"Papa? Are you in there? Can you hear me?"

Suzette knocked feverishly, but no answer came. Her hand trembled when she reached for the metal doorknob. Slowly, she turned it to the right. When the latch released, Suzette pushed the door open just enough to poke her head around the edge and peek inside. The curtains remained closed, and the room was dark and quiet. Suzette stood motionless for a moment, while her eyes adjusted to the lack of light. Finally, they rested upon her father's figure in bed.

"Papa, are you all right?"

After the silence persisted, she pushed the door wide open and hesitantly walked to his bedside. Dressed in his overnight gown, he lay prostrate, with his face buried in the pillow. She looked at him and realized his chest neither rose nor lowered. Frantic over the lack of movement, she knelt down at his side and placed her hand upon his back.

"Papa!" she cried. "Papa, wake up!"

The touch of his cold, stiff body spoke of death, and Suzette quickly withdrew her hand in horror of the discovery. She sprang to her feet, stumbled backwards, and brought both hands to her mouth, to catch her horrified scream.

Panicked, she fled out of the bedroom and ran down the hallway crying hysterically. Unsure what to do next, she paced back and forth in a distraught state of mind, until a moment of clarity returned. She exited the apartment and swiftly ran to her neighbor's door. With both fists, Suzette pounded on the wooden barrier, begging for assistance in a desperate, sobbing voice.

"I need help! Please, I need help!" Her hot tears burned her cheeks. A moment later, the door swung open.

"My word, child! What is the matter?" Monsieur Pelletier looked astounded over Suzette's frantic actions. His wife stood by his side wide-eyed.

Suzette gasped. "It's Papa. I can't wake him up!" Sobs choked her throat. "I . . . I . . . I think he's dead."

"Oh my God, Suzette!"

He wrapped his arm around her shoulder and swiftly headed toward their apartment. His wife, Adele, followed closely behind, shaking her head.

Suzette led them to her father's bedroom and then stood by the door, terrified to enter. She watched Monsieur Pelletier approach the bed.

"Edgar? Edgar!"

Monsieur Pelletier received no response and bent down to touch the cold, rigid body. He nodded his head and turned to Suzette with an empathetic look.

"He's dead, I'm afraid." Not wishing for her to gaze upon death, he took the wool blanket and pulled it up until it hid her father's body underneath.

"I'm terribly sorry, Suzette. He must have died in his sleep. God rest his soul."

He reverently made the sign of the cross, along with his wife, Adele. Suzette stood frozen in the doorway, unable to move. She sobbed loudly, and Madame Pelletier drew near to her side. Suzette buried her head in Adele's shoulder and lost herself in grief.

"There, there, Suzette," Madame Pelletier offered in motherly comfort, while stroking her back. "It will be all right. Your father is in heaven now. Don't despair."

Her words brought little comfort to Suzette's heart. Anxiety tightened her chest, choking the air from her lungs, and she wondered if she would perish, too.

Monsieur Pelletier placed his hand upon her shoulder. "It must have been a stroke or a heart attack. God is merciful. He probably died peacefully in his sleep. Your father was a good man."

"You should arrange for the body to be taken somewhere, William." Adele's eyes pleaded for her husband's help.

Suzette abruptly pulled from her embrace. "What do you mean take his body?"

"Well, he can't very well stay here, dear. We'll help you arrange for a parlor to attend to his remains." A look of panic spread across her face, and she inquired if Suzette had others to help her through this difficult time.

"Do you have family here, dear? Is there anyone who can help you?"

"No," replied Suzette, her face sullen and shocked. "There is no one except my aunt and her husband, but they moved to the Americas years ago."

"Oh, I see, dear." She turned to her husband and implored him to do something. "Go on, William. Get your hat and coat and take this child with you to the funeral parlor for arrangements. Please!"

"Yes, of course."

He put his arm around Suzette and encouraged her to get dressed. Suzette stood paralyzed as she looked at the body of her father. Her audible sobbing had turned to silent tears that rolled freely down her flushed cheeks. Overcome with shock, Suzette realized she could no longer inhale any air. Black spots danced across her field of vision, and she floated into darkness and into the arms of Monsieur Pelletier standing nearby.

* * *

Muffled voices, footsteps, and clanging noises echoed in the recesses of Suzette's mind, eventually bringing her back to consciousness. She opened her eyelids and blinked a few times, until she focused on the white plaster ceiling above her bed. After a quick glance down at her body, she discovered herself wrapped up in a blanket. Her pounding head rested upon a pillow.

Her first waking thoughts gave way to confusion. Why was she there? Like a cold bucket of water splashed in her face, the shock of her earlier discovery came flooding back.

She flung the covers off her nightgown-clad body and ran out of her room down to her father's bedchamber. She pleaded like a child the entire way. *Please, God, let it be just a terrible dream.* When she entered the doorway, an empty bed greeted her swollen eyelids, and the sick realization returned.

Suzette stood shrouded in grief for a few moments, and then turned and wandered into the kitchen. The floor shift beneath her feet, as she fought a sickening dizziness. Monsieur and Madame Pelletier were speaking to one another unaware of her arrival. She stopped in the doorway and exhaled in anger.

"Where is he?"

"Oh, dear, you're up." Madame Pelletier came to her side and gently brushed the unruly curls from her face. "Are you all right? We were worried about you. Grief overcame your senses, and you fainted."

"Yes, I'm all right. Where is he?" she demanded again.

Monsieur Pelletier placed his hand on her forearm in reassurance. "He's at the funeral parlor down the street, Suzette. I took the liberty of having their staff take your father's body from the apartment to a more appropriate place."

Gone. They had taken her father away, and Suzette felt lost.

"You'll have to go there later today, dear, and make the arrangements," Madame Pelletier informed her. "Don't worry, though. My husband will go with you, so that you don't have to do this horrible task all alone."

"I don't want to be alone," Suzette replied, as a tiny tear trickled down her cheek.

"Are you sure there is no one to help you, Suzette? Maybe a friend, perhaps, or your father's coworkers?"

"I don't think so," she answered, trying to think of anyone she knew. "Perhaps people at work, but my father never spoke of anyone in particular."

"Well, what about friends? You know, people your father visited."

"We rarely socialized with others. He said he was always tired when he came home from work, and we just kept each other company."

"The Parish, perhaps? What about Father Joseph? I'm sure he will help you during this difficult time."

"Yes, yes, I'm sure he would help me," she agreed. Suzette turned and looked at Monsieur Pelletier. "What should I do next?"

"I'm afraid, my dear, much needs to be done. You should dress, have something to eat, and then we'll go to the funeral parlor to discuss the matters that need to be arranged."

"All right, then," she responded, acting like an obedient child. She felt dependent upon her neighbors for help and guidance. Suzette had never dealt with such ominous matters before like funeral arrangements. Her mother died when she was a small child, and her father took care of all the details of her burial.

Bewildered, Suzette returned to her room to dress and closed the door for privacy. She stood in front of her long mirror with a blank expression upon her face. Her eyes were red, and her complexion looked pasty white. Suzette's wretched appearance confirmed what she felt inside—a part of her had died, too.

Her hands shook as she reached for the hem of her nightgown, pulled it over her head, and let it fall to her feet. Naked, cold, and alone, she stood shivering, stripped of all that she had loved. It would take some time before Suzette would be ready to accompany Monsieur Pelletier to the funeral parlor to take care of her father's remains, because once again hot tears streamed down her cheeks.

CHAPTER 2

"Mademoiselle, I am so sorry for your loss."

Suzette looked at the man who stood before her dressed entirely in black. His facial expression appeared sympathetic, but she wondered if he truly felt compassion, or if his words were merely routine in nature. Wary of his sincerity, Suzette refused to politely acknowledge his greeting.

Monsieur Pelletier had escorted Suzette to the funeral facility were they had taken her father's remains. Upon entering the building, she felt death greet her at the door. It felt reminiscent of the cold presence that followed her in the dream the night before. She shuddered over the similarities.

The surroundings, pleasantly decorated with palm plants, green settees, and landscaped art on the walls, did little to comfort or soothe her nerves. The manager appeared to notice her distrustful demeanor, and then attempted again to make her feel welcome.

"Monsieur Lefevre, at your service." He turned to Monsieur Pelletier and acknowledged his arrival with a nod. "Please, Mademoiselle Rousseau, follow me."

Monsieur Pelletier gave Suzette a reassuring look, and she followed the man clothed in black through a narrow hallway that led to his office.

"Please, have a seat," he said, motioning to a chair in front of his mahogany desk.

Still dazed, she sat and glanced around the room and then loudly inquired about the whereabouts of her father's body. "Where is he?"

A bit surprised by her demanding question, he cleared his throat before answering. "He is in our deceased holding area, Mademoiselle. I assure you we have treated his remains with the greatest respect."

Embarrassed over her loud outburst, she sheepishly replied, "Thank you."

"Now, let us talk of funeral arrangements, shall we?" The director opened a black notebook. He picked up his quill and dipped it in the inkwell on his desk ready to write the arrangements for the sale.

"Casket . . ." he said, in a businesslike manner. "We have a large selection of caskets, at varying prices."

"Prices?" Suzette squawked.

"Yes, prices, Mademoiselle Rousseau." After seeing the panicked look on her face, he replaced the quill in its holder, folded his hands on the desk in front of him, and leaned forward.

"Let me ask you a question before we go further. How much can you afford? If I know what you can spend, then I can show you items that are in that price range." He tilted his head and glanced over at Monsieur Pelletier with a smile.

Suzette didn't know the answer. Her father took care of financial matters, and she knew nothing about his private affairs. He gave her an allowance for clothes and shoes when she needed them. Other than that, the amount of money now in her possession was a complete mystery.

She turned to her neighbor and confessed her ignorance. "Monsieur, I do not know where my father kept his money or where he banked. I have nothing inside my purse but a few coins. What should I do?"

Monsieur Pelletier was not surprised. Suzette's naivety was quite evident, and no doubt her father shared nothing about household finances. Edgar probably never revealed any of his private affairs. As a matter of course, men never discussed money matters with wives or daughters.

He patted Suzette's clenched hands in her lap to give her reassurance.

"My wife and I will help when we return to your apartment. We'll look through your father's papers and see if we can find any financial records, money, or what bank he may have frequented." He looked at Monsieur Lefevre and offered a suggestion.

"Perhaps, Monsieur, you might show the lady your lowest prices possible for now. When we find more information about her financial situation, we will visit again to finalize the burial arrangements."

He sat straight up in his chair and reclaimed the quill in his hand. "A very good idea, Monsieur. Very well then."

After clearing his throat once more, he continued to discuss possible arrangements. "Mademoiselle, does your family possess a plot or crypt?"

"We have no crypt. My mother is buried in a plot, in the Père-Lachaise Cemetery."

"Is that a common grave or perpetual?"

"I don't understand," Suzette replied confused.

"When did your mother pass away, might I ask?"

"Twelve years ago, Monsieur."

"And do you still visit her grave today, or has it been removed?"

Appalled at the question, she responded in outrage. "No, Monsieur, her grave is still there, with a large marker."

"Ah, then your father must have purchased the plot in perpetuity." It was obvious by the look on her face that she was still confused over his statement, so he explained further.

"Those who cannot afford to purchase plots in perpetuity are buried in common graves that are exhumed after five years, and their bones relocated to the ossuary." Giving her a moment to take in the information, he continued. "Since your father purchased the plot in perpetuity, it means your mother will not be exhumed. That is a choice now you must make for your father. Do you understand?"

Suzette could not believe it! *Bodies were exhumed and bones were piled in heaps?* Of course, when her mother passed away, her father took care of the arrangements. They often visited her grave and brought fresh flowers or knelt and prayed.

"Yes, I understand, Monsieur. I did not know about these things."

He sighed and then stood to his feet. "Most do not, Mademoiselle. Death is not a subject that is often discussed, nor arrangements made ahead of time in many cases. Unfortunately, as you have discovered," he expressed sympathetically, "death visits us when we least expect its arrival, and difficult decisions must be quickly made."

He walked to the other side of his desk and suggested another course of action. "Perhaps it is better if Mademoiselle first inquires about your father's finances and then returns tomorrow. We shall continue to hold your father's body until I hear back from you. Would that be sufficient?"

Relieved that she did not have to make any immediate decisions, she nodded in agreement. "Yes, thank you. That would be more than helpful."

Suzette turned to Monsieur Pelletier. "Will you assist me with these matters?"

"Yes, of course." He stood up, held out his hand, and aided Suzette to her feet. After polite goodbyes, they returned to search out the matter of Edgar Rousseau's finances.

* * *

Suzette spent a sleepless night tossing and turning in bed. Her lack of rest did nothing to help her present state of mind as she sat before the solicitor's desk. Her body shook, and her knees bobbed up and down from nerves. She placed her cold hands upon her bony joints to suppress the movement, but failed to stop the jerking. It was a horrible nervous reaction she struggled with her entire life, which caused her to blush profusely with embarrassment.

The evening before, Monsieur Pelletier and his wife assisted Suzette as they rummaged through her father's desk looking for answers. To their dismay, they discovered little— only a few bank registers revealing miniscule funds. Bills from debtors were stuffed in drawers, which Suzette found disturbing. Her father's personal papers were stacked in no semblance of order. After an hour of searching every inch of Edgar's desk, they had only gleaned a bad case of frustration.

However, among the clutter they discovered a business card bearing the name of EDWARD DUPREE, SOLICITOR. Monsieur Pelletier hoped it was her father's personal solicitor, who handled his will and other financial matters. They set out the next morning to the gentleman's office in hopes of discovering answers to their questions.

Finally, after minutes of Suzette holding her knees down, a tall, young male clerk entered the waiting area. "Monsieur Dupree will see you now. Please come with me." He led the way to a large office, where an austere man greeted them with a stern expression.

"Mademoiselle Rousseau, it is a pleasure to meet you." He looked at her companion, because no introduction had been made. "And what is your relationship to the young lady?"

"Forgive me, Monsieur, but this is my neighbor, Monsieur Pelletier," Suzette apologetically clarified. "He has been graciously helping me, in order to ascertain my father's financial situation."

"Pleasure to meet you, Monsieur." He offered a weak handshake. "Please have a seat." After they had situated themselves, he continued. "So, how may I help you today?"

"Well, Monsieur," Suzette began in a shaky voice, "I found your card among my deceased father's belongings." Tears welled in her eyes, and she bit her quivering lips in an attempt to control her emotions. After inhaling a deep breath for composure, she continued. "My father passed away yesterday."

"My sincerest condolences," he interjected. A concerned look furrowed his brow as he waited for her to continue.

"I—we," she corrected, looking at Monsieur Pelletier, "have gone through my father's desk, checking his financial matters and found your card. We thought perhaps that you might know of a will he possessed or might have information about his finances." Suzette paused for a moment. "I need to bury my father, Monsieur," she spoke, lowering her gaze to her lap. "But I do not know where I can find my father's money in order to take care of the arrangements."

Monsieur Dupree looked at Suzette and then glanced at Monsieur Pelletier. He knew they both wished to hear good news; but, unfortunately, he would be the bearer of bad. He stood up and walked to the window and glanced at the street below to avoid the forthcoming pained expressions upon their faces.

"I'm afraid, Mademoiselle Rousseau, that your father has no money," he said coldly. He watched the numerous carriages passing by outside for a few moments in order to collect his thoughts before continuing to explain the sorry state of affairs. Finally, he turned around and faced Suzette.

"I have been hired by his creditors to collect his debts— one way or the other."

"Debts?" Suzette squawked.

"Yes, debts, Mademoiselle. It seems that some years ago, your father took out a rather large, unsecured loan, and in doing so, he became habitually behind on many obligations. My clients have been more than generous in giving him ample time to repay, but as time passed, it became increasingly clear that legal action needed to be taken."

"Oh." Suzette shoulders drooped over the revelation.

"Well," Monsieur Pelletier interjected, "I assume such debts are cancelled now that he is deceased."

"Not necessarily. The law requires that his estate be sold to pay those debts, and I assure you that my clients will definitely sell all of his possessions to obtain some return."

Monsieur Dupree's face turned dark, and Suzette could tell the man intended to carry out his threat. "We have very little," she pleaded. "What could his debtors possibly gain?"

"Satisfaction, I'm afraid," he replied with a grim face.

"But I will have nothing!"

"I'm sorry, Mademoiselle, but those matters are not my concern. I am only here to carry out the wishes of my clients. Now that I am aware of your father's demise, we will request a court order. The estate will be sold immediately in order to settle what he owes."

The solicitor sat back down behind his desk, picked up his quill, and turned his attention elsewhere. "My office will be contacting you shortly with an order from the court. Good day." He had done his duty representing his clients and preferred to say nothing further regarding the matter.

Frozen in her chair, Suzette turned to Monsieur Pelletier and whispered, "What can I do?" He only shook his head and stood up, offering her his hand.

"Nothing. Come now. We must leave." He held out his hand, which she took, and helped Suzette to her wobbly feet.

* * *

With no funds to give her father a proper burial, Edgar Rousseau, like other poor Parisians, faced eternity in a common grave outside the city walls. The spring day dropped cold rain upon Suzette's covered head. She insisted on accompanying her father's body to his final resting place.

His body, wrapped in coarse burlap, was placed in an uncovered wagon parked in an alleyway adjacent to the mortuary. Suzette sobbed as they lay his remains among other dead bodies. She followed the route of the wagon in a carriage hired by Monsieur Pelletier and his wife. It proceeded slowly down cobblestone streets, while onlookers gawked with curiosity as it passed by.

Finally, they reached the outskirts of the city and pulled up to the common grave area near the vast Père-Lachaise Cemetery. Suzette exited the carriage to watch the burial. She stood shrouded in her black-hooded cloak, appearing like a mournful angel that had fallen from the gray skies above.

The rain had thoroughly soaked the burlap bags, and the fabric clung to the naked bodies underneath revealing more than she cared to see. Suzette wished to turn her head away, but she kept her eyes upon the corpse that belonged to her father.

In somewhat poor taste, workers stood waiting for the wagon to arrive with joking grins across their faces and shovels in their hands. A large, freshly-dug hole for multiple remains gapped open in the wet earth.

Suzette watched while dispassionate men removed and tossed her father's body into the ground, alongside other nameless people. When he hit the bottom with a *thud*, she recoiled at the sight. No one else had come to join them as other nameless corpses were dumped into the muddy hole. When the last body was tossed, the men took their shovels and flung clods of wet soil on top of the burlap mass of death.

Suzette muttered, "Dust we are, and to dust we will return." She tossed a single white lily in the grave and watched until it disappeared in the earth.

Monsieur Pelletier tugged at Suzette's sleeve. "We should go now. No need to watch such sadness."

"No!" Suzette pulled away and stood her ground. She patiently watched the workers fill the hole. It was difficult to believe that her father's sacrifice had brought him to such a disgraceful end.

Edgar Rousseau incurred a large unsecured debt in order to purchase a perpetual plot for his wife inside the Père-Lachaise Cemetery. He commissioned a sculpted weeping angel for placement over her grave. Suzette never knew the financial cost of his expression of love. In addition, he had taken out several other loans to pay for her private education, a governess, and household expenses.

How ironic that he would never spend eternity alongside the woman he so ardently loved. Instead, in five years, his bones would be exhumed and thrown into a pit to rest with thousands of others, unmarked and unnamed until the day of resurrection. She thought the final destination a terrible price to pay just to give his departed wife dignity in death.

The men patted down the last clods of wet soil. The burial was over. Suzette felt a warm arm wrap around her waist.

"Monsieur Pelletier and I have been talking, my dear. We wish you to stay with us for a while until you get back on your feet."

"Yes, Suzette," he heartily agreed. "It's the least we can do, but I'm afraid it cannot be for long."

Suzette looked at her neighbors while drying her cheeks with her handkerchief. They glanced at each other with painful expressions.

"I appreciate your offer of generosity."

"You see, Suzette, before your father died, Adele and I made arrangements to move at the end of the month to Rouen to be with our daughter." He glanced at his wife and continued. "We can only keep you for two weeks, and then I'm afraid you'll have to make other arrangements."

Suzette felt dead and akin to the corpses underneath her feet. She merely accepted their proposal, afraid to think beyond the moment.

"Yes, of course, I understand. I sincerely appreciate your help. I'm sure I will find something soon." A feeling of dread clawed at her heels as she turned away from her father's grave.

* * *

After the burial, Suzette was plagued by sleepless nights and sickening grief. She cried for days, unable to receive comfort from her neighbors and refused any food they brought for her to eat.

A court order arrived setting a date for the estate sale. Suzette would be allowed to remove her own personal items, such as clothing and other essentials, but all other property was to be tagged, priced, and set for auction.

Employees from a Parisian auction house arrived a few days beforehand and began to inventory the contents of their apartment. Suzette insisted on standing nearby as they sifted through the household goods. She collected what she could keep for herself, along with a few pictures of her mother and father. Items deemed of value were set aside for auction, while those deemed as trash were hauled away.

By the end of the week, movers arrived to clear the apartment. The entire contents were stripped bare before her eyes, and what remained of her earthy belongings, fit into a small suitcase. The apartment landlord took the keys and made arrangements to rent out the residence she had once called home.

Totally destitute, her neighbors showered her in sympathy and gave her the divan in their parlor as a bed. To her chagrin, however, they had begun to pack for their move to Rouen. Suzette felt threatened and insecure. As the time drew closer to their departure, the hopelessness of her situation gnawed at her heart.

All her life someone had taken care of her. Somehow, she needed to find the strength to survive on her own, but she was frightened. Suzette listened to the kind advice of her neighbors, seeking wisdom on what to do next.

"I think it's time, Suzette. Perhaps you should talk with Father Joseph about temporary housing."

Monsieur Pelletier's sympathetic voice offered the suggestion in earnest. He had noticed that Suzette's depression and despondency worsened as the days progressed. She needed to take action soon, as he and his wife feared she would be on the streets alone as soon as they departed.

"Yes, of course," she agreed. "I know I need to speak with him, even if I do feel like a beggar."

"I'm sure Father Joseph can find you housing with the Daughters of Charity," Monsieur Pelletier counseled. "Don't be ashamed to ask for help, Suzette. They do the work of God."

"Why, yes," his wife agreed enthusiastically. "I've heard the Daughters of Charity are very helpful in these situations."

Suzette smiled and tried to reassure them both. "I will take care of it tomorrow. I promise."

The next day, she visited Father Joseph at St. Cecilia's, a neighborhood parish. The Father extended his sympathy, but Suzette purposely avoided discussing spiritual matters. She realized her anger toward God, about the death of her father, had poisoned her heart.

Suzette controlled her emotions during their meeting, as the priest told her about the outreach to the poor by St. Vincent de Paul and the Daughters of Charity. He would arrange for her to find housing under their roof, until she could find work and a permanent place to live.

When the day arrived for her to venture out on her own, sadness bore upon her heart like a heavy stone. She stood in the doorway of her neighbors' apartment, holding her life's belongings in a small leather suitcase. Crushed inside were as many clothes as she could carry, along with her rosary, pictures, and precious letter.

She looked gratefully at Monsieur and Madame Pelletier. Suzette loved them for their kindness and unselfish nature.

"Thank you for being here for me. I don't know what I would have done without your help and guidance." She gave each of them a tight hug, finding it difficult to let go.

"Please," Madame Pelletier implored with tears, "take care of yourself. There are bound to be brighter days ahead. I just know it!"

In a fatherly fashion, Monsieur Pelletier bent down and kissed Suzette on the forehead. "Be well, my child. God be with you."

Suzette forced a smile, said her final goodbye, and walked out of the apartment building into a frightening world of uncertainty.

CHAPTER 3

The walk to the Daughters of Charity proved long and arduous as she hauled her bulky suitcase though the city streets. Suzette's feet dragged as if weights were tied around her ankles. Her former life faded away with each step she took in the opposite direction of her former life. The foggy, grief-stricken days of the past weeks had lifted to reveal the cold, stark reality of her plight.

On the way to the shelter, Suzette nervously traversed the streets nearing the poorer sections of eastern Paris. Her entire life had been lived modestly, in a relatively clean and secure environment. Now, as she walked further into the bowels of the ancient city, the sights, smells, and sounds assaulted her senses. The streets, riddled with debris and garbage, merged with the stench of urine. Suzette battled nausea from the myriad of aromas and struggled with fear as she passed drunkards, beggars, and street prostitutes glaring at her along the way.

As she continued to walk down the crowded sidewalk, an odor of rotting human flesh grew stronger as the moments passed. She thought that she had experienced all that death had to offer, until Suzette found herself face-to-face with bodies in the picture window of the local morgue. Horrified, she gazed upon corpses displayed to the public for the purpose of identification. The awful smell turned her stomach. Quickly, she pulled out her hankie, covered her nose, and ran down the sidewalk to escape the stench.

Finally, able to breathe fresher air, she spotted her destination and sighed in relief seeing the sign of St. Vincent de Paul. It was housed in an old brick building. The façade appeared crumbling from age, which made the building look unstable. As she glanced around at the squalor surrounding her, she concluded it had to be better than the poverty of the cold and dirty streets.

Hesitantly, she closed the distance and stood in front of the open door. Not once in her eighteen years of life did she give thought to the struggle of the poor. Now, that she was among them, she felt ashamed over her lack of empathy. She hoped the Daughters of Charity would be her salvation and the nightmare of her circumstance would be short lived.

She took a deep breath and stepped over the threshold unsure of what to expect. Her heart beat thunderously in her chest. Suzette glanced around at the surroundings to get her bearings. A long corridor lay ahead with multiple doors extending to the right and left. One displayed a sign with the word "Enregistrement." She walked to the entrance and spotted a nun sitting behind a small desk. The Sister, engrossed in her paperwork, did not see her in the doorway, so Suzette cleared her throat until she caught her attention.

"May I help you?" Her eyes glanced at Suzette's suitcase, and the Sister returned a warm, welcoming smile that eased Suzette's anxiousness.

"Yes, I am in need of temporary shelter, Sister."

"Of course, dear. Come in and sit down."

Suzette approached a wooden chair, and the legs wobbled as her body met the seat.

"I'm Sister Mary," the nun said warmly. "What is your name?"

"My name is Suzette Rousseau. Father Joseph of St. Cecilia's wrote to you about me."

"Oh, yes," the Sister said. "I have his letter here somewhere." She shoved the papers around on her desk until she finally found the correspondence. She adjusted her reading glasses and perused it once more.

"My father passed away a few weeks ago," Suzette interjected, adding to her recitation of the letter. She paused for a moment as her knees began to bounce up and down, making her look like a frightened child. "They sold his estate to pay his debts, and I am now without a home. I need somewhere to stay until I can find work and housing." Her voice shook with desperation.

The Sister lifted her head and looked compassionately at Suzette. "I am very sorry, my dear, for your loss. It is always difficult when we lose someone we love, oui?"

Her sincere compassion touched Suzette's heart like a warm embrace, and unbridled tears fell from her eyes.

"We are here to help. Don't be dismayed."

Suzette wiped her wet face with the palm of her hands and tried to compose herself.

"We just need to fill out some paperwork. Do you feel up to answering a few questions for me?"

Suzette blew her nose in her hankie. "Yes," she mumbled.

"What is full your name?"

"Suzette Camille Rousseau."

"Ah, Suzette, I love that name. Lily."

"Lily?" she replied, quizzically.

"Yes, it's the meaning of your name. Didn't you know?" Sister Mary smiled warmly. "My favorite lily is the Lily of the Valley. It's a reference to our Savior in the Song of Solomon in scripture. The meaning of the flower is that *you will find happiness.*"

"That's lovely," Suzette responded with an insincere grin. "Lilies have always been my favorite flowers, but happiness seems far away right now." Her mind recalled the lily she threw upon her father's body in the common grave.

"I understand, Suzette, but have faith. All things work together for good. God will make sure you live out the full meaning of your name." The nun returned her focus to the paperwork. After finishing, she explained the regulations.

"I'm afraid, Suzette, we can only give you temporary housing for a short period of time. You are lucky that today, I even have a bed for you." Earlier that morning, one of the former female residents passed away from consumption. The Sister decided not to mention the cause, in case it frightened Suzette.

"The men, of course, are housed in a different building a block away. We keep strict rules. There is to be no consorting between male and females. Do you understand?"

"Yes, of course, Sister."

"Very well then. Follow me, and I'll show you the dormitory quarters."

She led Suzette down a long hallway to the entrance of a large room filled with bunk beds and cots. Suzette glanced around at the dark and dingy quarters and sighed, trying to be thankful it wasn't the cold pavement of the street outdoors. The Sister escorted her to an empty top bunk.

"You can sleep here, and there is room for your suitcase in the corner." She paused for a bit, and then gave a warning. "I'm sorry to say that not all the girls who are here are good hearted. Though we turn no one away, we have problems with thefts of personal belongings, so I suggest you keep an eye on anything you do not wish to lose."

"Yes, of course," Suzette replied, wondering why anyone would want to steal her meager belongings.

"There is a common bath chamber down the end of the hall with two bathtubs. We have chamber attendants who can help you carry hot water to the tubs. I'm afraid our plumbing is rather antiquated. Follow me, and I'll show you where that is located."

Suzette set her suitcase down upon her mattress and then followed Sister Mary. After a brief tour of the bath facilities, the Sister directed her to the dining area.

"We serve one meal a day," she announced, with a tone of sadness. "Unfortunately, our funding is limited, but we do try to give our residents one hearty meal."

Sister Mary then led her down the hallway to a wall board covered with pieces of paper. "You'll have your work cut out for you, dear, I'm sorry to say, in finding employment. We pray for all our girls that God will provide, but sometimes it takes time. Don't get discouraged."

She pointed to the pinned notices dangling from the board. "Occasionally, some of the larger washhouses or other industries hiring women post help wanted announcements here. I encourage everyone to look daily at the new postings. Of course, you should also go out each day and search for work on your own."

Suzette walked back to the dormitory, while Sister Mary continued to expound on life at the charity house.

"We have a chapel where you can visit for prayer and light a candle for your father, if you wish. All of the Sisters gather for vespers at six o'clock in the evening, and you are welcome to join us."

"Thank you, Sister Mary. You are most helpful."

"Very good then. I must return to my paperwork. You may come to me at any time if you need something."

After flashing a warm smile, she turned and walked back to her modest office. Suzette watched her bobbing, starched-white cornet flap up and down like the wings of a bird. She chuckled aloud at the sight. It was the first time she had laughed about anything in weeks, and it surprised her that she was able to find a morsel of humor amidst the bleak surroundings.

* * *

"So, what brings you here?"

The voice startled Suzette out of a sound sleep. Her eyelids shot open, and she turned her head to the right. A pair of inquisitive brown lashes flapped up and down. The stranger emanated a foul odor from her breath, which caused Suzette to wrinkle her nose.

"I beg your pardon?" she responded.

"Well now, what don't you understand, eh? What brings you here?"

Suzette sat up in bed and yawned. Alarmed over the brash introduction, she pulled her scratchy, wool blanket up to her neck to shield her body. "I'm homeless," she retorted, a bit annoyed. "What brings *you* here?"

"My lover threw me out on the street. That's what brought me here. Life of a lourette, you know," she slurred in a tone of disgust. "Now I'm out trying to find work and a place to live, but I swear I'm about to go out again and sell my body to the highest bidder. Can't stand all these nuns. Too much religion around here for my taste."

Suzette's eyes widened at her irreverent admission. "Is that necessary?"

"Necessary?" The woman laughed. "What? You mean to sell your body for food?" She studied Suzette more closely and then leaned into her face. "Well, you're a pretty little thing that would bring a good price on the street." She grinned and then whispered in a low voice. "You know, the Sisters can't keep you here forever, love. They'll give you 'bout a week and you'll be out on your derrière."

"Please don't speak of such things," Suzette snapped in disgust.

The woman threw her head back and laughed.

Suzette wanted to escape her taunting visitor, so she reached out to grab her robe, which she placed at the foot of her bed the night before. It wasn't there.

"Where's my robe?" she squeaked in surprise.

Her eyes darted to the floor, wondering if it had fallen off the bed. Most of the cots and bunks in the room were empty. The women remaining merely shrugged their shoulders and turned away with indifference.

"Don't know," said her neighbor. "Perhaps somebody took it!" She smiled deviously at Suzette.

Suzette shocked, didn't know what to say. She looked at her suitcase on the floor and discovered to her horror it lay open. Her belongings were strewn about.

"I don't believe it!" she exclaimed, jumping out of the upper bunk. Her feet hit the cold floor with a *thud*. She bent down on her knees and examined the remaining contents. The best of her clothes were gone, and only one old dress and a few undergarments remained. Frantic, she looked for her shoes and discovered them missing, as well. She stood up enraged at the thievery and glared at the occupants of the room, demanding answers.

"What are you, animals?" she snarled. Suzette shook from anger. Their attitudes were as cold as the chilly morning air of the dormitory. She picked up her suitcase, slammed it shut, and fled down the hall to the bath chamber carrying it underneath her arm. Clad only in her linen gown, she was too angry to care if anyone saw her hasty departure.

She burst inside and was relieved to find it empty. After slamming the door shut behind her, Suzette leaned against the stone wall, dropped the suitcase at her feet, and sobbed. Sister Mary had warned her, but instead of heeding her advice, she had trusted others. She scolded herself for acting like a foolish child and not taking the advice to heart. She could have kept the suitcase closer to her side. Unable to understand human cruelty, her first lesson left a bitter taste in her mouth that she would not soon forget.

After washing her face with freezing water, she attempted to brush the tangles out of her hair. She dressed in her undergarments and slipped on her one remaining dress. The thieves had stolen the best of her clothing, along with her cloak, leaving her with a modest blue, cotton day dress she wore when housecleaning. The sleeves displayed wear at the elbows, and the lace trim around the collar was frayed.

Without shoes, she made her way back down to the dormitory. She hesitated at the doorway and looked inside to see who remained. Everyone had left, and the room was vacant. As she walked over to her bed, a momentary panic filled her heart. She had forgotten in her haste to bring with her the one thing that was most important!

After frantically lifting the mattress, a sigh of relief escaped her mouth. Her small handbag was still there, safe from thieving hands. It contained all of her remaining valuables—a few francs that Monsieur Pelletier had given her upon departure, her rosary, a few pictures of her mother and father, and most importantly, her folded letter that she considered the one glowing treasure in her dark world.

"Thank God," she breathed in relief. She brought the purse to her chest and hugged it while her cold feet demanded shoes. Suzette left the dormitory clutching her purse and headed down the hallway to Sister Mary's office. She stood in the doorway shaking like a leaf in the wind, and once again cleared her throat to gain the Sister's attention.

"I'm afraid you were right, Sister," she said, the words embarrassingly seeping from her lips. "Someone took my things and stole my shoes."

"My word, child! They stole your shoes?" She jumped to her feet and came to Suzette's side for consolation. "I cannot understand what is wrong with some of the women we house. We give them the kindness of Christ, and they insist on acting like demons." She lowered her head and looked at Suzette's feet. "Well, at least they didn't take your stockings," she chuckled. "Come with me."

She took Suzette gently by the hand and led the way down the hall to a locked door. Sister Mary took out a key ring from her pocket, found the right one, inserted it into the lock, and pushed open the door. Suzette followed her into a room filled with shoes, hats, clothing, and undergarments.

"These are all donations, I'm afraid. Nothing new here," she spoke honestly. "But beggars can't be choosers, Suzette."

She motioned over to a line of worn women's shoes and encouraged Suzette to find a suitable pair.

"Help yourself. See if you can find something that fits."

Suzette went through the shoes, trying to find a pair close to her size. After numerous attempts, nothing fit perfectly. Either they were all too large or small. Suzette wasn't quite sure what size to pick. Only one pair felt fairly comfortable, and she opted for tight rather than loose, but later came to regret her choice.

"These will do, Sister Mary," she said, shoving her toes into a pair of black pumps. Thank you. I appreciate your kindness."

"Very good then. I'm happy to help. I'm sorry this happened to you, but you can't say I didn't warn you of the occasional riffraff finding shelter under our roof."

After adjusting to her new footwear, Suzette saw a shawl and wondered if she could ask for one more item.

"They took my cloak too, Sister. Would you mind if I took a wrap to keep warm while out on the street?"

"Of course not!" she replied, handing her a shawl of loosely knit yarn.

Suzette grabbed the gift without complaint and followed Sister Mary. The door was relocked, and the key replaced in the nun's pocket.

"Are you off to search for work, dear?"

"Yes, Sister."

"The Lord be with you and give you favor."

Suzette followed her back to her office and then proceeded to the front door of the charity house. The brisk morning air accosted her body through the thin cotton dress. She wrapped her shoulders in the thread-bare shawl to keep warm, hoping the sun would soon rise higher to warm the air.

Her stomach growled, and gnawing hunger pains reminded her that only one meal would be served later in the day. Thankfully, she had a few francs in her purse. She walked down the street, intent on finding a bakery and a piece of bread to silence the noise in her belly.

As she traversed the frightening streets once again, Suzette soon realized finding food would not be her only problem. The tight shoes she put on her feet minutes earlier, painfully squeezed her toes and rubbed her heels with each step that she took.

She wrinkled her nose again at the putrid smells in the gutter, as she began to limp along in pain. The awful sights of squalor and poverty filled her heart with fear. If she didn't find work quickly, the outcome would be disastrous.

Finally, she arrived at the entrance of a small bakery shop. The aroma of fresh baked bread caused her mouth to water, and she quickly slipped inside. A few people stood in line before her, and Suzette glanced at the goods lined up in the glass bakery case. The cost of each item was scrawled with chalk on a board behind the counter.

As she studied the items for sale, her eyes picked up the movement of little weevils crawling around the loaves. The thought of eating a piece of bread where tiny worms crawled around made her want to vomit. No one else in the store seemed bothered by their existence.

Appalled, she spun around and ran out the door looking for a bakery shop in a better part of town. Even though she was hungry, homeless, and in a horrible position, she wasn't about to eat bugs to appease her growling stomach. She had her limits, and this was certainly one of them.

CHAPTER 4

Suzette wallowed in discouragement after her first day searching for a job. She returned in the late afternoon, just in time to eat her one meal for the day. By the time she made it to the dining hall, she could barely walk from the blisters on her feet. A sympathetic Sister Mary took her back to the locked closet, encouraging her to consider a larger pair of shoes.

"It's better to flop down the street, dear, than limp in the presence of prospective employers."

Suzette smiled at the nun's humor and bobbing headpiece, which never failed to entertain her in the midst of hopelessness.

She ate her meal alone shunning the other women. It filled the emptiness of her stomach, but the food was bland and barely warm. Suzette decided to embrace solitude rather than choosing to befriend the thieves that had stolen the few items she possessed. They had taken what held value and discarded the remainder of her useless items. Her purse remained tied to her wrist, and Suzette refused to abandon it while in the presence of her roommates.

The second night in the dormitory afforded little sleep. The mattress was hard and reeked of stale body odor. She covered herself with the scratchy wool blanket and turned her face toward the wall. Secretly, she listened to the women in the dormitory spew their bitterness to one another. They complained about the food and the nuns asserting their religion. Everyone bemoaned their inability to find work.

Suzette on the other hand felt shy and angry in their company. She preferred to tuck her resentment in the recesses of her soul, rather than articulate it to a group of thieves. In her mind, there was no use complaining anyway. She only had one goal in life now, and that was to survive and stay off the streets.

After tuning out the bickering women, Suzette closed her eyes and thought of her father. She wanted to reminisce over his loving presence in the midst of her struggles. She tried to find strength in his spirit, but recognized it was his careless ways with money that had placed her in such a difficult situation. "Oh, Papa," she whispered, trying to forgive him.

Her aching feet reminded her of her tiring day. She had limped from store to store looking for work. Even though Suzette considered herself an articulate, young woman, she now knew that her life had been too sheltered. Obviously, her father had protected her far too much. She wasn't prepared to face the world on her own.

After the death of her mother, he provided for a governess. She had been bred to be a wife and caretaker of a home. Suzette learned skills to embroider, entertain, run a household, and remain faithful to God and her husband. Her stature was not one of high society, but her father had been a well-respected professor at the university. He held high hopes for her future nuptials.

Tomorrow will be a new day, she thought. She mumbled her first desperate prayer in weeks, asking God to provide for her needs. The heaviness of her eyes ushered Suzette into blissful sleep. At least for a few hours, she would find a reprieve from the challenges that threatened to destroy her life.

* * *

Relieved that the spring rains were abating, Suzette was greeted by another glorious morning filled with sunshine.

Determined to find work, so she could find housing, she took the time to bathe and dressed as neatly as possible. Rather than limping into prospective places of employment with tight shoes, she would flop down the cobblestone walkways in shoes that were too large for her feet. She learned that stuffing paper into the toes helped to close the gap.

After finding a small bakery along the way, which was weevil free, Suzette purchased a croissant and a cup of tea from the last bit of funds given to her by Monsieur Pelletier. She handed over the coins to the clerk feeling as if she were saying goodbye to her last friend—a silver franc. The morning tea and fluffy pastry brought satisfaction, and Suzette left the café intent on making it to her destination as soon as possible.

She made her way across town to the dress shops along the Champs-Élysées. The avenue, choked with busy shoppers, excited her senses as she passed by stores and restaurants of all varieties. Already her imagination pictured herself renting a furnished room inside a boarding house, after she received her first pay. Nothing would dash her hopes of finding work.

Nevertheless, her dreams quickly faded after hours of rejection. Store by store turned her away, giving every possible excuse. It was obvious that her plain dress, which showed years of wear and frayed seams, ruined her chances. All she received were the contemptible glances of shopkeepers and clerks, eyeing her up and down. She had been repeatedly shooed away like a fly, which fueled Suzette's anger over her stolen clothes. No doubt the thief had donned her best dress and found work.

By late afternoon, her stomach growled, and she worried about making it back to the shelter in time for her daily meal. After receiving the last shunning glance from a store clerk, she turned and walked across town as quickly as possible. Frustrated over the flopping shoes, which impeded her progress, she removed them and began walking in her stocking feet.

By the time she arrived, they were torn to shreds, but she had arrived in time for her portion of food. After eating another bland meal all alone, Suzette retreated to her bunk bed. She only wanted to hide beneath the covers again and find the strength to face another day.

* * *

Depressed and despondent after days of searching for work, Suzette felt pressured. Her search for employment was no better than most of the girls in the shelter. Bakeries, tailor shops, restaurants, and whatever else she could think of, turned her away one after the other.

Sister Mary warned the shelter residents that St. Vincent de Paul was at capacity and had been turning away other needy women. When housing became scarce, the shelter requested longtime residents to leave in order to make room for the incoming poor. Almshouses elsewhere in Paris were filled to the brim. An appalling number of homeless citizens wandered the streets, contributing to the crime and filth that Suzette witnessed daily outside the charity doors.

To make matters worse, the Parisian government conducted routine sweeps of the city streets, gathering homeless vagabonds and deporting them to remote, rural areas. In response to the aristocracy and bourgeoisie's request to rid beautiful Paris of what they termed the "scum of the earth," a new order had been released for roundups to begin within the next week. Suzette knew if she were unsuccessful in finding work, she would eventually be among those taken to the countryside and dumped like garbage without food and shelter.

Sister Mary recognized Suzette's good-hearted nature and took a liking to her. When she received word that a local washhouse had just a job opening, she told Suzette first before posting it on the board.

"Why don't you try to get a job as a laundress? One of the local blanchisseries is looking for a female employee. They will provide housing too."

Suzette had shunned the known sweat houses of Paris, mostly from fear and disgust. Becoming a laundress was a less-than-desirable occupation. Social stigma, long hours, and low pay—none of which sounded appealing—discouraged her from the thought. As Sister Mary wrote down the name of the washhouse and address on a piece of paper, Suzette caught the concerned expression on her face. Even she recognized that the prospects of finding work elsewhere were bleak. Suzette's options were dwindling.

"I suppose I can apply," she said, with resignation.

"It may be only temporary, Suzette, but it will at least provide you a place to sleep, work, and food for your tummy. We will only be able to keep you for another week, because there are others who desperately need our charity."

The announcement did not surprise Suzette. The benevolence of the order had done all they could for her. One door closed, and another appeared to be opening. Though Suzette thought bitterly of her choice, it was time to move on.

* * *

"Monsieur Brouchard," Suzette called over the noise of the washroom. She tried to get the attention of a tall, thin, gangly-looking man with greasy, shoulder-length hair. When he heard Suzette's voice, he swung around and looked disdainfully at her, sending a chill down her spine. Suzette was not pleased with the rude gawk.

"Yes? What is it?" He voice barked at her like an angry dog.

Taken aback by his abrupt response, Suzette hesitated a moment before speaking. "I am Suzette Rousseau. The Daughters of Charity said you are looking for workers," she screamed at him, over the noisy washroom.

His eyes squinted at her, as if he could barely see her standing a few feet away. Suzette raised her voice even louder.

"I'm here to apply for a job!" Her whole body shook as her exclamation carried throughout the room. Everyone heard her announcement, as workers bent over steaming washbasins lifted their heads to look in their direction.

He glared back at her and eyed her from top to bottom. "Very well then. Follow me."

He opened the door into a cluttered office and made his way to a small desk pushed up against a brick wall. His chair creaked when he sat down, and he growled his next request.

"Close the door, damn it! I can't hear a word over that cackling racket out there."

Suzette's heart raced over his brazen demands, but she dutifully closed the door. She turned around and approached the front of his desk. No chairs were available. She nervously clutched her purse like it possessed some magical power to protect her in that terrifying moment.

"So, you want a job as a laundress, do you?" He picked up a cigar, bit off the tip, and spit into a nearby trashcan filled to the brim with paper and rotting food. He lit the cigar with a match and blew a few puffs, while he continued to look at the size of her waist and breasts. His lingering gaze at her bosom caused Suzette to blush in embarrassment.

"Frankly, after seeing your stature, I don't think you can do the job." He took rapid puffs on his cigar, and then blew the smoke into the air above his head. For the remainder of the conversation, the cigar dangled from between his lips.

"It takes a strong woman to walk around the streets of Paris hauling baskets of clean laundry to our clients and dirty ones back to the washhouse. You need muscles! The baskets weigh twenty-five to thirty-five pounds apiece." His eyes roved over her body once more before asking her bluntly, "Do you think you can handle that?"

Suzette was unsure if she could, but desperation pushed a boldface lie from her lips. "Yes, Monsieur. I've carried heavy weight, though I am small. I'm sure I can handle anything."

"Frankly, I don't know," he mumbled, letting the doubt eat at her until he was satisfied she had suffered his indecision long enough. If her career as a wash woman failed, there were always other possibilities for her in the future.

He examined Suzette, who looked like a little bird quivering in fear. *Pretty and petite. Just the way I like 'em.* He imagined undressing her like a hungry wolf, and then decided to hire her just in case she came in handy for other purposes. Women would sell just about anything for food in their bellies.

"If I provide you a cot to sleep on, your hours will be from 5 a.m. until 11 p.m. each day. Your pay will be three francs per day. If I'm satisfied after a month that you are able to carry out your duties, I will raise it to three and a quarter francs per day."

Monsieur Brouchard doubted the young woman would last a month hauling baskets through the streets of Paris. She reeked of untouched innocence, which both disgusted and enticed him at the same time. The washhouse would toughen her up for whatever lay ahead. The women currently in his employ had been there for years and were rough around the edges, most of them morally loose and alcoholics. They'd spread their legs for a decent meal. He chuckled out loud over what the petite little creature was about to endure. It was time to give her exactly what she came for.

"Since you have no experience, I can only assign you to washing sheets, tablecloths, and curtains. Unless I know you have the ability to wash blouses or shirt fronts, you'll not be allowed to touch the clothes of my best clients."

Suzette pleaded, "Monsieur Brouchard, I would be most indebted to you if you would let me work for your establishment."

He liked it when people begged. "Fine then," he answered, standing to his feet. Brouchard crushed out his cigar next to other butts in the overflowing ashtray and began giving her instructions.

"Come with me. I'll show you where you'll sleep, and you can start work immediately. I'll introduce you to Flora, who will train you on what's to be done."

Suzette gasped. "You wish me to start now?"

"Yes," he sneered. "Do you want the job or not?"

"Yes, of course," she said, "but I thought I would have time to return to the charity to retrieve my belongings."

He looked at her in astonishment. "And what might those things be? Whatever they are, you can get them another time."

Afraid to disagree lest he change his mind, Suzette followed behind him like an obedient, frightened puppy dog. Once again, her life had turned upside down, and she hadn't been given the opportunity to thank Sister Mary for her kindness. However, as she walked through the facility following Monsieur Brouchard, she began to wonder if she would be as thankful a week from now.

The facilities were stifling hot from the rising steam of large washing bins on the lower floor. Suzette glanced at the working women as she passed by their stations. No one was talking in front of the manager, and there were only a few individuals who raised their eyes in her direction.

The air was moist and hot and filled with odors that irritated Suzette's nose. Tiny beads of sweat formed on her forehead as Monsieur Brouchard escorted her through the facility and up a narrow staircase to the second floor. Once upon the landing, he flung open a wooden door to a small, dark room. Inside were four cots pushed up against the wall.

"The one on your right is yours. The others are taken already. A bath chamber is down the hall on the left."

Suzette stared at the cramped quarters and the dirty mattress on wooden slats with a wool blanket and no pillow. "Do you have much in the way of clothes, shoes, personal belongings to get?"

"No sir. I'm afraid very little is back at the charity."

"Well, I suggest you retrieve what you do have when you can. Sometimes we have clothes that are unclaimed, and you can pick through the leftovers if you need anything. You won't need to dress in your evening gown to get the work done here!" His condescending laugh filled the hallway. "As you can see, most women around here strip so they can handle the heat." His lecherous behavior became obvious as he added, "And I don't mind the show."

He headed back and spewed out an order. "Follow me! I'll introduce you to Flora."

They walked downstairs, and Suzette followed him over to large piles of dirty linens that looked like mountains of white cotton. Upon closer inspection, Suzette noticed blood and other stains. The stench turned her stomach.

"This is where we sort the linens for our customers. You will serve the smaller accounts, and I have one in particular that will suit you just fine." He noticed her scrunched-up face over the odors. "Yes, dirty laundry stinks. What did you expect, perfume?" He turned and snarled orders at Flora. "Show her what to do." As he walked away with a smirk on his face, Suzette felt an immediate dislike for her new boss.

She looked at Flora. "Welcome to hell," she said. "Come here, and I'll show you what to do."

CHAPTER 5

Suzette spent her first night on a lumpy cot with a thin, wool blanket. Sleep quickly claimed her exhausted body. When she woke the next morning at 5 a.m., her back and feet ached.

"You best get up if you want to keep working here, dearie," Flora warned. "Monsieur Bouchard will dock your pay, if you're not at your station."

Her work companion was at least kind, though Suzette thought her a bit abrupt in her mannerisms. She looked like she was around forty years old, but Suzette couldn't believe it when Flora told her that she was only thirty. There was no refinement about her whatsoever. Her manner and features conveyed hardness and premature aging from years of work.

"Yes, of course," Suzette moaned. She heard soft laughter from another woman.

"Welcome to the life of a laundress!" she laughed. "Wait until you start hauling your first basket of laundry down the street. You'll wonder what the hell you've gotten yourself into."

Without further word, the women whose names she didn't know, giggled and left the room. Suzette slipped on her dress over her undergarments and wandered down the hall to the bath chamber. It was occupied, so she stood in the hallway until the door opened and another woman appeared.

"You must be the new one," she grumbled. Her face looked tired and sour. She lowered her gaze and pushed by Suzette. Everyone appeared miserable.

Suzette quickly splashed water in her face, and tried to brush the tangles from her hair. She pinned her long strands upon her head, away from her face, so it would be cooler in the heat of the washroom. Afterward, she ran downstairs to meet Flora, who she found sorting and tagging the incoming sheets.

She learned that once they sorted through the piles of dirty laundry from hospitals, clinics, and other establishments, other workers took them to the vats where they washed and dried the linens. Afterward, the sheets were returned to Flora and Suzette to fold and deliver back to the clients.

"There's a basket of folded and clean linens over there by the wall," she announced, pointing her finger to a white mound a few feet away. "Brouchard wants you to deliver them to the Chabanais immediately."

"Now?" she questioned, appalled at the timing. "It's only five in the morning. Will the client even be awake?"

Flora laughed. "Oh, yes, I'm sure someone will answer the door."

"Chabanais? I don't know what that is or where it's located."

As soon as the words left her lips, she could feel the manager's menacing presence behind her. Suzette clamped shut her mouth. When she felt his hot breath touching the back of her neck, she turned around to face his grotesque appearance. He looked no better in the morning than he had the day before.

"It's the brothel at 12 Rue Chabanais. You can't miss it. There's a sign right outside the door."

Suzette's eyes widened. Brouchard laughed.

"What, you've never been to the door of a brothel before?" He enjoyed every moment of taunting his naïve, young worker and walked off sporting a sly grin.

Flora stood up from her stooped position. "He's the most disgusting man I've ever known," she hissed, in his direction. "And you wonder why we drink alcohol in the afternoon on the job. It's because of his asinine attitude." She looked at Suzette and encouraged her to leave. "You better go now, or he'll come back screaming at you wondering why you haven't left."

Suzette walked over to the basket filled to the brim with clean sheets and pillowcases. She bent over and attempted to lift the basket, but failed to do so her first try. Flora watched her struggle, bending her back, and then walked over to her side.

"Here . . . do it like this." She bent her knees and grabbed the two side handles of the wicker basket. When she stood upright, she swung the load until it landed upon her right hip. "Carry it like this. Just think of it like a child on your hip, and you'll get the hang of it. It helps defray the weight."

After Flora lowered it back to the floor, Suzette took hold of the basket and did the same. She grimaced in discomfort. "How far is the Chabanais?"

"About two miles. Go out the door, turn to your right, and follow the street until you come to Rue Chabanais. When you reach the avenue, the brothel is on the left toward the very end of the street."

Flora returned to her duties, picked up another dirty sheet, and tagged it for washing. Suzette let out a deep sigh and went out the door toting her first basket of laundry. The heavy load challenged her strength, but she felt relieved that she was leaving the washhouse for a while. As soon as she walked out the door, the cold morning air accosted her thin dress. She had no shawl for her shoulders.

The wicker basket gouged into her hip, and the longer she carried it, the heavier it became. The weight pressed upon her waist, and every few blocks, she needed to stop, put the basket down, and rest. If Brouchard witnessed her weakness, she knew she'd never keep the job. Why he didn't deliver the laundry by cart was beyond her understanding, but she often saw women throughout the streets carrying large laundry baskets and sacks back and forth without a second thought. Once again, her sheltered life had turned into a painful lesson in reality.

Finally, after a long, arduous trek, her eyes fell upon a conspicuous sign above the entrance, WELCOME TO THE CHABANAIS. Thinking that it must at least be six o'clock by now, she wondered if anyone would be awake. As she approached the front door, a befuddled expression came across her face. The entrance looked like a cave.

She giggled at the absurdity of the situation. There she stood, in front of a brothel, with a basket of laundry on her sore hip at six o'clock in the morning. It was the last place in the world Suzette could have imagined herself weeks ago. Thankfully, Rue Chabanais was not a main thoroughfare and traffic was light in the early morning hours.

She examined the strange wooden door before grabbing the brass knocker. Suzette gave it a few strikes, dropping it against the metal plate with a *clang*. A few moments passed with no answer, so she tapped it again, only much louder the second time. The brass knocker dropped, and suddenly a small panel in the center of the upper door slid open. Startled, she stepped back and heard a voice but saw no face.

"We don't receive customers until seven o'clock at night. Come back then," snapped an irritable female, slamming the opening shut.

"But I'm here with the laundry," yelled Suzette.

The small panel opened again, and a pair of beautiful hazel eyes, with long lashes, peered at Suzette. "Laundry? Good gracious, woman, deliver it to the back door."

"Where?"

"Down the side alley," she spat, slamming the panel shut again.

Suzette glanced to her right and saw an alleyway. She turned the corner and proceeded to walk down the narrow, dark passage. Her nose caught the smell of urine, and a homeless drunkard lay asleep by a door with an empty bottle in his hand.

Carefully, she stepped around his snoring body and stood in front of a doorway with the name CHABANAIS etched on a small metal plaque attached to the door. She rapped with her knuckles, while balancing the full laundry basket on her hip. If she didn't put it down soon, she was sure it was going to dump on the head of the drunk that lay at her feet. Then she'd be in real trouble.

With no immediate answer, she knocked again, until the door finally flung open revealing a woman clad in a silken black robe. A cigarette dangled between her plump red lips.

"Come in," she grumbled, in a raspy voice. Suzette entered into a back room adjacent to a kitchen area and immediately released her burden by dropping the basket at her feet with a *thud*.

"Is there anywhere in particular you want these linens?" Her eyes darted around at her surroundings, and she spotted a small hallway beyond the woman standing in front of her. Suzette's curiosity piqued at the beautiful sight that lay beyond.

The woman took a puff on her cigarette, then took it from her lips and blew the smoke into Suzette's face, causing her to wince and cough.

"You're new. I can tell. Where's the other one?"

"The other one?" Suzette responded, still trying to clear her lungs from the irritating smoke.

"Yes, the other one. An old drunk who knew exactly what to do with the basket of linens." She gave Suzette the once over and quipped sarcastically, "It's apparent you haven't a clue what to do."

Ridiculed and exasperated from the walk, Suzette snapped back. "Can you just tell me where they go?"

"Nadine, leave the girl alone."

The deep, stern voice caught Suzette off guard, and her eyes met a tall, beautiful woman dressed in a dark blue brocade gown standing in the kitchen entranceway. Her brown upswept hair, flawless features, and dark eyes exuded power.

"Can't you tell she's new? Don't make her feel like a fool."

"Fine! You deal with her then," she said, spinning around and heading out the doorway.

The mistress's face turned dark as she watched her employee leave the kitchen. When they were alone, she returned her attention to Suzette, who stood motionless as she eyed her from top to bottom.

"I'm Madame Laurent, the owner of this brothel." She paused for a moment and raised her brow. "And you might be?"

Suzette, struck by the velvet coolness in the tone of her voice, nervously blurted out her name as she curtsied. "Suzette, Madame. My name is Suzette Rousseau."

"Good Lord, girl. There's no need to curtsy to me." Astonished by her visitor's formalities, Madame Laurent looked more closely, studying the young girl's regal face. "You appear much too pretty to be working in a sweatshop." Scrutinizing her once again, she finally gave her instructions regarding the laundry. "Follow me, and I'll show you where we keep our linens."

Suzette picked up the basket and followed the Madame. She watched her saunter down a long, carpeted hallway, while her hips swayed back and forth moving her bustle. Her deep blue satin gown trailed behind, and Suzette sighed with longing at the elegant dress. The woman's movements were poised and graceful.

While she was gawking at her clothes, it dawned on her that she was inside a brothel. Her poor, dear father would be horrified over her whereabouts, and a blush burst up her neck as she wondered what went on behind closed doors.

They arrived in front of a long line of closets built into the hallway wall and stopped. Madame Laurent opened one door and showed Suzette the interior.

"We keep our linens here. You can place what you have in the basket on the shelves. I expect the sheets to be arranged in a neat and orderly fashion." The mistress noticed Suzette's flushed face, and a hint of amusement sparkled in her dark eyes.

"I'm afraid there's a basket waiting for you to carry back too. You are to leave the basket you empty each day, then pick up the basket filled with dirty laundry for return to the washhouse." In a low, sultry voice she added, "Our customers come every night, so every day we have sheets to wash."

Suzette glanced away.

Madame Laurent sensed her teasing had gone far enough and decided to end the conversation abruptly. "I'll leave you to your duties. You may let yourself out the way you entered."

"Thank you, Madame," she answered in a low voice.

Suzette watched the woman depart and went about her job. Neatly, she lined up the pristine white linens, left the empty basket, and picked up the one filled with dirty sheets. With a sigh of relief, she retreated to the back door. Her feet stepped over the drunk on the stoop and quickly left the alley carrying another load on her sore hip.

The trek back to the washhouse was excruciating. She still wore the same floppy shoes stuffed with paper in the toes and her feet hurt. The physical activity caused sweat to bead on her brow as she struggled with the load. She realized how weak and out of shape her body had truly been, after boasting she could handle the weight. It would have to change soon, or there would be no surviving her new job if Brouchard found out.

When she returned, Flora said little, except to give her instructions on what to do with the sheets she had hauled from the Chabanais. The routine had begun, and Suzette tried hard to accept her new station in life. It wouldn't be easy.

CHAPTER 6

The weeks passed, and Suzette's depression deepened as she toiled in the heat and stench, learning the life of a laundress. Daily her boring schedule repeated itself, starting with tiring trips back and forth to the Chabanais. She hauled the laundry in all sorts of weather conditions. It made no difference to Monsieur Brouchard whether it was sunshine or rain; the items had to be delivered. If it rained, it was her responsibility to make sure the load did not get wet during the two-mile trek. She usually arrived looking like a drowned rat, but faithfully covered and shielded her basket, so that it would arrive dry.

Every morning, Suzette woke from a restless sleep on a lumpy mattress. Flora seemed to have an internal clock after years of toiling and would wake Suzette at four-thirty. With only a half hour to freshen for the day and barely time to take a bath, Suzette was required to be dressed and at her work station by five *"come hell or high water,"* as Brouchard so aptly put it.

After weeks of toiling back and forth and little interaction with anyone at the brothel, Brouchard suddenly announced that she could make her delivery to the Chabanais an hour later. Suzette did not question the change, but wondered if Madame Laurent had somehow found pity on her poor soul and requested a later time. Suzette was thankful nonetheless.

When seven o'clock arrived, she would throw her basket of laundry on her hardened hip and make the walk to the

Chabanais. As she had done countless times before, she entered through the back door, proceeded to the linen cabinet, and neatly restocked the sheets. Because her visits were early in the morning, she rarely encountered any prostitutes, except Nadine who was the rude woman she met the first day. Madame Laurent rarely said a word when their paths crossed, except to glide her eyes up and down her petite frame. It made Suzette feel uncomfortable.

On her return from the Chabanais, she hauled the dirty linens back to the washhouse. Her hips had become use to carrying the weight, and her arms grew stronger each day from hauling the baskets. It was easy, now, for her to pick up the heavy linens with little effort on her part.

As spring gave way to summer, conditions worsened in the washhouse. Between the hot air outside and the sweltering steam inside, there were days Suzette felt dizzy from the heat. She continued to push herself in fear of finding displeasure in Brouchard's eyes.

Flora was instructed to teach Suzette washing of the linens, so her duties expanded beyond folding and delivery. It was just more work to accomplish in the same amount of time, and Suzette could barely keep up with the demands.

The Chabanais and her other clients kept her workdays busy. When she sorted the laundry from the Chabanais, taunting thoughts plagued her mind about what transpired behind closed doors. Suzette knew little of the intimate ways of men and women. Her father never spoke of such matters, and her mother passed away too early to teach her anything about sex.

During her days of hard labor, Suzette learned that workers who ironed clothes possessed the better paying jobs. Experienced laundresses worked on high-end clothing such as shirts, pants, bonnets, and dresses. In addition, the washhouse employed a variety of seamstresses and lace makers, who repaired clothing.

Brouchard swore to her face he would never trust her with such delicacies and seemed content watching her hike back and forth each day hauling loads of sheets. His ill-gotten pleasure irritated Suzette. She decided long ago that if her life were relegated to a washhouse forever, she would work her way up to a higher paying position—*come hell or high water.*

Suzette's hands dried and cracked from the lye poured into the steaming water to whiten sheets. She often felt dirty, tired, and ugly. Her hips carried a continuous bruise from hauling the heavy baskets. To lessen the pain, Suzette learned to alternate hips each week to give the other time to heal. The routine of her employment turned into an endless, degrading cycle.

Her pittance of three francs per day barely purchased enough food to eat. She lost weight from her already petite frame, due to the strenuous physical demands and smaller portions of nourishment. Thirty centimes would buy a piece of bread, but if she wished for a piece of meat, it would cost two francs more at the café. Her daily diet consisted of soup and bread, but when she could afford to do so, she would splurge on cuts of beef or mutton.

Workers were allowed short breaks for lunch and dinner. Not everyone lived at the washhouse. The majority, who were married or made more money, lived in residences elsewhere. Only the lower-end employees, such as herself and Flora, kept residence in the small room, which began to feel more like a prison house than a comfortable place to live. The Daughters of Charity, as sparse as the dormitory had been, provided far more comfort.

Unable to save enough for clothing or shoes, she continued to wear the same worn-out cotton day dress and oversized shoes until they were on the verge of falling apart. She learned to stuff strips of old rags into the toes to make up for the excess size, after the paper she had used earlier fell apart.

Over the weeks, Suzette found the women of the washhouse crude in many ways but not necessarily mean. Most had worked there for years, obviously accepting their lot in life and conditions of poverty better than what the streets offered. As she feared, the reputation of laundresses lay low in the minds of men, especially during hot, sweltering days when the doors and windows were flung wide open. The women stripped and worked thinly clad to escape the scorching heat and avoid dehydration, which could lead to fainting.

Men, on the other hand, took advantage of the scene and stood in the open doorways watching bare-fleshed women bend over vats. The views, of course, from the front and back would burst a blush on any virgin's cheeks. Brouchard enjoyed the scene immensely, and he did not attempt to discourage the curious onlookers who came daily for the show of naked flesh.

To Suzette's surprise, most of the women were alcoholics, drinking low-grade wine during work each day, which was purchased and supplied by the owner. It was considered a benefit of the job, so they took advantage of the free drinks to relieve the stress of everyday life in the washroom.

Suzette shunned the practice, thinking it self-defeating, and refused to partake in the amble spirits of canteens strategically placed throughout the workspace. However, finding even a clean glass of water proved to be a chore, and on some days the heat and lack of hydration made her feel sick. She would succumb to a small amount of alcohol to quench her thirst when nothing else was available, but she despised the taste of cheap wine.

Her only comforts were the quiet evenings she found by herself as she lay on her cot. In her distress, she found prayer necessary to seek solace from a higher power. She was still angry with God for taking her father, but she tried to forgive

Him, and she prayed for forgiveness and grace for her bad attitude.

The one memory she clung to for as long as faith allowed her happened to be the folded letter that she had kept from her jewelry box. As delicately as she did many nights before, she unfolded the parchment, read the words, and returned it once again to its new hiding place within her purse. Of course, there was nothing of value in her purse any longer except a piece of paper, a rosary missing a few beads, pictures of her parents, and a few francs to show for her hard labor.

Suzette's reading of the letter gradually lessened as the weeks turned into months. Like dreams fade when one awakes, so did the words on the page. They held no meaning or encouragement, and Suzette finally came to a place where she didn't wish to feed her fanciful dreams any further. She did not have the strength to destroy the letter, but neither did she desire to read it again. It finally found a resting place of neglect in the bottom of her purse after the third month of her life as a laundress.

Her only reprieve was the Chabanais. The poverty and stench gave way when she entered through the brothel doors. As soon as she stepped inside, she inhaled the scent of perfumed air and held it in her lungs as long as she could retain it in order to replace the putrid smells of the washhouse.

One day as she made her way to the linen closet, Suzette walked past the opulent parlor. Her eyes always glanced inside, but she never stopped. Like a little mouse, she would scurry past the entrance, catching glimpses of red settees, gold-gilded furniture, ornate rugs, mirrors, and palm plants. She refused to linger and stare for fear of getting in trouble.

After returning all of the linens to the cupboard in a neat stack, she picked up the full basket of dirty laundry and flung it on her hip. She quickly sprinted down the hallway, but failed to watch her step. The toe of her foot caught on the edge of an area rug. Suzette stumbled and dropped the basket. She gasped when it landed full-force at the parlor entrance, strewing dirty laundry across the floor. Quickly, she lowered herself to her knees and grabbed the linens stuffing them into the basket. She bit her lower lip, as she glanced at the scene teasing her from the corner of her vision. Curious, she stopped and slowly turned her head to look inside the glorious room. Like a little girl in a candy shop, her eyes grew large in wonder.

"Like what you see?"

The voice of Madame Laurent startled her, and she jumped to her feet.

"Oh, Madame, I'm sorry. I tripped, and everything went flying. I apologize."

Suzette grabbed the last piece of laundry and shoved it in the basket as quickly as possible. She stood to her feet and hurled the basket upon her hip and darted for the door. Madame Laurent reached out and grabbed her arm, preventing her departure.

"Do you wish a tour?"

She wanted to see, but feared accepting such a daring invitation. Suzette hesitated, then slowly turned and faced Madame Laurent.

"It looks quite beautiful, Madame, but I'm sure Monsieur Brouchard would be quite angry should he find out. I don't wish to lose my job."

"To hell with Monsieur Brouchard," she said, empathically. "Put the basket down and follow me." The mistress of the house turned around and walked into the parlor, fully expecting her visitor to comply with her wishes.

Suzette dropped the basket at her feet with a *thud* and gave her curiosity free rein. She stepped cautiously through the entranceway. Once inside the forbidden world, Suzette stopped. The beauty of the ornate room took her breath away, and Suzette basked in the enthralling atmosphere of opulence.

Madame Laurent smiled at her reaction and motioned her to a red velvet settee. She sat down and patted the seat next to her.

"Come sit with me, Suzette. Rest a moment and take a look around."

Suzette walked over to Madame Laurent and slowly lowered herself onto the soft, cushioned seat. She hadn't felt such comfort since her father's passing, and the touch of softness to her tired body brought tears to her eyes.

Madame Laurent said nothing. She gave Suzette time to absorb her surroundings, while she studied her more closely. Suzette's complexion, albeit dirty, was flawless. Her auburn hair displayed a slight natural curl even though it was piled high on top of her head in messy tousles. Her body was far too thin, but she was certain that was only from too much hard work and poor nutrition.

It was easy to imagine Suzette with makeup to accentuate her features and fine lotions to smooth her rough skin. With a few dabs of enticing perfume to replace her obvious body odor, the young lady would be quite the attraction in her establishment. She needed a girl for the Louis XV Chambre to serve her aristocrats and rich businessmen. Suzette would fill the part perfectly—after a little makeover and training, of course. Her beautiful features and regal look would bring a high price.

Madame Laurent reached over and tenderly picked up Suzette's hand and held it in her own. She turned it back and forth examining the poor condition of her skin.

"My word, child, don't you have any cream for your delicate hands?"

Embarrassed, Suzette wanted to pull her hand away, but feared to spurn her touch. "I'm sorry, Madame, but I barely make enough for a good meal. Cream, I'm afraid, is a luxury I cannot afford."

"How did you come to choose the life of a laundress, Suzette? You seem intelligent and well bred," she inquired, after releasing her hand.

Suzette's wounded heart, still tender with grief, skipped a beat. For months, she had consciously chosen not to think of her father's death. In reality, there was no time to grieve either. The washhouse consumed her life, and each night she was too tired to think of anything except sleep.

"My father passed away four months ago." She paused for a moment letting out a sigh and then continued. "I didn't know, but he was deeply in debt. His estate was sold to pay the creditors."

"Well, I'm sorry to hear that. Am I to assume that you have no other family or friends to care for you?"

"No, Madame, I do not. I stayed with the Daughters of Charity for a while until they helped me find the position at the washhouse."

Suzette felt increasingly uncomfortable with time slipping by and begged to leave. "I need to be going. Brouchard will wonder why I am late returning." Suzette couldn't stand the thought of him reprimanding her upon a late return.

"Not yet, Suzette," she sternly replied. Madame Laurent looked into Suzette's eyes, and her serious gaze kept Suzette motionless in her seat. "I have a proposition for you, my dear."

Suzette swallowed a lump in her throat. "A proposition?" she repeated, wondering what she could possibly mean.

"I need a girl for my Louis XV Chambre." She softened her tone and conveyed her pride in her establishment. "This is no ordinary brothel, Suzette. I only cater to one type of clientele—the rich. The men who frequent my doors are royalty. We have Dukes, Marquises, Comtes, and Vicomtes, who visit my girls."

A prideful twinkle radiated from the Madame's eyes over her successful business.

"If you come to work for me, I can offer you a life of luxury. You'll be well fed, clothed, and housed in quarters that are a thousand times better than the filth you live in now. Instead of working eighteen hours a day, you'll only work four hours each night. You will be given one day off every week to do as you please."

Madame Laurent paused, giving Suzette a moment to consider everything she offered. It was obvious by the wide-eyed look on the young girl's face that she was in shock.

"I take good care of my employees, Suzette. I pay fifteen francs per night. With that type of income, you can buy as many new dresses as you please and all the hand cream you'll ever need." Madame Laurent's eyes travelled over the worn-out cotton fabric dress. "You are a beautiful young girl, and I hate to see you wither away in the filth of a washhouse."

She waved her arm pointing out the room gilded in gold, with hanging electric lights, potted palm plants, red velvet settees, and mirrors on the walls. "Would you join me here as one of my girls, Suzette?"

After Madame Laurent made her offer, Suzette sat motionless, barely able to breathe at the thought of what she asked.

"Do you mean you want me to be a prostitute?" The look in the Madame's eyes told her that was exactly what she inferred. Suzette jumped to her feet in horror.

"No! No, I could never do such a thing. I am a good girl!" With a quick bow of her head, she begged Madame Laurent's pardon. An overwhelming urge to flee the brothel washed over her. "Please excuse me, Madame, but I must return to my work."

Suzette sprung to her feet, leaving Madame Laurent on the settee. She retrieved her basket by the parlor entrance, flung it upon her hip, and swiftly headed for the exit. Just as she grabbed the doorknob and was about to turn it, she felt the tight grip of Madame Laurent's hand upon her upper arm.

"Think about it, Suzette. Do you really wish to live a life of poverty, hunger, and filth? For a small price, you can swallow your pride and live like a queen. The choice is yours."

Suzette wrestled her arm away from her grip, then flung the door open and ran down the alley. Madame Laurent watched her hasty departure and smiled, calmly assured this would not be the last of their discussions.

While making her way back to the washhouse, Suzette pondered Madame Laurent's brazen offer. Her confused mind screamed "no." But, her aching, exhausted, hungry body begged her to say "yes." The price was too great to pay, and she swore she would rather die in a back alley than sell her body to live in luxury. Her father would never forgive her for stooping to such a deplorable life, nor would she forgive herself.

Out of breath from her hurried return, she slowly made her way back into the washhouse. Fearful that Brouchard would scold her for the time she missed, she successfully dodged his keen eyes. Suzette reached her station, poured out her laundry basket from the Chabanais, and began sorting. She wanted to forget what transpired between herself and Madame Laurent, but touching the brothel linens made it impossible.

Angry and tired, she said nothing to Flora, who stood by curiously watching the odd behavior of her coworker. Suzette, grim and frustrated, flung the sheets from pile to pile. Each bend of her red and cracked fingers caused pain.

As she struggled to work, visions of the opulent perfumed brothel teased her resolve. Madame Laurent's invitation to live like a queen replayed in her mind. *It would be so nice to feel like a queen*, she thought, but the price was far too costly.

CHAPTER 7

As the weeks passed, Suzette felt like millstone hung around her neck, which she bore as a necklace of shame. Eighteen hours of work, sorting linens, washing, folding, and walking back and forth to the Chabanais became the entirety of her boring and meaningless existence. Each night, she returned exhausted to her cot for five hours of sleep in a room filled with drunken, snoring women who grated on her nerves.

In contrast, the opulence of the brothel would greet her with open arms. The scent of perfume filled her nostrils, alluring her from the stench of the washhouse. Suzette arrived at the shameful realization that she looked forward to her morning visits in a house of ill repute, if for nothing more than to breathe fresh air and enjoy a luxurious atmosphere where everything appeared soft and clean.

Her visits were often short and without conversation. As the weeks dragged on, she met more of Madame Laurent's employees. They rarely spoke to her. More often, they eyed her arrival through the back door and commenced whispering amongst themselves. Nadine always seemed to be the center of attention, giggling at her whenever she passed by.

At first, Madame Laurent stood silently observing Suzette as she carried out her duties. Eventually, she would bring up the subject once again, asking Suzette to join the ranks of her staff and become one of her girls.

"My offer is still open, Suzette, should you wish to take it. Leave the squalor and come live like a queen."

Madame Laurent entice Suzette's weakening resolve with offers of a comfortable bed, a belly full of food, new clothes, lavish creams, and perfumed hair. Suzette would shake her head and give the same timid response.

"No thank you, Madame."

After time, the cat-and-mouse game, as they often do, began to wear upon Madame Laurent's patience. Unable to convince an eighteen-year-old beauty to join her staff was merely a minor setback, which she would soon remedy by other means. It would not be long, and Suzette would be one of her new beauties of pleasure. When Madame Laurent wanted her way, she was sure to get it.

* * *

Monsieur Brouchard counted the 50 francs at least a dozen times. The bills were crisp, and he brought them to his nostrils and inhaled the alluring scent of money. The amount was more than what he made in three months.

He folded the bills for the last time and stuffed them into his pants pocket, after standing up from behind his desk. The clock on the wall indicated the end of the shift had arrived. He was about to earn his pay by performing one small task he would immensely enjoy.

The door to his office opened, and he walked out onto the washroom floor and observed the women finishing their work. Each night, he would bellow out at the top of his lungs, *"End of shift!"* and then stand aside and watch the weary ladies go their separate ways.

He meandered over to Suzette stooping over a basin scrubbing sheets, which should have been done hours ago. Both of his hands were shoved into the pockets of his trousers, and one fingered the crisp francs with greed.

"I need a word with you," he scowled. He purposely contorted his face into an angry scowl.

Suzette stood up straight and wiped her sweaty brow with the back of her hand. She frowned at him in return. "Yes, Monsieur Brouchard?"

"You're fired. Take what belongings you keep upstairs and leave. Your services here are no longer required."

Suzette dropped the sheet into the soapy water and wiped her hands on her apron. Dumfounded, she froze. He spat the words in her direction with such force that she could not deny he meant every syllable. His angry expression dared her to question him, but Suzette's shock would not allow her to remain silent.

"But why? What have I done?" she persisted.

"It doesn't matter," he hissed, as he took a step and shoved his face closer into hers. "It's my prerogative to fire anyone I please, whenever I please. I'm not happy with your work. These sheets should have been hung to dry hours ago." He shook his finger at her, inhaled a deep breath, and yelled, "Gather your things and leave now!"

Suzette could not believe what she heard. "May I at least spend the night here, Monsieur? Surely you don't expect me to sleep on the streets." Her voice shook from the fear. "I will leave in the morning." She wanted to kneel at his feet and beg for mercy, but before he would even give her the chance to plead any longer, he finished the deed he was paid to do.

"There'll be no sleeping under my roof once I fire an employee. Get your things and get out." He swung around and stomped back to his office slamming the door behind him.

Suzette turned to Flora, who was standing nearby. "Flora, he cannot throw me out on the street like this, can he?"

"There's nothing you can do. You best be going before he calls the police to have you forcibly removed. He's done it before."

Not wishing to bring his unbearable anger upon herself, Flora turned away from Suzette and finished her duties for the day. The other women who stood by said nothing. No words of comfort or help met Suzette's ears—only a cold silence and disregard that shattered her faith in humanity.

The unbearable cruelty caused hot tears to stream down her face as she ran upstairs to her cot and packed her few things into her small, tattered suitcase. She shook in fear as she walked down the wooden staircase, ignored by the women she passed, and exited the door to the street. Gas lamps lit her path, but only a few people and carriages traversed the avenue.

Afraid her life was in danger, she turned right and walked aimlessly down the sidewalk. Tears trickled down her cheeks, blurring her vision. She tried to keep her wits about her, as she wiped her eyes with the back of her sleeve to stop the flood.

Her feet carried her in the same direction she walked every day for months—straight toward the Chabanais. Almost blindly, Suzette headed for the only place she knew where others knew of her existence. She thought of the interior warmth and beauty of the brothel and wondered if Madame Laurent would be merciful enough to allow her to spend the night. She would make her way to the shelter tomorrow on the other side of town.

As she arrived at the Chabanais, she stood hesitantly by the corner of the building watching the brothel entrance. She spotted a few well-to-do men in black top hats leaving the establishment in waiting carriages. Fearful to approach until everyone departed, she stood in the shadows for fifteen minutes until everything went quiet.

When Suzette felt it was safe, she scurried down the dark alley until she came to the back entrance. She turned the doorknob, and to her surprise found it unlocked. Desperate, she opened the door and stepped inside hearing voices and activity in the kitchen. When she was spotted in the doorway, it grew silent. Every eye turned in her direction. Madame Laurent saw her shivering body and came to her side.

"Suzette! My God, what are you doing here? You look absolutely frightful!"

Unable to control the floodgate of tears, Suzette stood rigid, sobbing like a child. "They—he—he fired me, Madame. I have nowhere to go, to sleep—nowhere . . ." She couldn't finish the words.

Madame Laurent hugged Suzette and smiled at Nadine over the success of her plan. A few girls standing nearby giggled.

"You can spend the night here, dear. I couldn't bear to think of you sleeping in the alley. God knows you'd be raped by morning or found dead by the police, oui?"

Her words frightened Suzette so much that she stepped farther inside the ironic haven of the brothel, fearful of what was behind her back.

"Follow me."

She grabbed Suzette's hand and led her up a back staircase at the end of the long hallway that she had walked daily to carry out her duties. The narrow stairs climbed upward to the far end of the second floor. After a few short steps down another hallway, she opened a door to a room.

"Most of my girls live here at the brothel."

Suzette, frightened and uncomfortable, hoped that the brothel mistress wouldn't reveal too much about life inside a house of sin. Madame Laurent walked over to a closet and flung open the double doors to reveal a large assortment of beautiful clothes and nightgowns.

"There's a bath chamber adjacent to this room through that door. Take a bath, and you can use this for the night."

Suzette gasped at the beauty of the silken material, thanking her profusely.

"I'm so grateful for your kindness, Madame Laurent."

"Don't think twice about it. I only ask that you stay in this room the remainder of the evening. I'm afraid there are a few stragglers with some of my girls, and I don't wish them to find you wandering around. Wash up and get a good night's sleep. We'll talk in the morning."

"Yes, ma'am."

Madame Laurent smiled reassuringly. "Sleep well, Suzette. At least tonight you are safe, oui?"

She watched as the door closed behind her and felt relieved that she was off the streets. Suzette sat down on the bed and felt the softness welcome her tired body. Her hand brushed the white linen pillowcase, no doubt washed and carried by her own toil. When she pushed down on the fabric, the goose down feathers plumped at her touch, and Suzette began to cry.

She was surrounded by luxury. Two beds occupied the room, and Suzette wondered who slept in the other. Gorgeous coverlets, rugs, light fixtures, and framed artwork decorated the interior. It was nothing like the opulence she viewed in the parlor downstairs, but it held its own beauty and comfort. It was such a stark contrast to the dark room with four cots that she slept in for months.

Suzette enjoyed the momentary comfort, but knew it would not last forever. Soon, she would see the Daughters of Charity again. She had gone full circle, back to the beginning with no work and facing the prospects of living on the streets.

Unable to bear the uncertainties of the future, she buried her head in the soft pillow and sobbed. When she had finished pouring out her heart, she made her way into bath chamber and washed her face before climbing under the sheets in the silky nightgown. Finally, exhaustion won its battle, and Suzette drifted off into a deep sleep.

She woke early the next morning to find Nadine in the other bed. Not too keen on her roommate, she ignored her presence while focusing on her new-found comfort. For the first time in many months, she felt pampered. If it were not for the fact she was sleeping inside a brothel, she wouldn't have given it a second thought. It felt no different than a comfortable boarding house.

As she lay on her back, she stared at the ceiling above thinking about what to do next. Nadine's sleepy voice interrupted her pondering.

"I see you're awake." She sat up in bed and looked at Suzette wrapped like a baby in blankets pulled up under her chin. "Madame Laurent warned me that you were my new roomy."

Nadine heaved a sigh, flung off her blankets, and stood up stark naked. She stretched out both arms over her head and let out a loud yawn.

Suzette's eyes widened. Nadine's body curved in every direction, and at the sight of her unashamed nakedness, Suzette turned her face in the other direction. Her long, blond hair cascaded about her exposed breasts. *She looks like Lady Godiva, only without the white horse,* Suzette thought.

"Oh, for God's sake," Nadine quipped, disgusted over Suzette's reaction. "It's not like you've never seen a woman's body before. You look at your own every day!"

She snatched a black silk robe from the foot of her bed and slipped her arms through the sleeves. After pulling the sash tight around her waist, she warned Suzette.

"If you intend on staying here, you might as well get over your queasiness for naked bodies." Her feet slid through her open-toed slippers as she continued. "Believe me, you'll see them all the time . . . everywhere."

Suzette shot back in anger. "I have no intention of staying here."

Nadine smirked. "Oh? And where will you go? Wander the streets and sleep in alleys?"

Her roommate sauntered into the bath chamber and left Suzette stewing over her words. A few minutes later she came back insisting that she get dressed and head downstairs.

"We don't dilly-dally in the mornings around here either. Every one of us has chores to do in order to keep this place looking as nice as it is. Bridgette will wish to speak with you."

"Bridgette?"

"Madame Laurent. That's her first name, but she doesn't let everybody call her that."

Nadine dressed and then impatiently waited for Suzette to do the same. She looked at her in disgust, as she slipped into her dirty dress she had arrived in the night before. Annoyed over the smell, she spoke her displeasure.

"My God. Don't you have anything else?" she complained with a heartless sneer.

"No, I'm afraid I don't. You'll just have to deal with it."

Suzette opened the door and walked ahead of Nadine, hoping to get away from her, but then she realized she didn't know which way to go. Nadine grabbed her by the elbow and pulled her along toward the back staircase, causing Suzette to stumble.

"Come along. This way." Nadine pranced down the stairs and burst into the kitchen with Suzette in tow. "Look what the cat dragged in," she announced, as she hurled her into the middle of the room.

"Really, Nadine, is that necessary?"

Madame Laurent flashed a disapproving glare. Her action of protest in Suzette's defense surprised her. Three other women stood in the kitchen clad in robes, munching on pastries and drinking coffee.

"Did you sleep well?"

"Yes, ma'am." Suzette spotted a tray of pastries, and her tongue licked her lips. She hadn't eaten since noon the day before and was famished. Bridgette encouraged her to partake.

"Go ahead and have something to eat." She pushed the tray of pastries in her direction, and everyone watched Suzette reach for a croissant. She shoved it in her mouth and devoured it within a few moments. Bridgette poured coffee in a cup, added a bit of cream and sugar, and handed it to Suzette, who gratefully received its contents.

"I'm afraid not many of us drink tea, but if you wish, I can boil you a pot of hot water."

She shook her head no, while holding the warm cup between the palms of her hands. "No, this will do fine." After a few sips of coffee, she began to hunger for another croissant. "May I?"

"Of course, eat as many as you like and get your fill. When you're done, come find me in my office, and we'll talk," she said, while patting her on the shoulder. She flashed a sympathetic smile and then left Suzette alone in the kitchen with the other women.

"Madame Laurent is a nice lady." A thick Irish accent caught Suzette's attention, and she turned her head in the woman's direction. "We are all fortunate to live here."

Suzette looked at a fiery redhead whose porcelain fair completion accentuated the hue of her hair. She was gorgeous.

"I appreciate her taking me in for the night. Truly, I do," she replied, with a mouth full of pastry. She swallowed a lump down her throat. "I'm sorry. Forgive my rudeness. I'm really hungry."

Suzette turned and looked at the other woman who stood nearby, fascinated by her Asian appearance. She was petite in stature, and her midnight black hair shined like onyx. After staring at her for some time, the woman smiled in response and encouraged her, as well.

"You'd be a fool if you return to the streets. We have warm beds and plenty of food."

The free advice flowing Suzette's way began to make her nervous. Nadine stood silently by listening to the conversation with a silly grin on her face. Like a cornered animal, Suzette wanted to escape the glaring eyes of prostitutes, who were clearly trying to sway her decision. She warily looked at all three of them, and then swallowed hard, forcing the last bit of food down to her stomach.

"Could one of you show me to Madame Laurent's office?"

She expected Nadine to do the honors, but was surprised when the Irish redhead leaped forward and grabbed her hand. "Follow me. I'll show you the way."

Pulled out the kitchen door, through the parlor, and into the entranceway, Suzette had no time to protest her rash treatment. Before a word of displeasure could leave her lips, she suddenly found herself standing in the opulent foyer of the brothel. Suzette halted and pulled her hand from the woman's grasp with a quick jerk.

She stood stunned in the middle of the room, enthralled over its beauty. A broad, sweeping staircase with a plush red carpet, led to the second floor. Potted palm plants decorated the area, with mahogany side tables brimming with fresh flowers. A deep, rich oriental rug paved the floor for the arrival of royalty and aristocrats. However, the most impressive site was the enormous crystal chandelier hanging from the ceiling above.

"Oh, my God," she cried, "this is beautiful!"

The redhead laughed as she watched Suzette's head crook backwards to the ceiling, eyeing the dangling crystal orbs that sparkled overhead.

"I'm Annette, by the way," she said. "You've seen nothing yet, if you think this is pretty."

Suzette lowered her stare from the crystal chandelier and followed Annette to a closed door off to the right of the foyer. After a quick knuckle tap on the wooden door, Madame Laurent's voice called out and bid them entrance.

"Here she is," announced Annette with a smile.

Suzette found Madame Laurent behind a large mahogany desk sitting in a red leather chair, which surrounded her like a queen's throne. Annette closed the door, and Suzette jumped after hearing it shut. Nervous and alone, she turned toward Madame Laurent.

"Please, have a seat."

The brothel mistress pointed to the chair in front of her desk. Slowly, Suzette walked to a cushioned seat and sat down giving her derrière comfort.

Madame Laurent focused on Suzette. She smiled at the pretty, regal face. It looked as if she had washed it the night before, but she needed so much more. Her hair was filthy, and she smelled horrible. Suzette's nails harbored black dirt underneath, and her poor hands were cracked and red.

"So tell me, Suzette, have you thought anymore about my offer? Since you're unemployed, I would think you would be interested in becoming one of my girls." Madame Laurent carefully studied the movement of Suzette's body, which she noticed stiffened over her inquiry.

Suzette lowered her head and broke eye contact. She folded her hands in her lap. "I do not think, Madame, that this is an occupation I wish to pursue."

Madame Laurent flung back, "And what occupation do you think you can pursue? You were not exactly successful as a laundress. Without references, do you think you'll find work quickly anywhere else?"

Suzette shifted in her seat, which only encouraged her interrogator. "At least here, you'd have a comfortable and clean place to live, and a much better paying position."

"Yes, but not my reputation," Suzette interrupted, raising her eyebrows in protest.

"Reputation?" She grinned slyly. "I have one of the most revered reputations in Paris among the male population. There's something to be said, Suzette, about meeting the needs of men who cannot find satisfaction in their marriage beds. At least here, they find comfort and passion."

She paused for a moment to soften her tone and confidently leaned back in her red leather throne. Suzette said nothing for some time and then finally answered.

"Perhaps, but I'm—I'm a virgin, Madame, and I don't wish to give myself to strange men."

Madame Laurent laughed aloud at the absurdity of her answer. "I would think, my dear, it would be a small price to pay—the loss of one's virginity—when you weigh the dire consequences you face. I dare say, you are homeless, and will be crawling back to the Daughters of Charity again. I do hope they have room. If not, you'll end up prostituting yourself on the street anyway, as soon as your stomach continues to gnaw at you day and night. Your feet and hands will be cold from sleeping on the hard ground. You'll no doubt be raped within a week, because you'll have no one to protect you, diseased within a month, and dead within three."

The last words that fell from the mistress's lips were cold and cruel. Madame Laurent allowed the harsh reality of her situation sink in. Surely, it would produce the fear necessary to sway her decision.

"Do you really think losing your virginity is too great a price to pay in order to find safe shelter, a warm bed, clothing, and food in your stomach each day?"

She waited long enough without a response and stood up from behind her desk. Madame Laurent walked to Suzette's side and hovered above her shaking body, watching the young girl's knees bob up and down like apples in a barrel of water.

"Being a prostitute does have its rewards. You'll soon learn about fleshly pleasures you have no idea exist," she offered in a sultry voice. She curled a smile upon her red lips and reached out her hand to brush a stray curl from the Suzette's face.

"Don't be a foolish woman, Suzette. I dare say you have no other choice."

Suzette felt horrified. *Do I actually have no other choice? What about my future?* She looked up at Madame Laurent's face, wondering if her prophesy were true. *If I walk out that door right now, will I be dead in three months?* Her mind swirled with wicked possibilities that awaited her on the streets. She desperately tried to convince herself that she could find work elsewhere, and then wondered if there was another way around the Madame's offer.

"May I stay here and work in some other capacity for you? Maybe you need a housekeeper or cook—anything other than what you're offering me!"

"No," she replied emphatically. There was no room for negotiation. "In fact, if you do not accept my offer now, here this minute, you might as well get up and walk out the door, Suzette. I won't waste another night giving you a warm bed for nothing in return."

Madame Laurent unfeelingly turned away from Suzette, walked behind her desk, and sat down. She picked up her quill pen, dipped it in the ink well, and began writing notes on a piece of paper, determined to ignore the sniveling, foolish girl in her office.

"Why are you doing this to me?"

Madame Laurent remained silent.

"You are forcing me to make a decision I do not want!"

"I do it for your own good," she coldly replied. She lifted her dark, brown eyes and peered at Suzette in disgust. "Your foolishness astounds me, frankly."

Suzette sat shivering like a timid mouse in front of a cat. It was time to play her last card on the table to seal her fate.

"If you do not accept my offer, you can be assured I will make certain no one hires you in this city. I have connections in all the low-lying businesses who hire girls like you, and I will forewarn every sweathouse, restaurant, or store that you are useless. I will blacklist you, Suzette. You'll starve in an alley like the rest of the beggars who walk the streets of Paris."

Madame Laurent's anger pushed her to a new level. As she looked one last time at Suzette waiting for her to make a decision, she knew if the girl had half a backbone, perhaps she would have been less heartless.

Suzette looked into her eyes and believed every word spoken. Her shoulders drooped in defeat, and she raised her hands wiping tears from her face. It appeared fate had made the choice, and her life would be damned for the sake of survival. She was too weak to fight the inevitable and too afraid to protest her treatment. In a barely audible voice, she conceded.

"All right, then."

"All right, what, Suzette?"

She looked at Madame Laurent, who she now despised, and agreed to her proposal.

"I will become one of your prostitutes."

Suzette's surrender brought immense satisfaction to a woman who always got what she wanted. Her attitude quickly changed, and she responded with delight.

"Good! A wise choice." Her voice carried the victory of closing another business deal, and she proceeded with the details of the arrangement.

"You will need to comply with the law, of course, before you can enter the Chabanais. As soon as you are able, report to the Bureau des Mouers and register as a prostitute. I know it might be embarrassing, but my brothel is followed closely and licensed by the authorities. Unless I comply, they will shut me down in a heartbeat. Do you understand?"

"Yes, Madame," Suzette responded, unsure of what she was talking about.

"After your registration is complete, there is a one other requirement. You will be examined by a physician. Once he confirms that you are disease-free—which I assume you are, if you are a virgin like you say—they will release you to report back to me."

"I will do as you say, Madame."

"Good. Here is my card, which you'll need to present at the Bureau." After Suzette had taken it from her hand, she called out. "Annette, you can come in."

The door flung open, and the young redhead entered, waiting for instructions. As a co-conspirator, she had been patiently standing in the hallway anticipating new orders.

"Please, take Suzette upstairs. Give the girl a bath, wash her hair, and find suitable clothing. Then take her this afternoon to the Bureau des Mouers to register. You can hire a carriage." She opened up her drawer, drew out a few francs, and handed them to Annette. "Use this for your fare."

Annette took the money from Madame Laurent's hand and flashed a broad smile to her mistress over her conquest. She turned toward Suzette and offered a hand. "Come along, sweetie. It's time to take a bath and wash that nasty scum off your body."

Madame Laurent looked at Suzette, assured that she procured a valuable addition to her establishment. The poor girl fell into her trap—50 francs to a greedy manager, a late night dismissal arranged at the right moment, and a frightened rabbit coming to the only person who had befriended her pitiful life. The fly had flown into the web, and now she belonged to the spider.

There was one more piece of business left to attend to. She picked up her quill, dipped it in the inkwell, and began to write a note. A sly smile curled her red lips, as she thought fondly of the addressee.

CHAPTER 8

After receiving her instructions, Annette grabbed Suzette's hand once again and led her out the door. Suzette pulled hard to release her grip. It was obvious the new hire was a tad bit irritable.

"I can follow you without being dragged," she huffed. Angry over Annette's physical treatment, Suzette wasn't about to let anyone else tell her what she should or should not do, especially after the blackmail session that had occurred a few minutes earlier.

Annette raised a brow in return. "Fine with me." She walked through the foyer and invited Suzette to follow her up the grand staircase. "Come this way, and I'll show you what's up here."

Suzette placed her hand upon the curved cherry-wood banister and stepped on the pathway, whose center was covered with plush red carpet. Artwork of nude women lined the walls, strategically placed as a tantalizing foretaste of what lay ahead. Suzette cringed over the provocative scenes.

Once on the second floor, Annette stopped. "Nadine is supposed to give you the grand tour when you get back from the Bureau, so just follow me down the hallway to your quarters."

Suzette stood in the middle of a long hallway that stretched to the right and left of the staircase. As they began to walk, they passed multiple closed doors. Suzette only speculated briefly about what lay behind them.

It seemed as if everyone in the brothel was assured Suzette would succumb to Madame Laurent's invitation to join the staff. Annette led her to a bath chamber, where she had instructed their housekeeper to fill the tub with warm water. It sat ready and waiting for her to climb inside.

"Strip and get in, sweetie."

Suzette protested. "What, in front of you?"

"Yes."

"Well, I don't see the purpose," Suzette argued. "I can very well bathe myself."

"Can you? You can't reach your back. You stink like hell, and your hair looks like a rat's nest. Someone needs to scrub that scalp of yours." She reached for Suzette's head and began picking apart the matted strands. "There better not be any lice in there!"

"I don't have lice," she said, slapping away her hand.

The fiery redhead stepped back and put her hands on her hips, giving Suzette a dare-or-die glare. She could see the woman meant business, so she gave into her request and began unbuttoning her dress. It was filthy, and she did stink. There was no doubt about it. The steam rising from the warm tub looked inviting, but stripping in front of another person mortified Suzette.

After the last button, she let the dress fall around her feet and kicked it toward the wall. She took off her dirty chemise and bloomers, and then tossed them on top of the dress. A blush rushed up her neck, as she stood fully naked in front of Annette. With one leg, she quickly stepped into the tub, brought the other around, and settled down into the warm water. Just as she relaxed, a bar of soap hit the surface, and bathwater splashed in her face.

"You'll like the soap. It's scented. Madame Laurent buys the best of toiletries for us."

Suzette's hand reached toward the bottom of the tub and grabbed the silky bar beneath the water. She brought it to her face. The fragrance greeted her nostrils, and she couldn't help but sniff it repeatedly.

"It's nice," she admitted. "It smells like lavender."

Annette pulled up a chair alongside the claw-footed tub and sat next to Suzette. "Yes, it is lavender. We have all sorts of fragrant soaps, bath oils—anything a woman could want!"

Suzette took the bar and began to form suds in her hand to wash her body. When she finished, Annette dumped a bucket of fresh water on her head and added special herbs, fragrance, and soap shavings to lather through her auburn tresses that were tangled and frayed.

"My God," Suzette screamed in protest as the water hit her head and flowed into her eyes and mouth. "You could have warned me."

Suzette began to wonder if she would ever meet another woman with manners. Everyone was out to hurt her, from the roommates at the Daughters of Charity to the brothel. They were all biting flies she wanted to swat.

"I cannot understand what is with some of you women," she protested as Annette's fingers scrubbed her head harder than she wished.

"What are you complaining about?" she asked, scrubbing harder over her protests. "You need to toughen up or you won't make it in the world alone. Believe me, I know."

Suzette closed her eyes to the sting of soap and stopped struggling with the inevitable. The woman was not going to leave her alone until she finished clawing the daylights out of her. The fragrant scent of lavender brought some comfort, which made her feel pretty after months of smelling awful and looking ugly.

"There. That should do it. Close your eyes."

Annette poured another bucket of water over Suzette's head, slower this time, rubbing the soap residue from her hair until it squeaked between her fingers. Suzette kept her eyes and mouth closed until the ordeal ended.

When she finished, Annette rose, grabbed a large, fluffy white towel, and handed it to Suzette.

"Probably looks familiar, huh? From the washhouse."

She took the towel in her hands and stepped out of the tub. Suzette patted her hair, taking the moisture from her locks, and then turned to dry her body. When she was finished, she quickly wrapped the towel to cover her nakedness.

"Satisfied?"

Annette smiled. "Not quite," she announced smugly, leading her out of the bath chamber and back into her room. When they entered, Suzette saw Nadine propped up in her bed reading a book.

"Ah, the mouse has bathed I see," she drawled.

"Yes, but I'm not done yet," announced Annette.

She led Suzette to the vanity where she sat down. Annette picked up a brush to work the tangles from her hair.

"Ouch!" Suzette screamed, protesting her rough pulling of her wet locks.

"You know, your hair is quite pretty. I love auburn with a tint of red. We have all kinds here, as you can see. I'm the fiery redhead. Nadine over there is the blond of them all! The darkies from Africa and the Orient, their hair is black as the midnight skies."

"How many?"

"How many what?"

"How many girls does Madame Laurent have here?"

"Thirty," quipped Nadine. "Thirty whores and thirty rooms." She laughed. "You're number thirty!"

Suzette glared back at Nadine's reflection in the mirror, convinced she would never like her. In fact, she wondered if she would ever like any of them. They were no better than the hardened women of the washhouse. They only dressed better, smelled nicer, and drank more expensive alcohol.

With the final stroke of the brush, Annette pulled her hair behind her head and fastened it with a ribbon.

"There," she said, looking proudly at her creation, "It should be dry by the time we get to the Bureau."

"Mind if we borrow some undergarments?" she asked, walking over to a chest of drawers.

Nadine raised her brow in protest, but relented. "Sure."

Annette pulled open her drawer and chose a few items, along with stockings. She then walked to the closet and rummaged through dresses.

"Here, try this one. Madame Laurent will give you an advance, and you can buy some new clothes. For today, wear this dress." She laid the undergarments and dress on her bed, and turned to leave the room. "I'll go get ready and meet you downstairs in fifteen minutes."

Suzette looked over at Nadine, who was staring at her wrapped in a towel. She wanted to get dressed in her room, not on the wet floor of the bath chamber.

"Would you mind not watching me," Suzette implored.

"God, you're pathetic." She swung her feet around the edge of the bed, stood up, and headed for door. "You better get used to bearing everything."

After the door opened and slammed shut, Suzette mumbled, "Good riddance," and dropped the towel to the floor. She was determined to hold onto her last ounce of dignity as long as possible.

* * *

The carriage pulled up to the Bureau des Mouers located near the Prefecture of Police in the Île de la Cité. Suzette stepped out with Annette by her side and looked at the stark stone building looming upward.

Annette knew exactly where to go and what procedures needed to be followed. It was her responsibility to bring new hires for registration. She looked at Suzette and saw the uneasiness across her face.

"This is how it is, dearie. You'll be interviewed first by one of the brothel inspectors. He'll ask you questions, but I won't be able to accompany you during that process. It's no big deal," she sighed. "The usual stuff—mother, father, where you live, and so on."

Suzette nodded and willingly allowed Annette to take her hand as she led her up the steps. "Come on. Let's get on with it."

Once through the double doors, they stood in a foyer, and Annette stopped to give Suzette instructions before approaching the counter.

"They'll ask you why you want to be a prostitute, so come up with something good, will you? We don't want you getting rejected, now do we?"

Annette watched Suzette's frightened eyes widen. "After you answer all the questions, he'll give you a card to read with the restrictions, some of which are totally ludicrous, but we have to promise to be good little girls, or we'll visit the local jail."

Suzette felt like turning around and running out the door. The next bit of news nearly caused her to faint, while Annette, on the other hand, appeared to enjoy giving her the priceless details.

"After that comes the fun part. You'll have to go to the Bureau of Sanitaire for an examination by a doctor." She leaned into Suzette's ear and whispered. "He has to check your private parts to make sure you don't have diseases and such."

Suzette pulled away from her in horror. "You can't be serious?"

"What?" Annette laughed. "Never had a man look at you down there?" she teased, lowering her eyes to her pelvis area. "Every fifteen days, he comes to the brothel to take a peek at you. You best get used to it." She reached out her hand and playfully tickled her waist.

Suzette pulled back, appalled. "I can't do this," she pleaded, turning away toward the door. "Why doesn't she just let me work as a housemaid or something?"

Annette grabbed Suzette's wrist to prevent her from leaving. "Because, honey, you're a pretty one, that's why. She'll make money off you, and even more opening night, if you get my drift." Annette winked.

Suzette didn't quite understand her meaning at first, but then it became all too clear as they proceeded down the hallway to the counter. Madame Laurent was going to sell her virginity for a high price.

"She's here to register," Annette blurted out at the officer behind the desk. "You know what kind I mean, don't you sweetheart," she said, dripping seduction off her lips, leaning her elbows on the counter, and batting her eyelashes flirtatiously. The officer lifted his gaze and smiled, recognizing Annette.

"A new one, eh?" He looked at Suzette, enjoying the vision. "Have a seat then over there." The officer pointed to a row of chairs alongside the wall. "One of the inspectors will call you in a minute."

Annette grabbed Suzette's arm again and led her over to a chair to sit down. Suzette fidgeted the entire time, while Annette hummed an Irish tune underneath her breath, low and soft. A few minutes later, a man dressed in a blue police uniform walked out and handed a bundle of paperwork to the clerk behind the desk. He picked up a clipboard, turned his head, and glanced over at them.

"Both of you or just one?"

"Just her," Annette quipped, pointing her finger. "I already got my card! She took her card out of her pocketbook and waved it at the inspector like a flag. "See, dearie! Carrying it like a good little girl, I am."

He scowled at Annette and growled at Suzette. "Come with me."

Suzette stood up and followed nervously behind him until they came into an office. He closed the door and motioned for her to sit in a chair before his desk. She did, and then looked at the inspector, eyeing his appearance.

The officer looked bad-tempered and annoyed, as he fiddled with papers. Suzette concluded he was middle-aged due to his graying temples. His potbelly rested on top of his trouser belt, but his uniform was clean and pressed. A mustache decorated his upper lip and curled at the ends, meeting his long burly sideburns. On his lapel he wore a silver badge with large engraved letters, M. DUBOIS, BROTHEL INSPECTOR.

"Just have to ask you the usual questions," he announced, breaking the silence between them.

Suzette met his eyes, and she was thankful he had softened his harsh tone. The first question of many spewed out of his mouth, while Suzette's palms rested upon her bobbing knees.

"Name?"

Suzette was momentarily distracted by the office interior and didn't answer. The inspector bellowed to regain her attention.

"Name, I said!"

"Excuse me, Monsieur." She focused and swallowed the lump in her throat. "It's Suzette Camille Rousseau." She tilted her head as she watched the inspector dip his quill into the inkwell and scratch her name across the paper form.

"Age?"

"Eighteen."

"Place of birth?" He paused for a moment and then cursed. "Damn this pen." Clearly irritated, he tapped the end into the inkwell once again, not raising his head in Suzette's direction. He cleared his throat, indicating he was waiting once more for her to answer his question.

"Paris. I was born in Paris," she blurted.

"Are you married, widowed, or celibate?"

"I'm single," she answered, thinking it an odd sort of question, convinced a married woman would never prostitute her body.

He lifted his eyes and reiterated, "Are you celibate?"

"I'm chaste, if that's what you mean," she responded tersely.

"Are your parents living?"

"They are dead."

He blinked, and then raised his head to look at her. "Pardon me, Mademoiselle. I am sorry." He continued in a business-like tone. "What was your deceased father's occupation?"

"He was a professor at the University of Paris."

"Do you have any children?"

"No." She mused over the absurd question. *Does he think I'm like the Virgin Mary or something, able to conceive in a chaste state?* The suggestion, on the other hand, reminded her of the distinct possibility that her new occupation could result in that awful consequence. Ignorant of any means of birth control, she feared the possibility. *What will happen then? Will Madame Laurent kick me out on the street anyway?* Her anxious thoughts were interrupted by another question.

"How long have you lived in Paris?"

"I was born here, remember?" The irritated tone of her voice caused the inspector to lift his brow and glance at Suzette with a warning gaze.

"I've lived here all my life," she said softly.

"Have you ever been arrested?"

"No, Inspector, I have not."

"Have you ever practiced prostitution anywhere else?"

Silly damn questions, she thought to herself. She had just answered his question about never having been with a man. "I think I answered that earlier."

"Hum, that's right—chaste." He cleared his voice for the next question and looked directly into Suzette's eyes.

"I apologize, Mademoiselle, for the inconvenient question, but I must ask you the following. Do you have any venereal diseases?"

"I think you already know the answer to that one too. No." Suzette tried to be patient, but the questions were insulting and funny at the same time. A nervous giggle escaped her lips, thinking this entire process a sham.

The inspector raised a brow over his applicant's reaction. "Is there something funny?"

"No, Monsieur," she replied, quickly wiping the silly grin from her face. "Nervous . . . I'm just nervous."

"All right then." He dipped the pen in the inkwell once again for a fresh flow. "Education?"

"Yes, I have finished school. My father educated me well." For some reason, Suzanne felt compelled to emphasize her intelligence, trying to find an ounce of dignity in the moment.

"Final question." The inspector laid down his pen and clasped his hands together, resting them upon the desktop. "Tell me, Mademoiselle, what is your reason for registering as a prostitute? Since you claim you are still a virgin, perhaps I should direct you to a religious institution to, shall we say, convert your thought processes. However, you seem intent to pursue this course of action."

Suzette thought for a moment. This was the question Annette warned her about, and she needed a good answer. What if she told him that she had been blackmailed into joining the brothel? Perhaps squealing that Madame Laurent was forcing her to be a whore would get her out of the situation. However, when she remembered all the threats she was sure to carry out, Suzette feared the repercussions that awaited her for making such an accusation. If she did, she would be back on the streets, perhaps spending the night on a park bench or sidewalk or door stoop in some alley. Madame Laurent's words echoed in her mind telling her of the consequences.

"You'll no doubt be raped within a week because you'll have no one to protect you, diseased within a month, and dead within three."

"I'm hungry," she blurted out in a shaky voice. "I am also homeless, penniless, and alone. I have been offered a job that provides good food and housing. Is that reason enough?"

The inspector picked up his pen, jotted down a few lines, and said nothing further. Suzette wondered what he was thinking, but his face expressed no empathy, only indifference. No doubt, in his mind, she was just another throwaway like the hundreds of other girls who probably sat in the same chair. The only thing left of value in her life was her body.

"All right. Here is your registration card. Please take this back to Madame Laurent as proof of your compliance with the law."

He handed the card to Suzette. "A few more matters before you leave, Mademoiselle. There are the rules for prostitutes in Paris."

The inspector continued in what sounded to Suzette like a rehearsed speech. He droned on about the rules of her trade and instructed her in one last act.

"I am required to have you read the regulations to me aloud before you depart, in case you have any questions. It's imperative as a prostitute that you are fully aware of the law and consequences of disobedience."

Suzette looked at the small card and turned it over in her hand. Like a student reciting her lessons to her teacher, she began reading her obligations as a prostitute.

"OBLIGATIONS AND RESTRICTIONS IMPOSED ON PUBLIC WOMEN."

Stopping for a moment, she glanced up to see the inspector's eyes intently watching her performance.

"Public women are called upon to present themselves at the dispensary for examination, once at least every fifteen days."

Suzette continued reading the regulations. She must carry the card at all times, was forbidden to practice on the streets, and must dress modestly without bright colors. The lengthy directives read like orders to a criminal who was being locked up in a prison. There were regulations where she could stand, where she could walk, and how to look out a window. When she was finished with the recitation, she wanted to burst out laughing.

Finally, she came to the end and looked at the inspector.

"Well, do you have any questions?"

"No, sir."

"I hope you sense the severity of disobeying the law, Mademoiselle. I would hate for our next meeting to find you behind bars, oui?"

Frightened, she hoped to God that she could remember all the rules. "No, Monsieur, I do not wish to see you again either, I assure you."

"Next, you must go to the Bureau of Sanitaire to be medically examined," he announced. "When the physician has declared you free of disease, you are free to return to Madame Laurent and report for work. Every fifteen days, you must submit to a physical examination at the brothel whenever the physician arrives. Do you understand?"

"Yes."

Embarrassed and humiliated, Suzette stood up, curtsied in respect, and walked out of the office back to the lobby. She tucked her registration card into the bottom of her purse. Annette rose from the chair and came to Suzette's side.

"Makes you feel like trash. I know."

"I hate Madame Laurent," she spat.

"You just don't get it, do you? She's saving your life, yet you hate her?"

She took Suzette's hand. "Come on. The Bureau of Sanitaire is just around the corner. Now you can enjoy the next round of business."

* * *

When the last moment of unending embarrassment concluded, Suzette pulled up the sheet over her naked body, suppressing her tears in front of the physician. She sat on the edge of the examination table. There were no words to describe the shame burning through her veins.

A dreadful acceptance of her fate sickened her soul. She watched the physician write notes on a piece of paper and waited for further direction. The room was silent except for Suzette's whimpering. When he finished, he folded the piece of note, slipped it in an envelope, and handed it to Suzette.

"I see you are a virgin," he said, with a raised brow. "Make sure you do not skip the regular examinations like some girls do. Madame Laurent's establishment is fairly clean, but the clientele is not always guaranteed to be disease-free." He stood up and headed for the door. "You may get dressed," he instructed but hesitated leaving. "Has anyone spoken to you about birth control, Mademoiselle?"

"No, doctor, I have no idea what to do or if anything can be done."

"Well, there are methods the girls at the brothel will no doubt talk to you about. I suggest you have a heart-to-heart talk with another woman in the same profession about such matters."

"All right. I will."

Suzette watched the physician leave the room and close the door behind him. As soon as the latch clicked, Suzette burst into tears. A moment later, someone knocked. She tried to control her emotions as the door opened. It was Annette. Suzette slid off the examining table with the sheet wrapped around her shaking body.

"You survived, I see. You'll get used to it."

For the first time, she saw a glimpse of compassion on Annette's face, and Suzette took the morsel offered.

"It was horrid."

"Come on now, get dressed. You'll feel better."

Whatever virtue she possessed died at the hands of the doctor. Suzette dropped the sheet baring her naked body before Annette. When she finished dressing, Annette escorted her outside, waving down a carriage for their ride back to the brothel.

"Come on, we need to get back. We have business to attend to before seven. Besides, I'm hungry."

CHAPTER 9

Suzette, upon her return, was told to proceed to Madame Laurent's office. She rapped softly on the door until she heard the cold and unyielding voice bid her entrance. She approached the desk with envelope in hand and stood tall waiting to be told what to do. Suzette glared at her employer feeling no endearment for her whatsoever.

"Give me the report," she demanded.

Suzette handed over the documents angry over the smirk of victory written across Madame Laurent's face. She motioned for her to have a seat, but Suzette didn't budge.

"Relax, Suzette! It will be quite all right. You worry far too much about this entire matter. Now sit!"

She plopped herself in the chair and watched Madame Laurent open the envelope. After pulling out the papers, she read the contents.

"God! Bureau des Mouers. What a waste. I wish they'd shut the wretched office down."

She placed the certificate of approval in a pile of papers on the left of her desk and then glanced at the doctor's notes. "I see you have passed your medical examination," she noted. "My God, you *are* a virgin!"

"Did you think I was lying?" replied Suzette indignantly.

"Perhaps," she said, scanning over the doctor's report. "Most Parisian girls are quite anxious to lose their virginity as soon as possible. Frankly, I find it interesting that you have not." She lifted her eyes to Suzette. "So, did the good inspector try to talk you out of it or suggest referral to a religious institution?"

"He mentioned a religious institution, yes."

"Which inspector interviewed you, might I ask?

"Inspector Dubois."

"Ah, he's one of the better ones. A little more, shall we say, polite during his interrogation than some others."

"So, what is to happen with me next?" Suzette asked, curious to know when she'd be thrown to the wolves.

Amused over her question, Madame Laurent leaned back in her red leather chair and studied Suzette like a piece of merchandise. "Well, to be quite frank, Suzette, you're not exactly what I would term saleable at the moment. Your hair and the condition of your skin are atrocious and will need to be taken care of before I let any of my patrons touch you."

She picked up her quill and started to jot down a few words on a piece of paper. Suzette strained her eyes to see what it was, but couldn't tell.

"I have plans for you already. You might be surprised to know that you're a commodity that I must sell to the highest bidder. Virgins bring a pretty price, and I intend to use that fact to my advantage."

Suzette was not surprised that Madame Laurent possessed calculated and heartless plans regarding the sale of her virtue.

"Well, don't look so surprised. This is a business, not a boarding house. I run it as a business—to make money." She shuffled a few papers around then turned her attention back to Suzette.

"Let me go over a few simple things before I have one of our girls take you to your quarters. We have thirty rooms here in the Chabanais and thirty girls. By law, we are not allowed more girls than rooms. Foolish and stifling regulations indeed," she complained. "Otherwise, I'd have more girls if I could!"

Suzette remembered Nadine's words—*"thirty rooms, thirty whores."*

"All of my girls are provided room and board as part of their compensation, if they wish. I know you only have the borrowed clothes upon your back, but I do not pay for your personal clothing and incidentals. It must come out of your own pay. I'm more than happy to advance you money since you have none, but you will be indebted to me. I shall subtract what you owe me over the course of your employment during the next few months. Do we understand each other?"

"Yes, Madame."

"I do provide my girls a large assortment of lingerie, enticing gowns, and regional costume dress for work. However, I prefer to purchase the outfits myself that I think are best for my clientele's pleasure and the rooms where the girls are assigned." Leaning back in her chair, she eyed Suzette and then reiterated her good fortune.

"You are fortunate, Suzette, even if you do not realize it. You may not like where you are at the moment, but at least you are alive, warm, and fed."

Suzette still possessed unanswered questions, one of which was the curious opening that she now filled. "What happened to the other girl before me? Why do you now have twenty-nine instead of thirty? Did she quit or something?"

Madame Laurent raised one brow at Suzette's inquisitive question, but answered it truthfully nonetheless. "The girl before you, unfortunately, caught syphilis. I cater to the best of clientele so that my girls remain disease-free; however, one of my patrons apparently found pleasure in some street trash and was infected. It angers me when a perfectly good employee of mine contracts the insidious disease and is sent to the hospital. He, on the other hand, has been banned from my establishment."

She stood from her desk and came over to her side. Suzette found no compassion in her eyes—only superiority.

"As far as why I chose you, I have my reasons." Madame Laurent took her hand lifting Suzette's chin upward. "You have a sense of royalty about your demeanor. Once the rosebud is open, you will be perfect for the Louis XV

Chambre. I'll adorn you like a queen, and no doubt the men will treat you as one." Her gaze lingered on the innocent face she held captive. "Well, at least most of them will."

Suzette followed Madame Laurent out the door. "I'll have Nadine show you around and give you the grand tour."

As they entered the parlor, Suzette was surprised to see it filled with perfumed, seductive women waiting for patrons to arrive. The afternoon had slipped by, and it was nearly seven o'clock, the legal hour when the brothel could open.

A variety of prostitutes in the selection parlor lounged on divans and chairs, scantily dressed with low-cut bodices. The opulent room she had admired as a laundress turned into a scene of sirens waiting for their prey. Suzette's heart sank at the thought that she, too, would soon be among the group waiting to be picked and deflowered.

"Nadine, come here."

Nadine stood up and answered her mistress. She wore a Dutch-like purple gown. Her blond hair glistened, resembling the sun, cascading down her back and chest.

"Do me a favor, dear, and give Suzette a tour, will you, before the evening onslaught? When you are finished, escort her back to her room, but get her a quick bite to eat from the kitchen first. She missed supper."

Madame Laurent left, and Nadine smirked at her assignment who still wore her undergarments. She examined Suzette from top to bottom thinking even after her bath and washed hair, it was going to take some time to turn the sparrow into a swan. Nadine resented Suzette's intrusion into her room after having enjoyed a few months alone. As far as she was concerned, Suzette was an irritating bore.

"Don't look like such a scared rat. I'm just going to show you around," she snarled.

Suzette was tired of her roommate's constant demeaning tone. "Look," she said glaring back. "I'm not a rat, and I'm not scared. I'm just disgusted that I even have to be here with people like you!"

"You think you're better than us?" Heads in the room turned to watch the loud disagreement ensuing between the two women.

"Give it a couple of weeks, honey, and you'll be just like the rest of us whores—happy, satisfied, and not so high and mighty."

The girls in the room giggled, and Nadine smiled at the affirmation received from her coworkers. She turned and walked out toward the foyer. "Follow me and I'll give you the grand tour."

Nadine led the way upstairs, and Suzette peered once again at the nude artwork and magnificent crystal chandelier. When they had reached the top, she stopped and waited for Suzette to join her side.

"There are thirty rooms in the brothel, all quite unique and decorated differently. Madame Laurent has spared no expense."

Suzette wasn't sure if she wanted to know the detailed interiors of the rooms, but she braced herself as Nadine began to open doors one by one.

"Of course, her investors give her plenty of francs to decorate in the finest for their enjoyment."

Suzette couldn't help but notice the sudden radiance emanating from Nadine's face. It was obvious she enjoyed her occupation, appearing happy and satisfied.

"It's like traveling the world in a bedroom," she exclaimed. "There are a variety of designs—Moorish, Hindu, ancient Pompeii, Persia, China, Japan, and Africa, among others. Then if you prefer places instead of countries, there are rooms that resemble the cabin of a ship, private quarters on a train, or the Louis XV Chambre a king's bedroom— that's your room. Wherever and however the men prefer their fantasy, we provide a place for them to live it in the arms of a seductive woman."

Louis XV Chambre. The way Nadine spoke, "*that's your room,*" it sounded more like an office than a bedchamber. Suzette's curiosity piqued as Nadine continued.

"There are settees, large beds, pristine sheets, down-feathered cushions, mirrors, and bouquets of fresh flowers adorning each chamber. The men are given a supply of the finest tobacco and alcohol during their night of pleasure."

Nadine stopped in front of a large ornate entrance, and Suzette read the golden placard bolted on the outside, LOUIS XV CHAMBRE. Every door they passed displayed a name describing its interior contents.

"The least I can do is let you see where you'll be working."

Nadine placed her hands on the gold handles of two French doors, which were the only ones in the entire hallway. The other rooms had single-door entrances. The lock unlatched, and Nadine shoved both open, revealing a large, flamboyant, golden bedchamber.

"Gorgeous, isn't it?" A sly smile curled her lips. Once inside, Nadine turned around and saw Suzette's stunned facial expression. She laughed. "Come on in. You know you want to."

Nadine walked over to a side table and turned up the lamp, illuminating the interior. The light flickered and cast a soft glow through the stained-glass shade.

"So, what do you think, Queen Suzette? Not a bad place to make a few francs each night, oui?"

Suzette stood at the threshold to a king's room and gasped. She recognized the interior from paintings of Louis XV's bedchamber and could barely believe what her eyes beheld. It was an exact replica, only smaller in scale.

Mirrors covered the gold gilded walls, along with paintings from Francois Boucher depicting voluptuous naked women in seductive poses. As she looked at the pictures with interest, her face flushed red as a beet. Each piece rested in gold frames, emphasizing the color of their fair naked skin.

A large canopy bed rested brazenly in the center of the room, covered in gold silk fabric that draped down the corners of the bedposts. Suzette adored canopy beds, and the beauty was overwhelming. Unable to resist the temptation, she walked over and slid her hand across the smooth coverlet. There were numerous silk pillows, with gold tassels dangling from the corners, piled high at the head of the bed. She struggled with a horrible urge to jump in the middle and enjoy every inch of luxury.

Nadine smiled as she saw the unbridled pleasure Suzette displayed over her surroundings. "Come over here," she encouraged. "Look at the rest."

A settee and chair with gilded wood and gold velvet seat covers rested in front of the fireplace. A side table stood by the wall, filled with chilled bottles of champagne, wine, and brandy, and crystal glasses, as well as a cigar box, brimming with fine tobacco. A fireplace with a gilded hearth lay ready, with fresh kindling and wood to be ignited if the guest so chose.

Nadine spun around in the middle of the room, her purple gown swishing as she twirled. "I love this room!" she screamed. When she stopped, she looked at Suzette and confessed why. "I'm jealous, you know."

"What do you mean? Jealous of what?"

"Because when this room came open, I asked Madame Laurent if I could be the resident queen, but she turned me down." She made a face and spoke in the tone of Laurent's voice that made Suzette laugh. "Not regal enough," she said to me. "Your face isn't regal enough. You don't match the room."

Dizzy from her twirling, Nadine flopped down in the settee right behind her with a *thump* and bemoaned her fate. "So you came along with your auburn hair and regal look, and now you're the queen whore of the Louis XV Chambre."

"Don't call me a whore," Suzette said, looking at her with contempt. "I don't like being called a whore. It's an ugly word."

Nadine looked at her in disbelief at her self-righteous attitude. She stood up and walked over to Suzette. "Just wait. You may be all high and mighty now, but once Madame finds someone to do the job, you'll be a whore just like the rest of us."

Irritated over her roommate's attitude, she turned away and walked toward the bed. "I, on the other hand, work in the Nordic room. Madame Laurent thinks I look like a Swedish goddess with all my blond hair—Vikings and all that. Some men like that sort of thing," she said, flipping her hair up with the palms of her hands.

Nadine ran her fingers down the wood canopy posts. "You'll find the clientele here worth it, Suzette. If anything, you should be happy that this is not a slum whore house. The men here pay a high price for services. Most have titles—Marquises, Comtes, Dukes—or they've made their fortunes from business and are extremely rich. Many are private investors in the brothel too."

"Who?" Suzette asked out of curiosity. "Who comes here?"

Nadine's eyes twinkled. "Oh, you'll see. Men you've heard of, read about in the newspaper, or are known by the property they own and the titles they keep."

She walked over to the decanter of liquors and swirled her finger around the edge of a crystal glass, while gloating over the rich and famous men she had serviced. "They are all so unhappy. It's quite entertaining," she added with a smile. "They marry women to have children and produce heirs, but their wives are cold and pregnant all the time. So they come to our beds for the passion and sexual excitement they don't receive at home."

Suzette's countenance dropped, for she knew it to be mostly true. Mistresses were a way of life for Parisian men, though wives rarely spoke of such matters. They just accepted it as a fact of life. Her father never talked about it, and she was sure he had always been faithful to her departed mother. Perhaps not all men were like that, or at least she hoped.

As she stood in the room looking at the opulence around her, she began to wonder what would happen in the bed that her eyes admired. What would she be required to do and at what price?

"How much?" Suzette inquired. "How much do the men pay per night?"

Without hesitation, Nadine quickly answered. "They pay at least 100 francs." Pausing for a moment, but not wishing to go into other details, she added, "Sometimes much more, depending on special services they may require."

"What do you mean by special services?" Suzette couldn't imagine.

Nadine didn't want to spoil all the fun of her education, nor did she wish to frighten her so she'd run out the door. "Oh, things like taking champagne baths with royal men and a few other quirky fetishes some enjoy." She shrugged off the discussion and looked at the clock on the mantel above the fireplace. The time had slipped away, and she needed to get back downstairs to the selection parlor before 7 p.m.

"Come on. I need to get you something to eat."

Suzette watched Nadine as she turned off the lamp and headed for the door. Nadine took both handles and closed the French doors. Suzette felt confused. The room was opulent and enticing, but what happened behind closed doors she found frightful. She wanted to ask again about the so-called special services and what the word fetish meant, but was too afraid.

"Madame Laurent is smart, very smart. These rooms cost a fortune, as well as the decorative items. She visits the Jockey Club in Paris and obtains male investors. I've heard rumors, though she would never tell the girls, that she raised almost two million francs to build this house of love! Amazing, isn't it?"

"Yes, amazing," Suzette responded in a daze.

"I don't mind her as a mistress. She pays well."

"What about the other girls? Do they all live here too?"

"There are twenty of us who live here in the brothel. Up above us is another story with additional bedrooms. The other ten have been smart with their money. They have their own apartments in Paris and come to work in the evening and then go home."

"So they are able to leave?" Suzette felt encouraged.

"Yes," she replied, studying Suzette's face, then quickly dashed the girl's hopes. "They come back here because they love what they do, Suzette."

They walked down to the kitchen, and Nadine continued to explain what was in store. "You will soon meet everybody. We have some interesting girls who work here. There's a Negress from Africa, a couple of women from the Orient, Greek, Persia, and a variety of European women from France, England, Germany, Italy, and Spain. The women from the exotic places serve the rooms decorated from their countries, and they dress in their native costumes."

Suzette found it difficult to believe any woman would love this lifestyle. Who would want to come back willingly day in and day out to be ravished nightly by different men? If they were financially free, it made no sense.

Of course, she couldn't judge them any longer for their choices in life, for she had just made the same. However, she was convinced she would never love it the way Nadine and the others seemed to enjoy the pleasures they mentioned. She planned to leave as soon as she made enough money.

Nadine quickly made a plate of leftovers for Suzette from the dinner they ate earlier.

"You need to go now and get back in your room. It's seven o'clock, and I need to get to work. Scoot, little scary cat!"

It took very little encouragement for Suzette to depart, as she feared looking upon any of the customers. She took her plate and fork and ran up the stairs to their room. At least this evening, she would be safe and untouched, but she wondered how many more nights Madame Laurent would give her reprieve before insisting she earn her keep.

She ate her meal and then spent the rest of the night lying on her bed while the girls were at work. It was tortuous. The laughter and voices of men filtered from down the hallway into her room. Doors opened and closed, and Suzette shivered over what they might be doing with each other.

To get her mind off the moment, she opened her purse and pulled out her favorite piece of paper that had been scrunched in the bottom. She had ignored the letter since she left the washhouse, and holding it in her hands once again proved difficult. For the last time, she read the words.

The past needed to be destroyed, so she walked over to a lit candle, touched the corner of the letter with the flame, and dropped it onto her empty dinner plate. The fire quickly consumed the parchment. It was over now. No more dreams of what should have been.

For the remainder of the evening, Suzette sat in her bed with her back propped up against the headboard. She brought her knees to her chest and wrapped both arms around her legs while she pondered her predicament.

Shortly after midnight, Nadine returned, looking quite happy. "I thought you'd be fast asleep by now," she said, stumbling over to her bed.

Suzette said nothing. She watched Nadine undress down to her naked body. Quickly, she flipped back the covers of her bed and climbed beneath the blankets.

"I never have trouble falling asleep after a night's work. There's something about hours of pleasure that relaxes you like a drug. I come back, and I'm out like a light."

Suzette's curiosity was more important than her roommate's sleep. She had questions she had been pondering for hours, and now she wanted answers. *Whom had she been with? What had they done?* And there was one provocative question that needed to be answered.

"Did you enjoy it?"

Nadine's head lifted from her pillow. She looked at Suzette and sneered over the inconvenient question.

"Enjoy what?"

"What you did tonight in bed—I mean in bed with men."

A shrill laughter escaped her lips. "My God, Suzette, you are quite amusing."

"Well, I want to know. I've never done such a thing," she said, nipping back in defense.

Nadine looked at Suzette, thinking she was the snippiest female in the brothel. "Yes, I enjoy it. Tonight I had a good patron, but there are others who are not so good at the art of sex. They only want their own satisfaction. It just depends on who you get to . . ." Nadine stopped abruptly, about to use vulgar terminology but hesitated. "It just depends on who is your customer."

"And who bedded you tonight?" Suzette persisted.

"Tonight, Vicomte de Rieux visited my little Swedish haven. He's quite the ardent lover and funny man." Hoping Suzette was satisfied with her answer, she inquired, "Are we done now? I want to sleep." She returned her head to her pillow, pulled the covers up over her shoulders, and snuggled into a comfortable position.

"Turn the damn light off, will you, and go to sleep."

Suzette reached over to the lamp and shut it off. Tomorrow, she would ask more.

CHAPTER 10

Owning the most illustrious and expensive brothel in all of Paris did not come by chance for Bridgette Laurent. She was a wise and intelligent woman, who was as good as any French businessman. When she wanted something, she knew exactly how to get it. After all, she single-handedly raised two million francs from investors by selling shares to sex-starved aristocrats, who wanted the pleasures of discreet brothel visits.

Bridgette loved horses and frequently attended the horse track to satisfy her occasional taste for betting. In doing so, it opened the door to becoming a member of the prestigious Jockey Club in Paris. She purchased a membership, which turned out to be one of the wisest business decisions she ever made. It opened the door to meeting a variety of famous aristocrats and wealthy men. The Grand Café on the ground floor of the exclusive club became her second office, as she flirted and struck deals with the hungry male population.

Everyone loved Bridgette, except for the women, of course. Beautiful, bold, sassy, and outrageously dressed, she was the talk of the male patrons and the disdain of the fine ladies. When she entered the Café, heads turned and men drooled. Her charisma was her power, and men succumbed to her wiles at the bat of an eyelash and a flattering word from her brilliantly painted red lips.

Thanks to her endeavors, the Chabanais was the most famed brothel in all of Europe. Painstakingly decorated and housing the most beautiful prostitutes in Paris, men repeatedly frequented her establishment. Even the Parisian government sent her visiting dignitaries to entertain, as perks to their arrival in France. Her high prices and notable clientele kept the riffraff at bay—just the way she liked it.

Bridgette was determined to have Suzette perfumed, softened, and ready for work as soon as possible. Even though her hardened exterior exhibited a lack of compassion, she was not totally without feeling—though it often appeared that way. Today, she had come to the Grand Café to have lunch with one of her clients and make a proposition on Suzette's behalf.

Not long after her striking entrance, the host escorted Bridgette to the location she often requested to do business, which consisted of a nice table for two tucked away from the hustle and bustle of the restaurant. She delivered correspondence the day before to a particular gentleman she considered a possible match for Suzette.

After ordering a cup of tea and leisurely waiting for a few moments, she spied the tall blond male making his way over to her table. A smile spread across her face, for she always enjoyed looking into his dark blue eyes and admiring his sex appeal.

He approached the table, smiled, and then teased her about the note. "Why is it when you French need something done, you call an Englishman?"

Bridgette laughed as she held out her hand, which he quickly accepted to plant a rather long kiss upon her delicate fingers.

"Madame," he said, his eyes flashing with a twinkle. He took a seat opposite his luncheon guest and proceeded to pull off is black gloves finger by finger, while enjoying the view on the other side of the table. The waiter approached moments later, and they both ordered a cup of tea.

"How have you been, Lord Holland?" Bridgette asked, smiling broadly at the handsome man a few feet away. "It's good to see you. You're here for a long holiday, I hope."

A pot of hot water and tea arrived, and Lord Holland poured each of them a cup while answering. "I've been here far too long already. I'm due to return to London this Friday."

Bridgette grimaced. "Friday? Why so soon? I was hoping you would be around for a few more weeks, but I guess it will have to do."

He took a sip of tea and then asked why he had been summoned. "So why the cryptic note enticing me to tea?"

"I'd like to entice you for more," she said, with a wicked smile. "I have something special for you."

He looked at her gorgeous body, admiring her curves and full bosom, while he waited to hear about the special offer.

"I've asked you to join me today, because I have a special task for you to perform—one I thought you'd be quite interested in accomplishing. However, I'm afraid my price might be a little higher than usual for this event."

"Special? Why am I not surprised you wish to charge me extra for *special*," he said with a warm smile. Money being no object, he encouraged her to continue. "Go on. You have my interest."

"Her name is Suzette." She lowered her voice and leaned forward, so no one would hear. "She is a virgin, my dear."

Lord Holland's eyes widened in disbelief, and a broad smile parted his lips. He sat up straight, giving Madame Laurent his undivided attention. "You must be joking," he exclaimed. "A virgin in France?" The only reason he enjoyed visiting Paris was for its lack of moral compass.

"Yes, the doctor confirmed it, and I was frankly astonished myself." She picked up her china tea cup and sipped the brew. Once she lowered it upon the saucer, she feigned an empathetic look. "She's a young woman, like many of my girls, whom has fallen on hard times. You know what it's like out on the streets of Paris, Robert. At least they have food and decent shelter under my roof and good pay for their services."

He nodded in agreement, but questioned the obvious reason for the girl's state. "She must not be the prettiest, I would imagine."

Madame Laurent laughed. "Oh my, dear! Do you think me such a poor business woman that I would bring in someone not as lovely as the rest of my girls?" She paused for just a moment, before enticing him further. "She's an unspoiled flower, darling, that needs a gentleman to break her in. I can think of many men who grace my establishment that I would not want to touch her for the first time." The thought made her shudder, picturing a few overweight, rich buffoons who irritated her to no end—especially the Marquis Barone.

"I thought you'd do well to teach her since you're so charming." She curled her lips in a sassy smile, knowing every word contributed to building his over-inflated ego.

"So, how much will it cost me, Madame Laurent?"

"For you, a bargain. Only 300 francs."

He agreed to the price without protest. It was a trifle amount to pay.

"It's a bargain, my dear!" She thought for a moment and then added, "I warn you, Lord Holland, she's not like the others. You'll find her quite interesting and articulate, though she may be a bit timid upon your meeting. She hasn't stopped shivering at the thought of her first time."

A little hesitant about the young woman, Lord Holland inquired further. "How did you come upon her?" he asked seriously. "I wish to know. Is she there of her own free will?"

Taken aback by his inquiry, Madame Laurent answered him truthfully. "As I stated before, she came upon hard times. Her father passed away, and apparently, the man was grossly in debt. They sold his estate, and Suzette found herself with the Daughters of Charity until she found a job as a laundress, slaving away for eighteen hours a day. As fate would have it, she happened to be delivering our sheets each day, and then the poor girl was fired from her job for poor performance in the middle of the night. She came to me seeking refuge. I offered her a position. Rather than sleeping on the cold pavement on an empty stomach, she decided to stay. It's that simple."

"It never ceases to amaze me," he said, with a serious frown, "how easy it is for French women to let go of their chastity. In England, she probably would have starved first, but I'm no judge of character."

"I don't usually get attached to my girls," Madame Laurent said musingly, while looking at Lord Holland's concerned face. "It's bad business. Yet this one is different. I'm afraid I like her quite a bit, though I haven't revealed my sentiments."

She held out her hand, palm up, in expectation of the full price. "That will be 300 francs, paid in advance." Madame Laurent pondered for a few moments and then added, "On the other hand, since you're only here in Paris for another three days, you can have her for the next three nights for 600 francs total. Would that suit you?"

Lord Holland pulled his wallet from his chest coat pocket and counted the bills. "Here you go, Madame." He counted each franc aloud for her enjoyment. "Here's 100 . . . 200 . . . 300 . . . 400 . . . 500 . . . 600. That's 600 French francs, not English pounds." He placed his wallet back in his inside vest pocket and sipped his tea, while watching the shrewd brothel mistress put away the bills.

"She has been assigned to the Louis XV Chambre, so you can make yourself feel like a king."

"You're such an enticer, Bridgette." Robert enjoyed his frequent trips to the brothel, and years ago, when Bridgette first opened, he was one of her early investors. When duties in London and at home became burdensome, he would cross the English Channel to sow a few wild oats away from the prying eyes of his stoic family.

His current holiday had passed all too quickly, and he had promised his father he would return by the end of the week. The next three nights at the brothel would be grand entertainment. All too soon, he would be back in London living the life of propriety that was fully expected of him.

"Well, I shall be there tomorrow evening seven o'clock."

"It's always, a pleasure, Lord Holland. Always a pleasure."

After finishing the business deal, they chatted about inconsequential matters until both departed their separate ways. Bridgette, however, lingered behind to greet a few of her other fine investors, who were dining on lunch. She considered herself the dessert.

After she was finished with business, she returned to her brothel intent on speaking with Suzette. She found Nadine sipping coffee in the kitchen with a few other girls and greeted everyone with a nod.

"Where is Suzette?"

Nadine responded. "She's upstairs in her room pouting, no doubt."

"What did she think of the establishment last evening when you gave her the tour? Did she like it?"

"Oh, yes," Nadine answered enthusiastically. "Like a little girl in a candy store. I thought she'd faint when I took her into the Louis XV Chambre."

"Good, good. She'll come around. I have no doubt of it." She walked over to the carafe and poured herself a cup of coffee.

"I've just come from the Jockey Club and tea with Lord Holland. I thought he'd be a good gentleman to do the deed," she said to Nadine standing nearby. "Englishmen are far gentler than some of our brutish Parisians with a virgin underneath." She sipped her coffee and then smiled at Nadine. "See, I'm not a heartless bitch as some think."

"Well, when he's done with her, send him my way, will you?" Nadine laughed. "He's no gentleman with me!"

Everyone in the room burst into laughter, and Bridgette shook her head. "Why am I not surprised?" she replied, laughing with the other girls. "He'll be here tomorrow evening, but unfortunately, he's returning to London in three days and shall be gone again for months. It's a shame. I find the man quite amusing, to say the least."

"Well, then I guess I won't get to romp around with him between the sheets this time around, eh?"

"No, I'm afraid not, Nadine. I talked him into Suzette for the next three nights. I thought after he's enjoyed himself enough with her, she won't be so skittish with the others that come her way."

She drank the remainder of her coffee and then gave orders to Nadine. "You have your work cut out for you. Today, I want you to make sure she is ready. Give her a bath in oils, and for heaven's sake, cream those rough hands and arms of hers as much as you can. Her hair needs to be trimmed, brushed, washed, and curled. Clean and cut her nails. Make sure she knows she's not to pin her locks up in a tight bun like an old maid, will you? I want some of her auburn tresses flowing freely about her shoulders."

"I'll take care of it." Nadine thought for a moment about the task ahead. "Of course, it's going to take some work turning a common sparrow and into a swan."

"Still jealous, I see," said Bridgette, flashing a disapproving glance. She was about to return to her office, when Suzette entered the kitchen.

"Ah, Suzette. I was just talking with Nadine. She's going to spend the day with you. I've asked her to help you with your appearance, your clothing, and other matters. Tomorrow evening will be your first day of work."

"Already?" she gulped.

"Yes, already," Madame Laurent confirmed. "Time is money, my dear, and I'm not going to waste it. You can't put it off forever."

With a sigh, Bridgette had other matters to attend to and left the kitchen. "Nadine, take care of it," she said, passing her on the way to the office.

Suzette inquired, "So, where do we start?"

Nadine smiled and reached out to her dry hair. "Well, let's try with this mop on your head. That should keep us busy for a while."

"But I just washed it yesterday," she protested, remembering her torturous hair episode with Annette.

"Too bad! It still looks like straw."

Suzette reluctantly followed Nadine back their room. During the next few hours, she received lessons in the fine art of allurement by pampering her body with oils, creams, perfumes, and cosmetics from around the world.

Nadine insisted Suzette bathe again and filled the tub with warm water and fragrant bath scents. Pouring water over her head, Suzette braced herself for the deluge. Nadine applied herbs and oils to her hair, which made her strands soft as silk.

"Some of these tricks we learn from the girls from the Orient and Persia. Beauty is different around the world, Suzette."

After massaging the oils in, she let them sit and soak into the hair, while the remainder of her body relaxed in the fragrant soaps soothing every rough spot. After months of filth and neglect, Suzette enjoyed the relaxing moment.

Nadine pulled up a chair next to the tub and watched Suzette melt in the waters. "You look as if you're enjoying this." For the first time, Suzette heard a hint of kindness in her voice, as if she was truly taking an interest in her life. She smiled warmly in return.

"Each day, you need to bathe in the morning. Madame Laurent wants her girls clean, especially after we spend time with men. We can pick up disease very easily. I don't know if it helps any, but she seems to think sitting in a hot tub does. It certainly can't hurt."

She stopped and examined Suzette's petite body underneath the water. "Besides, it makes you clean and fresh for your next patron. They love the touch of smooth, tender flesh and fragrant hair next to their bodies. Most of their wives don't bother to take the time to care for themselves like we do."

Nadine sensed Suzette wished to know more. "Does the little virgin want to know what to expect?"

Suzette turned her head in Nadine's direction in response to her question. She met her glowing eyes and mischievous grin. "I don't know what to expect," she said, turning away, picking up a strand of hair and playing with it between her fingers.

"You mean to tell me that you've never been touched by a man in any way? Not even a beau who slipped his hand over your breast or up your skirt?"

"Well, there was someone once, but he was a gentleman. He never tried to touch me like that." Suzette pushed away the memory. "My father was very strict and protective of me. I was not allowed to be in the presence of a young man without a chaperone or Papa nearby."

"Well, you're a rarity then, which brings me to my next question. Do you know anything about sex? Did your father teach you anything, or did you talk with a girlfriend about it?"

Suzette bit her lower lip and then confessed. "I have no idea what it means to have sex, Nadine. My mother died when I was very young. My father raised me, and he never spoke of these matters. There were no other women in my life to teach me either. My single governess never talked of it. I can only imagine," she said, pausing to think how ludicrous she must sound. "I don't even know what to imagine."

"Well, I'm not shy. I'll tell you what it's all about and what to expect."

Nadine sat for the next twenty minutes, while Suzette lounged in the tub, and discussed the intimacy of the human body. Her explanations were a bit crude, yet effectively communicated in detail. Suzette listened to her description of the sexual act until the bath water grew cold. Her fingertips shriveled like prunes, and goose bumps ran up her spine by the time she was through.

Suzette's facial expression during her detailed prose brought amusement to Nadine. It fueled her manner of speech, which became graphically descriptive regarding the male appendage and where it would be placed. When she had done the deed, she left a shocked wide-eyed virgin shivering from more than cold water.

"Any questions?" She couldn't help but laugh seeing her student's face turn white as a sheet. "Well, then, you'll find out the rest by yourself, I imagine!"

She stood up and grabbed a nearby towel throwing it at Suzette, who caught it before it landed in the tub. "You better get out before you look like a prune," she said, stepping away. "Dress and come back to the room."

Nadine went into their room and waited for her pupil. She was amazed that the young mouse knew nothing about the ways of a man and woman. It was unlike her own life, as she recalled her rude awakening at the tender age of sixteen, when a friend of her father stole her innocence.

On that day, she lost her virginity in a crude fashion when he raped her by lifting her skirt and bending her over a table. Rather than being a tender first-time experience, it was crude and horrible violation, and served to create the rough edges of Nadine's personality. The screams that escaped her throat during the painful ordeal were ignored by her drunken father, who had passed out in another room. Without a mother in her life, there was no salvation.

After years of abuse from an alcoholic parent, she ran away and found herself alone on the streets of Paris. If it were not for Madame Laurent discovering her one day in a café, she would have perished with the rest of the whores.

Madame Laurent offered her work when the brothel first opened, and Nadine had been there ever since. She certainly had no innocence to lose, so she was happy to take the job in return for housing and a full stomach. Truth be told, she had found an odd sort of adoration from men by giving them her body on her terms. She fed her self-esteem by being desirable and wanted, even if it only lasted a few hours each night. Nadine had grown to love the act she once despised and hungered for it like opium.

Unknown to Suzette, she had given birth to a baby girl the year before, after becoming pregnant by one of her frequent customers. She gave the child up for adoption without an ounce of remorse and never spoke of the incident again.

Suzette came through the door wrapped in her towel, jolting Nadine back from old memories she had buried long ago.

"I understand from Madame Laurent she's giving you an allowance. You're free to choose what you wish in the way of clothes. Let her know what you want, so she can add it to your account." With a sigh, she gave Suzette a word of warning. "Take it easy, Suzette, on how much you become indebted to your employer. Debt is a tactic she uses to keep the unwilling girls here for years. The foolish ones who want to leave can't, because they still owe her money they can't repay. Their greed for clothing and finery has put them into an endless cycle of debt."

She walked over to the closet and opened it up. "There are things I like very much about Bridgette Laurent, but she can be shrewd when it's to her advantage." She looked at Suzette and added, "I guess I don't need to tell you what you've learned already." Nadine hesitated before continuing. "You know that she arranged to have you fired, don't you?"

"What?" Suzette squawked.

Nadine nodded in affirmation. "Don't tell her that I told you," she said nervously. "She'll have my hide, she will."

Suzette wanted to know more. "I promise, Nadine, just tell me. What did she do?"

"Well, she got tired of asking you if you wanted the job. She knows Brouchard at the washhouse, so she paid him a large sum to fire you. She figured you'd come running here on a cold night at eleven o'clock, with nowhere else to go."

Suzette didn't know whether to scream or cry.

"But I think she did the right thing. Your life here is much better. You'll see. It has its advantages."

Nadine led Suzette toward the full-length mirror and held up one of the dresses.

"Tomorrow will be your big day—the queen of the Louis XV Chambre. Madame Laurent has a special surprise for you. It won't be as bad as you think."

Suzette didn't know what to think. All she knew was that the clock on the wall was ticking away, and her virginity would soon be lost, as well as her soul.

CHAPTER 11

Suzette's nerves frayed as she contemplated, what she called, her "evening of impending doom." The day passed far too quickly, even though she spent the majority of it hidden behind the closed door of her room. She emerged briefly for a small mid-morning snack but had no appetite the remainder of the day.

Her wish to avoid Madame Laurent entirely went unfulfilled when she called her to report to her office at five o'clock. Nadine, sensitive enough to leave the dreadful pouting virgin alone, only came into the bedchamber to announce Madame Laurent's summons.

Obediently responding, Suzette wandered down the grand staircase and knocked on the door before entering. She found Madame Laurent sitting reposed and confident behind her desk. She looked ready to give her instructions for the evening.

"Ah, Suzette. Come in, close the door, and have a seat." After completing each task as requested, Suzette walked to the chair and sat down. She studied Madame Laurent's face searching for an ounce of mercy and regret but saw none. Instead, the usual cold and calculating business stance prevailed.

"Yes, Madame, you wanted to see me."

"We need to talk about your first night, oui? Are you nervous?"

"A bit."

"Understandable." Rising from her chair, she walked over to a side table and poured herself a glass of brandy. "Do you want one? It might ease those jitters."

"No, thank you."

After pouring a glass, she sauntered over to the front of her desk and rested her derrière upon the surface, causing her bustle to billow like a balloon. A nervous chuckle escaped Suzette's lips. While Madame Laurent took a sip of her brandy, Suzette fought with her bobbing knees.

"I've procured for you Lord Holland for this evening. You shall not be disappointed, my dear. The girls tell me that he is one of the more satisfying and kind patrons we have." She smiled in amusement over Suzette's jitters.

"He's an Englishman, which should give you some comfort. Your first time won't be with some hungry, lecherous Frenchman." Bridgette brought attention to her kindness in Suzette's eyes. "See . . . I am not without some compassion."

Suzette looked at her with disdain, convinced if Laurent possessed an ounce of compassion, she would have given her a job as a housekeeper. She would have gladly cleaned the toilets and changed the sheets, than to soil them nightly as a floozy upstairs.

"Don't look surprised, dear. I'm a mistress, not a monster. There are other wolves who could have ravished you. Believe me when I say you'll be thankful that Lord Holland is your first. In fact, you're lucky he happens to be in Paris this month. He lives in England and only frequents our establishment when he's on holiday."

"I don't know what to say, Madame."

"*Thank you* might be appropriate." She gulped the remaining alcohol in her glass. Suzette's persistent silence irritated her, especially when no thank you was forthcoming. She raised her brow and gave her a warning.

"Do your best to please him in spite of the circumstances. After all, this is my livelihood, and if my customers are not satisfied, they will not be happy." Madame Laurent drew her lip back into a threatening smirk. "And if they are not happy, I am not happy. Do we understand each other?"

She returned to her red leather chair and sat down before giving her parting words. "I hope to keep you here for some time, Suzette. Do your best. If not, I will be forced to let you go, especially if Lord Holland finds displeasure in you."

She didn't actually intend to let Suzette go that quickly after her first night, no matter what the outcome. However, a small veiled threat on her part would serve to give the girl incentive to carry out her duties with more vigor.

"That is all. I suggest you ready yourself for the night. Nadine has been given the dress I chose for you to wear. I've already spoken to her about it. I expect you in the parlor at six thirty sharp!"

"Yes, Madame."

Suzette rose and left her office, closing the door behind her. She took every word of warning to heart. If she failed this evening's performance, the woman would kick her out of the brothel. Not wishing to spend the remainder of the night curled up in the alley, she decided to do her best. She only hoped she wouldn't die of fear beforehand or that her first time wouldn't hurt like her roommate warned.

She returned to her room and was greeted by Nadine. Lying upon Suzette's bed was an ivory-colored French gown, decorated with pearl beads around the bodice. The shoulders draped low, the sleeves were short, the cut was revealing. A long row of satin buttons lined the back of the dress. Suzette, stunned by its beauty, couldn't resist picking up the garment. Though it was ivory in color, it looked like a queen's wedding gown. She brushed her fingers across the smooth fabric.

"It's quite gorgeous. Did you choose the color?" Her voice shook as she asked the question. *Scarlet red would have been more appropriate for the occasion*, she thought.

"No. Madame Laurent did."

Reluctantly, she looked at Nadine. "You'll need to help me with the buttons in the back." Suzette undressed down to her corset and slipped into the dress.

"I heard she procured Lord Holland for you," Nadine replied softly, buttoning the back of the dress. "He's a good man. His father is a Duke, but Robert visits here often."

"Robert?" Suzette questioned. "Is that his name?"

"Yes. I've been with him a few times. Madame Laurent did well arranging him for you. There are some who turn your stomach."

Finished with the long row of buttons, Nadine turned her around and arranged the curls of Suzette's hair. She fluffed her auburn tresses on the sides for a little more volume, and then smiled at how pretty Suzette looked adorned in ivory like a porcelain wedding doll.

"You look like a scared rat, honey. You need to relax. It's not all that bad, believe me. He'll be gentle, if I know him."

Suzette shook her head, unable to speak. Her throat had closed minutes before, and she wondered if she would even be able to utter a word to the man when the time came.

Nadine took a bottle of perfume from her vanity and gave Suzette a few drops in strategic places. She also dabbed a bit more rouge on her white cheeks drained of blood. On the other hand, red blotches started to creep up her neck from nerves. It was hopeless. Pale or red, nothing was to be done. A familiar twinge of jealousy over not being queen of the Chambre crept into Nadine's heart.

"We should go now. It's almost six thirty. Laurent wants us in the selection parlor before seven o'clock. She'll come and get you when the time comes to meet your patron."

Suzette followed Nadine out of their bedchamber and down the long corridor to the grand staircase. The closer her feet came to the foyer, the more feeling drained from her legs. Her entire body grew numb. The trip felt like a death march, and Nadine had been chosen to lead her to the executioner.

They entered the parlor, and she observed the entire selection room filled with voluptuous women. All the girls lounged either on the settees or on chairs. Some stood in groups chatting. Adorned in their finery, the stifling scent of perfume gagged Suzette as she entered. She admired how gorgeous they appeared, most carrying fans, fluttering about like butterflies. Some wore exotic costumes to match their rooms, and Suzette was fascinated by the variety of ethnic women, most of whom she had not met.

Madame Laurent appeared to be examining each like goods on a shelf for sale. Suzette's stomach churned from nerves, and a slight wave of nausea flowed through her body. Too nervous to sit, she stood with Nadine by a large potted palm next to the wall. Mindlessly, she reached out and began fiddling with one of the beads on her bodice.

When she took a closer look at some of the woman, Suzette couldn't help but notice some wore practically nothing. The kitchen staff wandered out to speak with Madame Laurent, and Suzette nearly died. They were topless. Nadine quickly caught a glance of Suzette's astonished face and chuckled.

"Oh, sorry," she whispered apologetically. "I forgot to mention the men are served by topless waitresses."

The nakedness appalled Suzette. It was then, however, she noted that she was the best dressed in the entire room. Indeed, she was clothed as a queen in order to play her part, and others were dressed to play whatever fantasy their room provided.

The clock on the fireplace mantel chimed seven o'clock, and Madame Laurent opened the front door. The hour arrived, and men started pouring through the entrance way. Hostesses greeted the patrons with smiles, took their hats, canes, and coats, and one by one, they entered the selection parlor drooling like a pack of wolves.

Suzette observed the scene with interest. Some went directly to certain women. A few words were spoken between them, and then they disappeared from the parlor and ascended the grand staircase together. Other girls giggled and flirted with the patrons, who seemed content to wander among the perfumed beauties, with drinks in hand, before choosing one that caught their fancy.

The fear of what lay ahead shot another wave of nausea through Suzette's stomach. She saw an empty chair and scurried over to sit down. Nadine had already been spirited off by some aristocrat, leaving her alone to fend for herself. As soon as she sat down and lowered her gaze to the floor, she saw two booted feet standing in front of her. Suzette slowly lifted her head and beheld an overweight, middle-aged man whose appearance made her skin crawl. She prayed to God it wasn't Robert Holland.

In the meantime, Madame Laurent lingered in the foyer greeting guests and collecting payment. She wanted to welcome Lord Holland personally, but he was running a bit late. She glanced into the parlor taking a quick assessment, happy to see girls were already off servicing the men. She quickly returned her attention to the doorway when her favorite voice rang out.

"Good evening, Mademoiselles!" Lord Holland walked over to Madame Laurent and lifted her hand to his lips. "Madame." Giving her a wink, he teased her as usual. "It's been quite some time since we've met."

"Oh, you jest, Robert!" She laughed at his antics, which were his usual routine. He flung his overcoat from his shoulders and tossed it, along with his cane, to the waiting hostess. She ceremoniously caught it as usual with a giggle.

"Fine catch, my dear!"

Bridgette noticed that he was obviously in a gregarious mood. When he had finished handing them to the hostess, he turned his attention to the parlor for a quick peek. The usual faces smiled enticingly at his arrival, but his eyes searched the room for a new one.

"I can see you are curious, Robert."

"Where is she?"

"There, dear, sitting on the settee with the look of horror across her face. She's in the ivory gown."

Robert squinted, trying to capture a clear sight of his purchase. He caught a glimpse of her attractive, but distraught face.

"She's gorgeous, Madame, but she looks not yet sixteen."

"She's of age, I assure you." She pulled him to the side away from the view of the parlor. "You have the Louis XV Chambre. Why don't you head upstairs and wait for her? I'll pry her away from the Marquis and send her up."

"That sounds reasonable." He turned around and quickly strode up the staircase and disappeared out of sight.

Madame Laurent returned to the selection parlor to pry Suzette's current admirer away. Marquis Barone was undoubtedly one of her least liked patrons. The girls found him revolting, and so did she. His character was that of a fat buffoon, whose ability to care for his physical appearance lacked considerably. However, Bridgette was not one to send away those with money. He had richly invested in her brothel and deserved service just as much as the other aristocrats— no matter how unpleasant that task might be.

"Marquis, good to see you this evening," she said, touching him on his arm and diverting his stare from Suzette's breasts.

"Madame, I see we have a new Mademoiselle tonight," he smiled.

"Oui, but I'm afraid you're too late for this beauty, Marquis. She's already spoken for."

A look of disappointment flashed across his face, and his shoulders drooped in a dejected manner.

"Very well," he said. Before searching out other pleasures, he reached out his hand and touched Suzette's chin. "Such a shame," he said, looking down into her frightened face. He bent down and whispered in her ear, "Perhaps next time, I shall ravish your body, oui?"

Madame Laurent heard his whisper and answered for Suzette. "Perhaps. Pardon us, if you will, Marquis. I shall return shortly, and we can talk about your choice of one of my other fine ladies. I need to escort this lady to her waiting patron."

She took Suzette by the arm and led her out of the parlor to the bottom of the grand staircase. "I'm sorry, my dear. The Marquis is not one of my favorites."

Suzette watched Madame Laurent take one last assessment of her appearance before leading her up the grand staircase to her waiting patron. Her hand brushed a stray curl from Suzette's cheek and arranged a few strands strategically by her plump breasts that spilled over her bodice. Unfortunately, it was too late to do anything about the red blotches creeping up her neck from nerves.

"As I stated earlier, I've procured Lord Holland for this evening. You shall not be disappointed. He's one of the more satisfying and kind patrons we have." Madame Laurent grasped Suzette's cold hands in reassurance before announcing her last instructions.

"I know you're apprehensive, Suzette, but this is your job. I have done my best to provide for you. Do your best to gratify him, in spite of your obvious fright. After all, this is a business. If my customers are not satisfied, I will not be happy." Madame Laurent released her hands and turned to climb the stairs ahead of Suzette. "Come along now. He's waiting."

Suzette sighed, reluctant to follow the brothel mistress to the waiting patron. She was dressed as a French queen and heading for the Louis XV Chambre, but her legs felt like lead weights with each step she took. Her deflowering had arrived, and Suzette was terrified.

CHAPTER 12

Robert entered the dimly lit room illuminated by a small electric lamp on a side table and lit candles on the mantel. The lighting created a golden hue throughout the entire chamber, emphasizing the French king's favorite colors.

He felt like getting comfortable, so he untied the cravat around his neck and pulled the irritating cloth across his flesh until free. The tie was tossed onto the nightstand, and he loosened his shirt collar until it flopped open revealing his wide neck. A few chest hairs were visible over the first button of his white linen shirt. He revealed much more after he slipped the second button through the eyelet. The coolness against his skin felt refreshing. Robert took off his black suit coat, and draped the garment over the back of a nearby chair.

He definitely needed a drink, so he walked over to the crystal decanter and poured a glass of red wine. After a few sips, he could taste it was a rare vintage. Madame Laurent spared no expense for her guests. The brothel was luxurious entertainment for Robert while in Paris and a well-needed escape from his stuffy life in England. The gold-gilded, flamboyant Parisian décor surpassed his dull Tudor-style estate. It was a king's room indeed, and Robert felt like one for the moment.

His stay in Paris had neared its end, and though he was looking forward to the next few hours of relaxation, he found himself consumed with thoughts of home. A few days ago, he received a communiqué from his father requesting his immediate return. The old man always had a way of dampening his holiday spirit.

Since his routine in life would soon return, Madame Laurent's invitation to spend his last three nights enjoying the pleasures of the flesh arrived at a good time. A mischievous smile burst across his face as he thought of the horror his mother would exhibit if she knew of his present whereabouts.

"600 francs," he mumbled aloud. "You would think she'd pay me for my services." After all, he was about to do her a service, wasn't he?

Robert patiently waited for his guest to arrive, but couldn't shake an underlying concern about his purchase. The girl he saw in the parlor appeared much younger than eighteen. Though he had no reason to distrust Bridgette's assurances, he couldn't shake a feeling of uneasiness. Her face held an innocence that made him question why she resided within these walls, even though the explanation he was given at the Jockey Club seemed quite reasonable.

The women he had enjoyed in the past—especially Nadine—were experienced and hardened to the life of prostitution. He felt no guilt whatsoever in seeking pleasure from their bodies they willing gave. They enjoyed their profession and shared his bed for whatever pittance Madame Laurent gave them. It dawned on him, as he stood pondering over his glass of Chardonnay, that he had never asked what the women were paid out of the francs he so freely spent each tryst.

He shrugged off the thought and sat down on the settee facing the fireplace to relax. The silence of the room was deafening, except for the *tick tock* of the clock on the mantel. His eagerness to take a young girl's virginity grew by the minute, until finally a knock came at the door. He jumped to his feet in an attention stance, surprised over his foolish reaction over their arrival.

After clearing his throat and running his fingers through his blond hair, he walked over to the door and swung it open. There on the other side stood Madame Laurent with his purchase at her side.

"Lord Holland, may I introduce to you Suzette Rousseau."

Suzette turned and looked at Madame Laurent, who gave her a little push with her hand. Robert watched the young woman, who was stiff as a board, take tiny steps inside. Before he had the opportunity to bid her goodbye, Madame Laurent grabbed the doorknobs and closed the double door behind her. The latched clicked.

Awkward and tongue-tied, he watched Suzette stare at the floor, obviously afraid to lift her eyes or take a step in his direction. He felt like an ass, so he just stood there for a moment. She didn't appear quite as young as he had thought earlier. It was obvious by the makeup and style of hair that Madame Laurent had done her best to make the Suzette look older than her years. However, Robert was keenly aware, innocence was innocence, and it permeated the room with its stifling presence.

Still holding a glass of wine in his hand, he knew he had to do or say something to break the silence. He reached for her hand, and as with any other woman, he grasped it and brought it to his lips. Finally, her timid eyes lifted to look at his face, and he saw her astonishment.

"I believe a Frenchman would say to such a beautiful woman, 'Enchante, Mademoiselle.'"

His English accent did nothing to help his charismatic, French-like behavior appear authentic. He kissed her tiny hand and held it for a moment until he finally glimpsed a small accepting smile rise from Suzette's quivering lips. Her cold hand trembled in his own, so he tried to assure her. "Don't be nervous. I won't hurt you."

Her eyes latched onto his, while he admired with fascination her curly auburn tresses that cascaded over her shoulders. Enticed to reach out and touch the glowing silken locks, he picked up a few strands between his fingers. Suzette flinched.

"Your hair is gorgeous," he whispered. He smiled while looking at her flawless complexion. "And you are very attractive."

"Thank you."

Finally, the frightened Mademoiselle spoke! He reached for her hand again, grasping it gently, and led her to the gold velvet settee in front of the fireplace.

"Please sit down," he said softly, hoping to relieve her fears. He walked to the side table and poured another glass of wine, refilled his own, and brought it back to her.

"Here, drink this. I insist. It will help you relax."

Suzette reluctantly looked at the wine. Her indecision was obvious, so he moved the glass closer until she finally took it in her hand.

"Thank you, my lord."

He couldn't believe she called him *lord*. He sat down next to her, and immediately put a stop to formalities of any kind.

"Please, drop the titles. I'm Robert. You have my permission to call me by my first name."

She grinned, then slowly brought the glass of wine to her lips and sipped the liquid. Her endless gaze into his blue eyes told him that she was fascinated by what she saw. Most Parisian women were taken by his fairness of skin, blond hair, and ocean-colored irises.

He leaned back at the other end of the settee. Suzette scooted in the opposite direction. Robert sat quietly for a few minutes, taking small sips of wine, while he observed the beautiful creature that he would soon know intimately. He studied every feature of her face and delicate demeanor. Her unblemished quality pained him, and he began to question why she had chosen to become a prostitute. Though he sat within a brothel, he wasn't a brute by any means. Deep down inside, he was still an English gentleman. Surely, she deserved some respect.

"So tell me, Suzette, where are you from? Have you always lived in Paris?" By the look on her face, his question startled her. He felt somewhat offended that she perhaps thought he would take her virginity without any civility beforehand.

A meek voice answered. "I was born and raised in Paris."

"And your family? Where are they?" Though Lord Holland knew the sad story of her father's passing, he felt compelled to inquire further, hoping his questions were not too prying.

"My father passed away four months ago." As soon as the words left her mouth, a sorrowful expression snatched her beauty. He felt remorse for asking and apologized.

"I'm sorry. I should not have asked such a question. Madame Laurent mentioned the matter of your father. Please forgive me for such an intrusion into your private mourning. My behavior is uncalled for, and I see it has brought you pain to think of his passing again." A forgiving gaze met his confession.

"No, that's quite all right. One day I know I shall answer the question and will not feel grief. It will pass."

They both brought their glasses of wine to their lips to take a sip. Each looked at the other. Robert witnessed the flickering candlelight dance off her hair, and he admired the reddish-brown color resembling a late-autumn leaf. He desired to know more about her background and hoped that she would share on her own. To his surprise, she spoke once more, this time with more assured calmness.

"I have no other family here. My aunt and her family moved to the Americas, and when my father passed away, I found myself in a bit of a predicament."

"Well, I'm truly sorry to hear that," he offered. "You are a lovely young woman, and I can see you're quite, shall we say, innocent in many ways. I'm just surprised you are here."

He paused, lowering his voice. "Frankly, my dear, it doesn't become you."

"It probably does not," she responded quietly, "but I must take care of myself in some fashion. There were few options for me."

Her attempt to justify her choice did not surprise Robert in the least. He could tell from the few short minutes they were together that her character was not that of a prostitute. He dropped the subject and took another large sip of wine. Finally, when he couldn't control the urge to touch the softness of her perfumed skin, he took her glass in hand, along with his own, and set them on the side table. A sudden look of panic crossed Suzette's face.

Robert noticed her demeanor change. He moved closer to her body at the end of the settee and raised his hand to meet the side of her face. With a tender touch, he softly stroked her skin. He let the warmth linger with the hope it would calm her apprehension and stop her poor knees from bobbing up and down. It was all he could do from laughing at the poor girl's nervous response.

"You are quite beautiful," he softly whispered. Robert slowly traced the lines of her jaw with his hungry desire. He moved his hand underneath her soft hair and wrapped his fingers tenderly around the back of her neck. Gently, he pulled Suzette toward him and leaned into her lips. Her body grew rigid, and Robert struggled whether or not to object to her resistance.

He decided not to force her in any way. Instead, he closed the distance until his lips rested upon their destination. He gently kissed her, enjoying the flavor of her moist flesh, and immediately the rush of desire flooded his body. Her lips tasted of unspoiled innocence, and the longer he enjoyed the moment, the more she trembled.

He had hoped his infamous tenderness in foreplay would eventually melt her coldness, but it was obvious he needed to do more. The kiss ended, and he stroked the side of her face with the palm of his hand, while the other moved down her back. Robert fondled the curves of her body and played with the satin buttons of her dress that he couldn't wait to undo. The smell of her perfume drugged him, and he began to lose restraint.

His enjoyment of the beautiful creature in his grasp was tainted by Suzette's unresponsive and frigid manner. Robert's disappointment grew. Her fear was palpable, and he knew that she would not be a willing participant in anything that lay ahead from this point forward. It was apparent he could very well leave a virgin intact, while he throbbed unfulfilled.

He released his grasp of her body, sat up, and then leaned his back into the corner of the settee. His response to the situation startled him. As much as he wanted to take her to the tantalizing soft bed only a few feet away, he could not bring himself to do so. He desired to undress her like a beautiful flower, slowly plucking each petal until it revealed its bud for the taking. Disappointed and fighting his own animalistic urges, he abruptly stood from the chair and walked to the liquor table for another refill. As he left Suzette's side, he heard a sigh of relief.

Silence passed between them, and Robert couldn't speak a word. He was frustrated and confused. Hadn't he just paid 600 francs to take the beauty that now sat alone?

"Have I done something to displease you?"

He poured the glass of wine, but didn't turn around in response. While Robert tried to think of an answer to her question, she apologized. It sounded more like a plea for mercy.

"I'm sorry if I'm nervous. I've not been with a man before."

Finally, Robert turned around and flashed a smile for her sake, though he didn't feel like it inwardly. He saw Suzette's distraught face. Her worrisome countenance broke his heart, and he didn't have the desire to cause her further distress.

"Yes, I know," he said softly in a low tone. "I am not mad. On the contrary, I'm enthralled with your presence. Perhaps soon, my tenderness will melt your resistance, but I doubt it will be tonight."

"I'm sorry, Lord Holland. I do not wish to disappoint you," her voice begged.

"Nonsense. It's not you. You have not disappointed me, rest assured."

He returned to the settee with drink in hand and sat close to her side. Robert boldly placed his arm around her shoulder, drawing her near to his chest. The least she could do was give him a hug.

"There's something about you I find most adoring, and frankly, I don't wish to ravish or frighten you for quick gratification." He hesitated. "Though I must admit at this point, I'm in dire need of it." He chuckled, wondering if Suzette even understood the meaning behind his words.

Robert decided to leave the flower intact for the moment. He didn't want Suzette to earn her keep—not like this. Instead, tonight, he would merely settle for the enjoyment of her company. To pass the moments, he played with her silken hair between his fingertips, yearning for more but controlling his urges. If circumstances were different, and he came upon her elsewhere, she would have certainly caught his interest.

"I don't understand." Suzette's voice shook as she watched his fingers playfully toy with her curls.

"You're not ready, and I will not force myself on you," he replied emphatically.

"Don't I please you?"

"On the contrary, I am quite pleased, but being pleased has nothing to do with it. After paying Madame Laurent a hefty price to even be in this room, I still think it's been worth every franc."

"Lord Holland, I'm afraid that if I do not satisfy you this evening, I shall lose my position here with Madame Laurent, and I will be homeless again!"

Suzette's desperation upset Robert. "She'll never know," he assured. "Don't worry, my sweet." For now, he would settle for a few moments of a petite lady held tightly in his arms. "The least you can do for me is let me hold you. That's all I ask."

Robert inhaled her perfume, softly stroked her cheek, and whispered tenderly in her ear words of comfort. As he continued, he could sense the tenseness release from her body, because she no longer felt pressured to perform.

For the next half hour, hardly a word was spoken. Robert held her, and Suzette sat quietly while he made occasional small talk and sipped his wine. Her only responses to his words were an occasional "uh-hum," and Robert wondered if she even listened to anything he had to say.

When he finished his drink, he sighed. He wanted her, and each time he thought of the bed behind him, his body responded. His unsatisfied urges were becoming increasingly difficult to curtail, so he decided to proceed with the necessary deed and get the hell out of there before doing something rash.

"I'll be right back," he announced, standing up. He walked over to the perfectly made bed, grabbed the corner of the coverlet, and flipped it back into a heap. His hands pulled the sheets into a tangled mess, and he flung one pillow off to the floor. He then scrunched the bottom sheet until it looked as if it had been used.

He returned to the side table, opened the decanter of red wine, and poured a small amount in his glass. After returning to the tousled bed, he strategically poured a few crimson drops in order to leave feigned evidence of a woman's lost virginity. Suzette blushed profusely, understanding the full meaning of his actions. Nadine had warned her of the possibility ahead of time. He drunk the remainder of the wine, and then set the crystal glass back down on the silver tray.

"Hopefully, this shall be proof enough that I've deflowered you," he said, laughing. He picked up his cravat from the nightstand and draped it around his neck leaving it untied at the end. With his waistcoat on his arm, he walked over to Suzette on the settee and bent down, ceremoniously messing up her hair with one hand and laughing the entire time.

The relief in Suzette's soul spilled over, and she laughed along with him. Robert took his index finger, wiped the lipstick from her lips, and smudged a bit along his lip line.

"If anyone asks, Cheri," he jested in a French accent, "I am the greatest lover you've ever known." He paused as he corrected that thought. "Though some will think I do my deed far too quickly!" He turned to walk to the door, and Suzette stood up and ran to his side, grabbing his forearm.

"I'm very sorry if I've disappointed you."

"No, you've not disappointed me, I assure you." He gave her an endearing wink in an attempt to allay her fears. "On the contrary, I'm quite pleased." A longing look entered his eyes, and he spoke in confidence what he hoped would be true. "I will be your first when you are ready, and it will be when you want me as much as I want you." He took his finger and touched the tip of her nose. "Perhaps tomorrow night, eh?"

Hesitantly, Robert opened the door and stepped out, closing it quietly behind him, leaving behind a stunned, untouched virgin. He ran down the grand staircase trotting like a stud and burst into Madame Laurent's office. She sat in her chair behind her desk, and he loudly announced his arrival. "I wish to speak with you!" He stood in front of her and peered intently into her surprised face.

Madame Laurent thought the worse and spoke in defense. "Did she not please you, Robert? I'm very sorry if that's the case. I shall deal with it immediately."

Robert corrected her misconception. "On the contrary, Madame. She is the most enjoyable creature I've ever had the pleasure of knowing." He continued with a serious look upon his face and began to lay out his proposition. "I've come to thank you for the next two nights of ultimate bliss before my return to England. I want to make sure our deal stands, and you will not sell her to another before the end of the week." He would not leave the premises until she assured him of their agreement.

"Yes, Robert, you have my word, and you've paid in advance."

"Good. It's agreed then. I will arrive tomorrow evening at seven sharp!" He turned toward the door, but made one last request before departure. "Don't have her come to me until after I've arrived. I'll wait for her in the room."

"Very well."

"Good! Au revoir, Madame."

He left and walked back to the foyer to retrieve his hat and topcoat. Feeling quite pleased with himself, he hailed a cab, and climbed inside for the trip back to his townhouse. As the carriage lurched forward, the sound of the horses' hooves on the cobblestone pavement echoed in his ears like the beat of his own heart. Something stirred deep within, as he struggled with a mixture of yearning and desire. Suzette was one of a kind, and he felt concern for the young woman's wellbeing and safety. The only problem he faced was how to deal with the matter before leaving Paris and returning home in two days.

CHAPTER 13

Suzette watched Robert walk from the room and close the door behind him. Alone in the Louis XV Chambre, her heart released its apprehension with a loud sigh from her lungs. Her nerves had been on edge for so long that she felt dizzy. She made her away back to the settee and flopped.

She giggled like a schoolgirl. The mirrored room reflected her silliness back to her, but she couldn't contain her joy that she was still a virgin. Suzette thanked God for sparing her from damnation for another night.

It was hard not to relive what had just transpired. She closed her eyes and pondered the moment Madame Laurent walked her to the door. When it opened and revealed a most agreeable man in appearance, she felt relieved. His shocking golden hair and deep, blue eyes beguile her so much, that she quickly hastened her gaze to the floor. He was handsome and different in manners from typical Frenchmen.

Lord Holland stood at least four inches taller than her own father did, and she felt weak when he looked down upon her shaking frame. When she finally lifted her eyes to look at him, they were level with his open linen shirt at the collar line. Just gazing at a portion of his bare skin brought a queasy feeling. Suzette had never seen a man's exposed chest and taunt muscular physique. She found it shamefully fascinating and began to wonder if these were some of the pleasures that Nadine mentioned.

Suzette's emotions ran rampant from relief to worry. Her greatest concern was Madame Laurent and what she would do to her if she found out. Should she check the room, the evidence placed by Robert would hopefully convince her that he had accomplished the task. Suzette stood to her feet and walked over to the bed to examine the crimson stains that had dried on the sheet. It represented the loss of her virginity, but Suzette still kept her precious virtue intact.

There was nothing more to be done, except return to her room and lie about what transpired. She opened the door slowly and poked her head out into the hallway looking down the corridor both ways. All was quiet, so she quickly closed the door of the bed chamber behind her and tiptoed down the hall to her room. Another swift turn, and finally she was behind the closed door, safe and sound for the remainder of the night, or at least she hoped.

Overcome by relief, she felt the need to let it all out, so she ran to her bed, fell upon her pillow, and bawled like a baby. It felt good to sob and let the threads of her pillowcase catch her tears.

Before she finished the task of completely emptying her burdens, the door flung open, and Nadine walked into the room. Upon seeing her sobbing figure bobbing up and down, she came over to Suzette's bedside and sat down.

"Good Lord, sweetie. Are you all right?" Her hand gently lay upon her shoulder. "I didn't think your first time with Lord Holland would cause such a sorrowful reaction. He wasn't mean or anything was he?"

Suzette blurted out through her blubbering tears. "No . . . no . . . he wasn't mean."

Nadine sighed with relief, but was shocked at Suzette's behavior over her first night of work. She quickly pulled back her comforting hand and rose from the bedside. "Well, losing your virginity surely isn't worth all those tears." She walked over to her bed and sat down as Suzette continued to wail.

"If you're hurting down there, it will go away soon. By tomorrow night, you'll be good as ever, and each time you allow a man to have his way with you, it just gets easier. The pain leaves, and then you'll learn about the pleasure."

Suzette didn't wish to lift her head and discuss the matter further, but Nadine seemed intent on finding out every little detail of her experience one way or the other.

"So, how was Lord Holland? Did you like any of it?"

"He was fine," Suzette said reluctantly, finally raising her head and wiping her nose with the back of her hand. "I don't wish to discuss the details."

Nadine shrugged her shoulders. "Whatever, dearie. I've shared his bed a few times myself. I know what he's all about down there. Nothing new to me." Yawning, she stood up, undressed, and prepared for bed.

"I'm tired," she said, stripping nude. She left her clothes in a heap on the floor and crawled under the covers. "Turn the light out, will you!"

Suzette was exhausted, as well, having spent every ounce of emotion from the evening, but she still needed to undress. "I will in a moment," she said, standing up. "But I need your help with these buttons."

"Damn, you're such a pest!" Nadine flung the covers off and walked behind Suzette, undoing the buttons one by one. As she did, she wondered how the dress got back on her body so neatly again. "Don't tell me Robert took this off and then buttoned you all back up!"

The act of redressing Suzette seemed a bit odd to Nadine. She knew Robert loved the sexual tease of undressing women. He was great at taking his time with her corset, slowly pulling the fabric cords through the multiple eyelets one by one with his long, slender fingers. He drove her crazy by his actions, and she often felt like ripping it off her body so they could get on with it.

"Yes," Suzette muttered. "I asked him to button the dress for me."

Accepting her answer, Nadine returned to her bed and slipped back under the covers. After placing the dress on a hanger and putting it in the closet, Suzette slipped into her nightgown and crawled into bed.

As she lay there in the dark, Lord Holland's entrancing eyes teased her imagination, and a thousand questions about his life plagued her thoughts. He acted kindly toward her, but she knew she had not escaped the inevitable. He had paid a price to take her innocence, and no doubt, very soon he would collect what he was due.

* * *

The morning arrived, and Suzette woke to find Nadine gone. Her bottled-up fearful emotions had drained her the night before, and she had finally fallen into a deep sleep. She slipped from bed, donned her robe and headed downstairs for morning coffee.

Suzette quickly learned that the brothel was like any other home. There were routines. Each morning, the girls who boarded in the brothel congregated to talk about the night before, like one huge sisterhood sharing their secrets between the sheets. Between the hours of 7 p.m. and 11 p.m., the men owned their bodies. The remainder of the time, they did as they pleased. The opulent brothel was their home, and the camaraderie of the prostitutes passionate.

Madame Laurent maintained two housekeepers on staff, who arrived in the mornings, and a cook who took care of the meals. The girls helped by keeping their own rooms, changing their bedding, and cleaning their quarters. Madame Laurent supervised the housekeepers, who tended the various rooms. Each day, except Sunday when the brothel was closed, she ensured the thirty rooms were in tip-top shape for the patrons. Like a drill sergeant inspecting barracks in the Armée de Terre, she would personally stroll through the halls, examining the conditions of each fantasy suite.

Though she implicitly trusted her housekeepers, there were days minor mistakes occurred, such as a decanter of brandy on a side table left empty or clean crystal glasses missing from the tray. The bedding, above all else, was especially fussed over. Each pillow had to be fluffed to perfection, and satin bedspreads were to be smooth and straight across the bed.

Madame Laurent, an obvious perfectionist, made sure that all was in order before the doors opened. Cleanliness, excellent service, and comfortable surroundings would entice returning clients. Aristocrats demanded attention, and she knew exactly how to cater to the egos of the various men who walked through her doors seeking the pleasures of the flesh.

Bridgette paid careful attention to the health of her girls, making sure they were well fed, but maintained their figures. She spared no expense providing the best perfumes and lotions to keep their skin smooth and delicate.

After arriving in the kitchen, Suzette poured a cup of coffee and expected the mistress of the brothel to corner her at any minute to begin interrogation about the events with Lord Holland. It didn't take long. After her first sip of coffee, she heard her voice.

"And how was your evening last night, Suzette?"

Nearly choking on her drink, she quickly swallowed and spun around, feeling a slight blush rush up her neck.

"Fine, Madame."

"Come with me. We need to talk . . . now."

Suzette's body ran cold with fear, wondering if Lord Holland had discussed what happened. If he did, surely Madame Laurent would be furious. She set her coffee cup down on the counter and followed her to the office. As soon as they entered, Bridgette closed the door and instructed her to take a seat.

Suzette shifted uncomfortably over her stern facial expression, bracing herself for a lecture.

"Well, well, I must congratulate you, Suzette. Lord Holland was quite satisfied with your services last evening. As soon as he left your bed, he approached me in my office for a private discussion. At first, I was expecting, what I thought was the inevitable, but to my surprise, he told me he was quite pleased with your performance."

"He did?" Suzette's eyes widened. "He was?"

"You are his for the next two nights as well."

"Yes, he mentioned he would return," Suzette replied, relieved.

"He's returning to London by the end of the week, so I granted him a three-night visit. Of course, he paid dearly, let me tell you." She pondered his departure. "He'll be bored, no doubt, when he returns to England. There's not a brothel across the channel that compares to mine."

Suzette was relieved her little secret was safe.

"I don't usually make such bargains, but we came to an equitable price. So, my dear, you are his for the next two nights, and then you'll be back on the block to the highest bidder who walks through our door."

"I don't know what to say," Suzette replied, extending the lie.

"Whatever you did with him last evening, do it again. That's all that matters. The next few days, you are to focus on his pleasure only in the Louis XV Chambre. Be dressed and ready for his arrival promptly at seven o'clock each evening. You can use the same dress. However, do not ascend the stairs until I tell you to do so. Stay in the parlor and consort with the other gentlemen until I summon you to go directly to the room. Do you understand?"

Suzette acknowledged her understanding of the instructions. "Yes, Madame."

"That's all. You may go."

She left Madame Laurent's office, closing the door behind her. A devious smile spread across her face over the dangerous little game she played with the mistress of the house. Perhaps tonight she would be safe once again.

* * *

The remainder of the day, Suzette pondered the strange man who had refused to take her virginity the night before, even though he had paid for the privilege. His motives and apparent kindness were confusing, and she tried to understand what he could possibly gain by waiting until she willingly gave her virtue.

She followed the required preparations and took a bath in scented oils, brushed her auburn hair until it glimmered, and dabbed perfume in all the spots Nadine had taught her the night before. After dressing with Nadine's help, she stood in front of her mirror and smiled. In all of her anxious worry over what lay ahead, she hadn't even taken the time to consider how she had changed into a beautiful woman.

Being a laundress made her feel worthless and dirty, with old clothes and shoes that didn't fit. Not once did she miss the heat, long hours, or uncomfortable living conditions. Since Suzette arrived at the Chabanais, she had tasted the simple pleasures of a comfortable life. It was nice to be pampered like a queen and turned into an attractive creature—only she had not yet paid the price for any of it.

Obeying Madame Laurent, she arrived in the selection parlor with the other women. The experience standing among the waiting bodies felt no easier than it had the evening before. Nervously, she glanced around for the Marquis, hoping to be spared his repulsive presence. Relieved he was nowhere in sight, Suzette found Nadine and clung to her side.

"So, the queen receives another evening with the lord," Nadine drawled as she puffed on a cigarette.

"Yes, tonight and tomorrow."

"Well, isn't that just peachy? You're so lucky."

Suzette wondered why Nadine was in such a foul mood. "Why do you care?" she retorted. "You said that you didn't get involved with any of them, so why the jealous undertones?"

Nadine's gaze narrowed. "Perhaps I just love doing him," she said snidely and walked away.

Suzette dropped her jaw at the crude remark and glanced around the selection parlor. Earlier, she had considered the comforts of where she lived, but the snide remark slapped her hard, reminding her of the grim reality of her plush surroundings. The scantily clad bodies and the topless servers would soon welcome the lecherous men through the doorway. She closed her eyes and fought the sickening feeling inside her gut.

"Suzette."

Madame Laurent demanded her immediate attention. "Now."

There was no need to question the order. "Yes, Madame," she answered half-heartedly. She left the parlor and headed for the grand staircase. The beautiful crystal chandelier lighted her path to Lord Holland. Resolutely, she placed each foot before the other climbing the stairs. The opulent room and its customer waited for her arrival to perform her job.

Conflicting emotions cluttered her thoughts. Part of her looked forward to seeing the handsome man again, and the other abhorred the thought of what it meant. She had to admit that the touch of his hands on her body the evening before elicited a strange sensation. It was foreign, but delightfully pleasant. After months of toil and abuse, it felt comforting to be treated so kindly by an attractive man.

She stopped in the middle of the hallway on the way to the Chambre, as she realized where her foolish thoughts were leading. *You're a prostitute*, she reminded herself. Nadine warned her not to take to heart any of the men that treated her kindly. The aristocrats came for one thing—sex. There was no life waiting outside these doors with any rich man who paid the fee to bed a whore. Quickly, she thrust the foolishness from her mind.

She reached the room and hesitantly stared at the golden doorknobs, wondering if she should knock first. Since he was waiting for her arrive, she took a deep breath, and entered the dimly lit room. As soon as she crossed the threshold, she felt a child-like shyness steal her courage. Her eyes focused on the floor beneath her feet. A moment later, the greeting of his smooth, enticing voice met her ears.

"Good evening, Suzette."

She looked up and saw Robert sitting in the settee holding a single white, long-stemmed lily in his hand.

"Hello," she said, nervously. She closed the door behind her, and then stood motionless waiting for his instruction.

"Come here," he beckoned. "Sit next to me." His hand patted the seat next to him, and Suzette walked slowly forward and sat down. His kind face smiled, and Suzette stared at the lily in his hand. It was a fresh bloom, and the strong fragrance greeted her nose.

"I see that you like the flower," he said, responding to her bright eyes.

"You have found a weakness in me, Monsieur. I love flowers."

Suzette wanted to reach out and touch the petals. He extended the flower within her reach. With her shaking hand, Suzette's fingertips moved closer until they slid across the white rim of a single petal. She smiled.

"Here, take it. A lily for beautiful Suzette." A satisfied smile curled his lips. "Do you know why I brought you a lily?"

"Because it's the meaning of my name?"

Her voice sounded like a curious child in Robert's ears. He adored her at that moment. She appeared like a fragile flower herself, beautiful and fragrant. Once again, her innocence filled the room, and her pure demeanor and lovely face struck him.

"Ah, you know then!"

"Yes. I didn't know until Sister Mary at the Daughters of Charity told me, after I first lost my father." Suzette brought it to her nose and inhaled the fragrance. "She also told me lily means *you will find happiness*, but . . ."

"But what?" Robert asked, seeing the light disappear from her eyes.

"I often find that hard to believe."

"Well, I'm . . . I'm glad that you like it," he said, stumbling over his words. The room grew silent as they both sat pondering what to do next. Robert watched Suzette, closely analyzing her behavior and looking for telltale clues whether she would succumb to his charms that evening.

Suzette wondered if tonight he would take what he had paid for, but then she remembered his words the evening before. *"I will be your first when you are ready, and it will be when you want me as much as I want you."* What he suggested seemed impossible. Convinced their little game couldn't continue forever, she resigned herself to the inevitable.

"Tell me more about yourself, Suzette. You have stirred my curiosity." He lowered his voice to a smooth, gentle tone to allay her fears. "That is, if it's not too painful for you to speak of such things."

Suzette clenched the lily in her hand a bit tighter and inhaled its calming fragrance once more. She looked into his kind eyes and let out a sigh. He was truly empathetic over her plight, and she instinctively knew she could trust the stranger sitting next to her. It wasn't just idle conversation, but she wondered about his motives. Nervously, she soothed her skirt with one hand, rearranging the creases as she gathered her thoughts.

"Well . . . I was born eighteen years ago."

A smile crossed his face, and Suzette let out a girlish giggle over her absurd statement.

"I'm sorry. I should be more serious. I couldn't help it." A flood of relief flowed through her veins, slowing her rapid heartbeat.

"No, no. I enjoy your humor," he replied, still chuckling himself. His smile remained while he waited for Suzette to continue.

Finally, feeling relaxed, she mindlessly twirled the lily around in her hand. "I've lived in Paris all my life. My mother passed away when I was a young child."

His smile faded, but his attention stayed focused.

"My father raised me alone, except I did have a governess during my younger years."

It appeared the mere mention of her father's name still held the power to produce the threat of burning tears. Suzette blew a puff of air from her lungs, suppressing the urge. She was determined to continue without becoming emotional.

Robert sat graciously, still and quiet, waiting for her composure to return with no intention of pushing her beyond what Suzette could easily share. He could not bear to cause her pain, because his conscience would reprimand him terribly if he did.

"My father was a professor at the University of Paris," she managed to announce proudly. "He taught history. He was a wonderful man, and I miss him very much." The grieving thoughts were less painful than before, but still more than Suzette wished to feel.

"When did your father pass away, Suzette?"

"It's been four months now. He died in his sleep—a stroke or heart attack, I think, but no one really knows." The vivid memory of his lifeless body appeared. "I found him dead in his bed one morning."

The vision had done its work, and Suzette's lower lids filled with tears, in spite of her attempt to push them back. Quickly, they spilled over the edge and ran slowly down her cheeks. Embarrassed, she turned her head away from Robert and wiped them away with the back of her hand.

He had succeeded in causing her grief, and regret filled his heart. "I am truly sorry. I should not have intruded. You don't need to talk anymore. I can see the loss is still fresh in your heart. Forgive me."

Robert's hand lightly touched her chin and turned her face back. With the tip of his thumb, he gently removed the tears from her cheeks. His deep blue eyes apologized for his intrusion.

Suzette found the warmth of his touch distracting, yet comforting, and she wondered how one small thumb could contain so much tenderness. The strange feeling of longing she had struggled with the evening before returned, and she shifted uncomfortably in response.

"You don't need to apologize. Talking about my father brings me comfort too. He was a good man—a very good man. I just miss him and haven't finished mourning his loss."

"Madame Laurent told me how you came to be in her employment. It appears that you lost more than just your father," Robert continued with curiosity.

Her father's debts were shameful, and she had not reconciled his actions in being so careless with his finances. Biting her lower lip, she hesitated before speaking. "Yes, I'm afraid his entire estate was sold by the court to pay his creditors." She fiddled with her gown and continued. "I was not privy to my father's financial matters, so I was quite shocked at the outcome." Suzette noticed his face turn pensive and anticipated his next question.

"But why here, Suzette? Why choose this life? Surely you had other options, didn't you?"

Suzette's heart pounded in her chest with anger, remembering the blackmail and frightful words of Madame Laurent. Still intimidated by her power, she didn't dare to speak of what really transpired between the two of them.

"You must think me horrible," she said.

He said nothing, but let the intensity of his stare examine her soul for truth.

"You are right. I lost everything. The Daughters of Charity cared for me for a few weeks. I then found a job as a laundress. As fate would have it, the Chabanais happened to be one of my assigned customers to service." She paused, assessing his reaction looking for signs of disdain. "Madame Laurent showed kindness to me during my delivery of the linens."

Even though she knew it was a setup, she felt like a failure. "They fired me from the laundry house at a most inconvenient time, very late at night. I was afraid, and with nowhere to go or no one to turn to, I came here."

Suzette looked at Lord Holland with pleading eyes, wishing to end the discussion. Almost irritated at the situation, she began to wonder why he was so insistent on finding out about her past.

Robert sighed heavily and stood up to obtain his own release from the uncomfortable conversation. He walked over to the side table and poured himself a glass of wine, mulling over her words and tone of voice.

"Do you want one?" He kept his back to her.

Suzette hesitated, as she felt the atmosphere in the room grow cold. "No, thank you."

"Very well." He poured a full glass and then returned to her on the settee. His countenance changed dramatically, and his eyes turned from calm blue pools to dark stormy oceans, which frightened Suzette. Robert sat next to her and remained quiet for a minute before speaking.

"I'm no fool, Suzette." He paused while keeping his gaze upon her lying face. "The moment I met you, I knew you were not meant to be here. You're no prostitute." He took a drink and then continued. "Believe me, I've had my share."

Robert studied her broodingly, dealing with his irritation over the entire matter. Had the circumstances been any different and she was a woman of title, he would have gladly courted her to marriage. However, that was not the case. There was no doubt in his mind that his arousal each time they neared confirmed how much he wanted to lose himself in her embrace. She was captivating, petite, fragrant, and attractive. There was something about her heart and demeanor that stirred him deeply.

"You're beautiful, well-spoken, obviously well-educated. It makes no sense."

Suzette's behavior changed over his comments. Though they were kind, she felt a need to defend her choices.

"People do strange things to survive. I never imagined I would end up here, frankly, but when you're faced with a choice between the streets, possible death, or disease, you tend to make difficult decisions that you would not have done otherwise." Out of breath from her defensive stance, she sat erect in her seat, feeling the need to posture an ounce of pride in light of her situation.

"I'm not condemning your judgment, Suzette. That's not my intention," he assured her. He set the glass on the side table. "Life can do cruel things to us, and we are sometimes forced to make difficult choices. I understand." His hand reached toward the side of her rosy cheek and lightly brushed her delicate skin.

A soft, tender smile and a look of longing filled his gaze. Suzette's heart pounded in anticipation. She closed her eyelids, avoiding the look of hunger in his expression. When she felt the warmth of his breath next to her face, she stiffened. His hand gently rested upon her cheek. Suddenly, Suzette felt flushed, as if she had gulped an entire glass of wine within a few seconds.

She kept her eyelids tightly shut and allowed Robert to claim a kiss. When his lips touched her mouth, she did not fight the moist sensation nor did she attempt to kiss him in return. He seemed content to touch her gently without making further demands. Suzette's frustration rose. His hand did not grasp any part of her body, and she wondered if he was going to forgo taking her virginity another night.

Finally, he released his lips from hers, and Suzette looked at him. She was greeted with adoration, rather than lust, which confused her.

"Why are you doing this? Why do you wait and not take what you have paid for?"

Robert merely chuckled in return. He reached out to the lily that lay in Suzette's lap and picked it up. His hand twirled it around between his fingers, while he looked thoughtfully at the flower.

"You are like this lily, Suzette—perfect, beautiful, fragrant, but innocent. Like any flower, one must not pull its petals off too quickly or the flower will lose its beauty." He set it back in her lap. "I don't wish to do that to you."

Robert stood and walked over to his chair, where his outer jacket lay resting on the back of the seat. He grabbed it and slipped it on.

"I will leave you once again tonight. It's still not time." He glanced over at the bed and reminded her, "Don't forget to mess the bed up and make it look like there was a rousing time between the sheets." He laughed at his words, but winked as he saw a faint, silly smile curl across her face.

"I shall see you tomorrow night, which I'm afraid, shall be my last."

The door closed behind him, and Suzette sat stupefied, holding the lily in her hand. The worrisome weight she carried on her heart lifted. For one more night, she had kept her virginity.

She set the lily on the settee and walked over to the bed. A quick pull of the coverlet revealed the pristine white sheets, smooth and untouched. As she looked at where she should have been naked with Robert at her side, a strange physical frustration teased her inwardly. Furious, Suzette flung her body into the middle of the bed, grabbed a nearby pillow, and thrust her face into the feathers and screamed. As her body heaved, she wished he were only a few feet away, so she could toss the pillow at the good-looking English aristocrat to express her frustration.

When she was through releasing her irritation, she sat on the edge of the bed. Suzette messed up her long locks with her fingers and afterwards stared at her reflection in the mirrored wall. For two nights, she mentally prepared herself for the biggest event of her life, only to be toyed with by a man. She decided she despised him. A moment later, she adored him. Tomorrow would be the last night, and she would make sure he'd do the deed one way or the other.

* * *

Walking out the door, Robert closed it quietly behind him and headed down the hallway. He felt pressured for time. In two days, he was scheduled to catch a coach to Calais, where he would board a ship and return to England. Precious days and nights were passing by, and he still agonized over what to do about Suzette. If he didn't play the gentleman and gently take her as Madame Laurent wished, she'd be left with God-knows-who-else to do the deed. He shuddered at the thought.

Angry, he descended the staircase, grabbed his hat and coat, and left without speaking to the mistress of the house or anyone else. His visit was short, and he hoped Madame Laurent wouldn't think Suzette hadn't satisfied his needs, but he was in no mood to speak with the woman. Something was not right, and he began to wonder if Suzette had been pressured into prostitution. It was obvious the girl didn't belong there.

I don't have time to get involved, he told himself, as he climbed into his waiting carriage. Robert snapped at the driver to take him home. He felt slightly remorseful for his irritation afterward, but recognized the source. Suzette

Rousseau was touching his heart in places he did not wish to be bothered.

Tomorrow night would arrive, and that would be the last time he would see the girl. He would do the deed and be done with it, no matter how sorry he felt for her plight. Afterward, he would wipe her out of his mind and return to England. Even though it was the only rational course of action, Robert felt wretched over the entire matter.

CHAPTER 14

"Wake up, sleepy head!" Suzette felt Nadine's hand push roughly against her shoulder, and she moaned in response.

"Too tired, eh, after another romp in the sack with the English rogue?"

She opened her eyelids and gave her roommate a disgusted look before rolling back over.

"What's the hurry? Can't I have a morning to sleep in?"

"Not today, sweetie. The physician is due here in the hour to take a look at your . . . well, you know."

Startled, Suzette shot up out of bed with a frightful look. "What do you mean the physician? I just got examined the other day!"

"Don't matter. He comes every fifteen days, and today it's been fifteen days. You still get to have the lucky look right along with the rest of us." Nadine gave her advice. "Best to wash up first so you smell decent."

Nadine put on her robe and then headed into the bath chamber. Suzette in the meantime thought she would die. Once the doctor looked, he would know! Madame Laurent would know! Panicked, Suzette started to pace the room, her body shook uncontrollably. Nadine came back and stood in the doorway wondering what in the world she was doing.

"What the hell is wrong with you?" she squawked, dumbfounded over Suzette's actions.

Swinging around wide-eyed, she blurted out, "He didn't do anything!"

A puzzled look crossed Nadine's face. "Who didn't do anything?"

"Lord Holland, that's who!"

"You mean he hasn't—?"

"My God, Nadine!" she interrupted with a scream. "What am I to do? Madame Laurent will find out, and she'll kill me."

Laughter was the inappropriate response, but Nadine found it hard to suppress. She roared out loud and then burst out her question. "What have you two been doing the past two nights?"

Suzette stood motionless, thinking of how absurd her next words were going to sound.

"Talking."

"Talking?"

"Well, he did kiss me."

Completely flabbergasted at the announcement, Nadine walked over and flopped on the edge of her bed. "I don't believe it. I just don't believe it!"

Suzette raced to her side, grabbed her hands, and knelt in front of her. "What am I to do? If the doctor tells Madame Laurent, she'll dismiss me. I just know it! I'll be back on the streets again."

"Well, I guess you could ask the doctor not to tell." Nadine looked at Suzette and understood the problem. It was quite clear. "He likes you, Suzette. You've caught the interest of Lord Holland, and he likes you!"

"I don't think that's it," Suzette said, dismissing the possibility. "I think he plans to do it tonight. In fact, I know he will or else I'll make him!"

"Well, all I can say is you better convince Madame Laurent of that. Otherwise, I'm afraid you will be out the door on your derrière."

Suzette felt sick.

* * *

The physician assigned by the Bureau to make rounds at the Chabanais, arrived at ten o'clock to examine the girls. Afterward, he would submit a report to the Bureau des Mouers for their records.

Adhering strictly to the law, he inspected each girl's genitals for a total of three minutes, which included the physical exam and paperwork.

After he had concluded examining all thirty employees, the doctor took his findings back to Madame Laurent for her perusal. He handed over the paperwork, and she took it from his hand hoping there would be no more bad news. Already, she had lost one girl to venereal disease and wasn't in the mood to lose another.

"Have a seat, doctor," she said, pointing to the nearby chair. "Anything out of the ordinary? Hopefully I don't have to send another one off to Saint Lazare Hospital."

"No, Madame. I'm happy to report all are clean and disease-free. Your clientele, no doubt, does keep the rate of infection low."

"Oui, oui. Nobility unfastens their trousers only in the best of places." While laughing and perusing the papers, suddenly her countenance changed, and a grim look replaced her gregariousness. "My God, man! Is this right?"

The physician grimaced knowing exactly why Madame Laurent had just screamed loud enough to wake the dead.

"Suzette Rousseau is still a virgin?"

"Yes, Madame. I was about to ask you about the strangeness of the situation. The young lady begged me not to tell. Of course, I had to refuse the request. I could lose my job or even my license for falsifying records."

"Well, frankly, I do not understand. She's been a private purchase for one of our best patrons the past two nights."

Bridgette stood to her feet and threw the papers down on her desk. She was angry as hell and paced back and forth musing over what to do next. She needed time to clear her head, so she dismissed the physician.

"I'm sorry, doctor. Thank you for visiting today. I shall see you again in fifteen days for your next scheduled appointment."

She bid him goodbye and quickly closed the door behind him, so that she could consider her next course of action. Bridgette needed to deal with Suzette's treachery. It was not only the young woman's betrayal; it was Lord Holland's unexplainable actions she found hard to believe. Had he taken a personal liking to her?

Madame Laurent seethed with anger. She had purposely gone out of her way to find Suzette a kind patron—yet she remained a virgin. The man hadn't even taken what he paid for, and it made absolutely no sense whatsoever. She couldn't phantom what in the world had transpired between the two the last few nights behind closed doors. The only conclusion she could come to was that Robert had taught her to satisfy him by other means.

Angered at his inability or refusal to complete the task, Madame Laurent was intent on taking matters into her own hands. She had gone out of her way to be kind to the little wench by arranging the sale of her body to kind Robert. She could have very well been a cruel bitch and broken her in with an unkind patron. Suzette had just played her for a fool and sealed her fate over her ungratefulness. It was time to put an end to their little game.

After formulating her revenge, she justified her decision easily. The Chabanais belonged to her, and so did every girl under its roof. Her desire to deflower Suzette and keep her indebted at the brothel would require action on her part. It would be risky but worth the satisfaction in the end.

She sat down at her desk and penned a note for delivery to a certain male, suggesting that he arrive early using the side door off the alley. Even though she was confident he wouldn't refuse the invitation, she asked for confirmation of his pending arrival beforehand.

Satisfied with her correspondence, she left her office and found her housekeeper. "See to it immediately that this letter is delivered to the addressee. Instruct the courier to wait for a reply, and have it delivered back to me as soon as possible."

She left her side and then went to take care of the remaining business by giving Suzette instructions for the evening ahead. Bridgette strode up the stairs stomping the entire way to the betrayer's room. Upon reaching it, she spared no courtesy and flung open the door to the bedchamber. Suzette was alone, sitting in front of her vanity mirror brushing her hair.

"I need a word with you, please."

Suzette lifted her frightened eyes over the intrusion. Madame Laurent said nothing, and simply walked to the wardrobe. Thrusting aside each hanger in anger, she found an extremely attractive black gown, outrageously low-cut, see-through, and highly seductive. Approaching Suzette with the garment, she gave her orders.

"Stand, please."

Suzette rose to her feet with trepidation written across her face, and Bridgette held the garment next to her body. She gave an approving gaze, and then shoved it at her so hard that Suzette flinched in response.

"I expect you to be ready and waiting in the room by 6:30 p.m. Do you understand?

"Yes, Madame, but—"

Madame Laurent interrupted her protests. She smirked and continued with her instructions. "Lord Holland will be arriving early this evening. He's anxious to spend his last night with you before leaving for England, and I granted him the luxury of an additional half hour as a parting gift."

"Yes, but—"

"Do as I say!"

She turned quickly around, causing her satin skirt to swoosh through the air as she flung her body toward the doorway. After slamming the door behind her, she walked down the hallway past the Louis XV Chambre on the way to the staircase. An unwelcomed surprise would be waiting for the girl at six thirty, and one sorry little deceiver would lose her virginity at the hand of another.

* * *

Suzette pondered the entire afternoon over Madame Laurent's behavior and instructions, while fighting a sickening feeling inside her gut that told her something was terribly wrong. As the hour approached, Suzette did as instructed. She put on the black gown and combed her hair, allowing it to cascade down around her chest and back. The lace covered her breasts, but this gown was terribly revealing. Suzette felt ashamed as she gazed at herself in the mirror. The reflection was not one of a beautiful woman that had greeted her the day before. Instead, a prostitute stood before her eyes—a whore. Suzette shuddered as her nipples turned hard and were visible through the dress.

Nadine sat like a purring cat on her bed, watching Suzette preen for the night ahead.

"So, Laurent told you to wear that?"

"Yes. She's mad. I can tell. The doctor must have told her."

"Probably did. He meets with her afterwards to give his reports before he leaves the brothel." As she looked at Suzette in the seductive dress, she saw its purpose. "She's making you into an irresistible woman so he'll take you tonight. That's the only thing I can think."

"Well, she's doing a good job. I feel like a whore, not a queen."

Resigned to the fact that her mistress was onto her secret, she knew in her heart that tonight would be the end. Robert would take her virginity for the price he paid and leave. Her initiation into the world of prostitution would be complete, and there would be no turning back. From that point forward, her body would belong to the lechers downstairs.

Suzette didn't know whether to be angry or mourn. She felt empty inside and void of life.

* * *

Madame Laurent examined his repulsive figure, as he entered through the back door. Taking his coat and hat, she forced a smile over his arrival.

"Madame Laurent! Good to see you this evening." He leaned into her face and winked. "A rendezvous through the back entrance . . . how intriguing!"

"Good to see you, Marquis. Thank you for accepting my invitation."

"Tell me, please, where is the little angel?"

"She's upstairs waiting for you in the Louis XV Chambre." She motioned him with her finger to follow. "Please, come with me to my office. I have something I must tell you first."

The fat man waddled behind Madame Laurent, brushing the sweat from his brow, already excited at the thought of the little creature upstairs. She closed the door for privacy and went right to the point.

"She will cost you a little extra. I've found out today she is still a virgin, if you can believe that. You may have her, but at a slightly higher price." Always wanting to get the best money for the flesh sold, there was no crime asking to receive what she believed was fair.

The Marquis took his handkerchief and dabbed the sweat from his face. Bridgette could barely look at the buffoon. "Of course," he said, taking out his wallet bulging with bills. "How much?"

"It's 300 francs."

"Done." He counted the amount and placed the francs in her waiting hand. His face dripped with sweat. "Tell me, how in the world is she still a . . ."

"Don't ask. Some foolish treachery between her and another patron who apparently fell for her charms, I'm afraid. Though he paid well for her, I didn't hire the girl to be kept as a virgin. She's yours."

He turned and put his hand on the doorknob. "It's always a pleasure doing business with you, Madame. I shall enjoy this immensely."

"She is in the room waiting for you, but don't be surprised if she reacts negatively. She's expecting another."

A wicked smile spread across the Marquis' face. The entire intrigue caused his arousal even before he set foot on the staircase. It was exciting to be stealing the little woman from another. It might cause her to protest beforehand; nevertheless, he enjoyed rough foreplay.

Finally, at the top of the stairs, huffing and puffing from the climb, he wiped his brow one more time and made his way to the door. His eyes bulged with excitement as grabbed the doorknob. Marquis Barone slipped inside to his waiting purchase and locked the door behind him.

* * *

Robert felt exhausted as he prepared for the evening ahead. He had spent the day overseeing the packing and making last-minute arrangements for his return to England. Everything had been taken care of, and he was nearly ready for his noon departure the following day. All that remained was his last visit with Suzette.

The girl's situation did not sit well with him, and a disappointing distrust of Madame Laurent raised its ugly head. She had never given him cause for concern in the past, but Robert had a sixth sense about people, and something was definitely not right.

His plan for the evening was to arrive precisely at seven o'clock and head straight for the room to wait for Suzette's arrival. If she showed any signs of wanting him that evening, he would take her and be done with it. That way, he could leave and forget the entire matter, which he felt at that moment was the best course of action. Then with a clear conscience, he would board the carriage for Calais at noon and be on the ship back to England. All would be over and forgotten.

When he arrived that evening, he proceeded as planned. He checked his hat and coat with the hostess. It was Friday night, and every aristocrat in Paris seemed to be crowded into the selection parlor. He glanced quickly inside, spotted Madame Laurent with her back turned, and took advantage of the situation. He had paid his fee already and had no further business with the woman, so he climbed the stairs two at a time, anxious to reach the Louis XV Chambre.

As he approached the door, he heard the sound of Suzette's whimpering voice and halted. Someone was inside the room with her, so he placed his ear near the door to hear the conversation.

"Come here, damn it!"

A man yelled, and then her piercing scream met his ears. He grabbed the doorknob but found it locked.

"Please don't," her voice pleaded.

The horrid sound of her begging sent Robert into a rage. An animalistic urge to protect Suzette rose inside his chest. He stepped back, lifted his booted foot, and kicked the double doors. They jolted slightly. With another thrust of his leg, his heel hit it again, and the doorjamb split.

Suzette's terrified scream reached a peak, and her pleas for help were enough to force the adrenalin through his veins to finish the task. The next thrust of his leg broke the frame, causing the French doors to fling wide open and hit the opposite wall with a *crash*.

To his horror, the Marquis' naked fat body was firmly planted upon Suzette, attempting to force her legs apart with his knee. Suzette's hands clawed at his back, and he angrily grabbed her arms and pinned them above her head. Torrents of tears flowed down her cheeks. The Marquis, ignoring Robert's arrival, was about to gain successful entrance into Suzette's purity. The scene appalled Robert to such a degree that he lost all control.

The moment the Marquis was about to thrust his erection into his purchase, Robert wrapped his arm around the man's neck and jerked him backward off her body.

"Get your filthy hands off her, you pig!"

Terrorized, Suzette screamed louder as she wiggled her torso away from the Marquis. Her vision caught sight of Robert's seething face, and she screeched, "Robert, please, help me!"

It was all Robert needed to finish the deed. With every ounce of strength, he flung the Marquis' naked body off the bed. He landed on his back with a *thud,* which shook the floor. The Marquis moaned in pain.

"I should kill you for this!" Robert growled.

Immediately, he turned his attention to Suzette. When he saw her nakedness, he pulled a sheet up over her body. The groaning buffoon rolled on the floor at his feet, and Robert continued his angry rant.

"You're a disgusting animal! I should thrust my knife in your fat gullet and be done with it!"

"I paid for her, you know," he huffed, out of breath. "She doesn't belong to you. I want what is due me," the Marquis argued indignantly, trying to stand up.

Suzette turned away from his grotesque, naked body and clung to the sheet. Robert took out his wallet, grabbed 300 francs, and tossed them into the Marquis' face.

"Here's your refund—the price Madame Laurent charged you for a virgin, no doubt."

"You English trash!" the Marquis growled. "I will not be treated in this fashion. I'll see that you pay for this!"

Robert was about to pull out a knife from his pocket and carry out his threat. When Suzette's uncontrollable sobs filled the room, he relented, realizing she had suffered enough.

"Come with me," he said, holding out his hand to her. She quickly grasped it, and Robert led her shaking body, wrapped in a sheet, to the door. A crowd had gathered outside, other patrons and prostitutes drawn by the noise of screaming and splintering wood. Nadine was among them, and Robert asked for her help.

"Nadine, do me a favor," he said softly, knowing he could count on her assistance.

"Yes, whatever you need," she answered, looking at Suzette in his arms.

"Take Suzette back to your quarters, dress her, and bring her downstairs to Madame Laurent's office as quickly as possible. Whatever you do, don't let that fat ass touch her again. If he tries, fetch me immediately, and I'll finish the job."

Suzette clung to Robert. "Don't leave me! I'm afraid."

With sympathetic eyes, he instructed her gently. "I need you to trust me, Suzette. Do as I ask. Dress quickly in whatever you can find and meet me downstairs. Do you understand?"

She nodded, and he released her into Nadine's care. He sped down the staircase in search of Madame Laurent. Apparently, she had heard the commotion coming from upstairs and was about to ascend the staircase. Robert glared at her and bellowed a command.

"Madame Laurent, a word with you . . . NOW!"

As soon as the word "now" left his lips, the entire parlor within earshot of his voice fell silent. Madame Laurent, well aware of what the discussion was about to entail, answered him tersely.

"Very well. My office then."

She entered first and quickly walked over behind her desk, in order to put distance between the two of them. Robert slammed the door behind him and stood in front of her. He placed both his hands on the desktop and leaned forward. With clenched teeth, he demanded answers.

"How much, damn you? How much to buy her out of this whorehouse?"

Madame Laurent fell back into her chair aghast over Robert's frightening demeanor. She had never seen him in such a state of anger. Even a formidable woman such as herself had the good sense to respect the ire of a man when she recognized it.

"I suppose 5,000 francs," the words spewed from her mouth without thought. "That's three months of profits I'd gain from her body."

"Fine, then 5,000 francs it will be. She's worth all of it. I am taking her with me this instant."

He opened his coat pocket, pulled out a small checkbook, and flipped it open on her desk. He dipped her feather quill pen into the ink well, scrawled her name on the check, and signed it forcefully. After placing the pen back in its holder, he picked up the check and blew on the ink until it dried. His stare bore into Bridgette with disgust over her cruelty to Suzette, and he threw the check on her desktop.

"You betrayed my trust, woman, and I refuse to return to your establishment again."

He stomped toward the door and flung it open. Suzette stood at the end of the hallway wrapped in the arms of Nadine. He approached the hostess and asked for his topcoat and hat. The night was chilly, so he took his coat and wrapped it around Suzette's trembling shoulders.

"I owe you, Nadine, but I'm afraid I shall not be returning here again."

Suzette grabbed Robert's arm, afraid of where he was taking her. "Robert, where are we going?"

"Don't worry, Suzette. Trust me." He led her out the door to his waiting carriage parked a few yards down the street. As he approached, his driver opened the door with a curious look upon his face.

Robert helped Suzette inside and gave orders to be driven to the Hotel du Louvre. Robert climbed into the carriage and closed the door. Suzette, obviously in shock, sat motionless and pale. Her condition broke his heart, and he sat next to her and drew her into his arms.

The carriage gently rocked to its destination, and Robert stroked her hair with his hand. "It will be all right. I promise you." As he consoled Suzette, the rapid beating of his angry heart subsided. Finally calm, he explained his violent reaction.

"I have despised that fat pig for many years. He's been a thorn in my side, and when I saw him on top of you, I could have killed him." He paused, considering his words. "I should have killed him."

The realization of what he could be capable of on her behalf shocked Robert. He held in his arms a beautiful, delicate creature that deserved so much more than a life of prostitution. His path, for whatever reason, had crossed a damsel in distress, and she had captured his heart. He felt endearment toward the French Mademoiselle. Unsure of what to do next, he only knew that Suzette Rousseau was never meant to live inside the Chabanais.

* * *

The carriage pulled away, and a shaken Madame Laurent walked back into the hallway to calm down the upset patrons. The Marquis limped down the staircase, his face red as a beet, spewing his rage.

"I damn well expect a replacement," he growled. "I nearly got killed by that mad Englishman."

As much as she hated to say the words, she offered her condolences. "I apologize for Lord Holland's intrusion." She leaned in and whispered in his ear. "By the way, were you able to accomplish the task?" she asked hopefully.

The Marquis lied. "I damn well did," he said, puffing his chest out like a male peacock. He wasn't about to admit defeat in the area of his sexual expertise.

"Good," Madame Laurent said, satisfied all had not been lost on her behalf. She glanced around the room and saw that her petite Asian prostitute was still available. "May I offer you a trip to the Orient this evening Marquis for your trouble? I'll even give you a refund."

He looked at the little Asian beauty, who fluttered her black eyelashes at him, and his arousal returned. "Yes, that will be fine," he said. He wasn't about to tell Madame Laurent that Robert had already paid him a refund. As far as he was concerned, it was merely restitution for throwing him on the floor.

His purchase sauntered over to the Marquis and began stroking his forearm. "You wish to come with me?" she purred. The Marquis wasted no time. He followed her up the staircase, puffing the entire way.

Madame Laurent watched the two depart and let out a long drawn-out sigh. Nadine approached with a smirk across her face, determined to ask one more time. "So, does the Louis Chambre XV belong to me now?"

Madame Laurent smirked. "Fine," she reluctantly agreed. "You may assume your role as queen of the brothel."

Nadine smiled.

CHAPTER 15

Suzette, shaken from the last hour, listened to the *click clack* of the horses' hooves on the cobblestone pavement. For the moment, she felt safe in Robert's strong arms. In extreme shock, she remained speechless as the haunting visions of what had transpired returned.

As requested, she arrived at the room on time, spending only a few moments thinking of what lay ahead. She struggled with her attraction for the likeable Englishman, so she played a game in her mind to prepare for the night. She would pretend they were married and it would be their wedding night. The fantasy would allay her fears, and if he stayed true to the tenderness he had expressed beforehand, all would be bearable.

She escaped into a make-believe world, feeling calm and ready as she sat inside the beautiful Chambre. When the door opened to reveal Marquis Barone, Suzette jumped to her feet in protest. He smiled wickedly and locked the door behind him.

"Monsieur," she boldly protested. "I'm waiting for Lord Holland. I believe you have the wrong room."

He merely shot a grin in return and began approaching with beast-like lust in his eyes.

"No, it's not a mistake. I've just purchased your services from Madame Laurent. Apparently, your lord has been a bit remiss in taking what he paid for and won't be here this evening."

The next few minutes turned into a fiendish nightmare. Gone were her visions of a wedding night. Instead, they were replaced by the aggressive Marquis. He aggressively stripped her of her gown and then disrobed in front of the locked door, which Suzette had tried numerous times to escape through. Fully naked, he dragged her to the bed, threw her down, and climbed on top. She was helpless under his mass. It was then she heard the pounding of Robert's foot against the wooden barrier.

Suzette clawed and screamed, and when the Marquis had pinned her arms above her head, Robert burst into the room with fury. It frightened her. She never witnessed such intense anger in a man's eyes before and fully expected him to kill the Marquis.

It happened all so quickly and now she was here, in the carriage, with Robert holding her tight. She wanted to thank him but couldn't form the words. Instead, she began to worry what would happen to her next.

A few minutes later, the carriage halted. Suzette recognized the hotel. Robert released his arm from around her shoulder and brought her chin up with his hand to meet his eyes.

"Mademoiselle, I am putting you up in a hotel for the evening. However, I don't wish you to enter the lobby looking like such a fright."

He was quite right. Suzette had grabbed her old dress from the laundry house, which she secretly kept after having it washed. Her hair was a mess and her makeup smudged. *I must look terrible*, she thought.

"I shall procure a room, and the driver will take you around to the servants' entrance down the alley. I will meet you and then escort you to the room up the back stairway."

He gave her a quick kiss on the cheek, and then opened the carriage door and exited. Suzette heard him mumble instructions to the driver, and Robert disappeared inside the foyer of the hotel.

The carriage lurched forward, turned down a side alley to another entrance, and came to a halt. Suzette anxiously looked at the door, waiting for Robert to arrive. A few minutes later, it opened, and his head popped out. The driver jumped down, opened the carriage door, and escorted Suzette to the servants' entrance. Suzette pulled Robert's topcoat tightly around her due to the cold outdoors.

As she approached, he smiled warmly, attempting to alleviate her fears. When she reached his side, he put his arm around her waist and led her inside.

"Follow me, sweetheart." He escorted her three flights up a small staircase, and then once through the stairway door, he inserted a key into the first room on the right. It opened, and she entered a room illuminated by a small lamp. He quickly locked the door behind them and made his way to the side table to turn up the light.

Robert walked over to the window and drew the curtains shut. A housekeeper had started a fire per his request to the desk clerk. It was beginning to take the chill out of the air. He walked around surveying the quarters, while Suzette stood motionless in the middle of the room. Robert sighed.

"It will do for the evening until I decide what to do next." He walked over to her, taking his coat off her shoulders, and pulled her closer to the fire.

"Stand here for a moment and let the fire warm you. I will pour us a drink."

Robert pulled the stopper off a crystal decanter filled to the brim with brandy and poured two glasses. The reality of the situation bore down upon him, for now he was faced with a difficult choice. He looked over his shoulder at the petite figure that stood facing the fireplace. In his zeal to save her, he had done so without thinking of the consequences. A hard decision would need to be made.

He remembered when he was a little boy how his father had scolded him for bringing home a stray puppy, and Robert admitted how much he loved to rescue anything in need. It was his weakness. He felt terribly responsible for her predicament, especially now that she was practically homeless again. *Bloody awful timing,* he thought to himself.

He walked over to her side and handed over the glass. "Drink. It will warm you."

"Thank you," she mumbled, eying the brandy. She hated the taste, but needed something to calm her down.

"You're welcome," he said, while tenderly pushing back her messed-up hair from her cheeks. "Even with a tear streaked face, you are quite the most beautiful woman I have ever known."

Suzette felt secure and safe with Robert by her side. She owed him her life, and she wanted to thank him. He had shown her true kindness and mercy, when others had not. She placed her glass upon the hearth of the fireplace, then turned and looked into his blue eyes.

"I owe you a kiss," she said, leaning into him. Suzette unashamedly placed her lips on his and kissed him deeply. The sensation of his warm touch felt marvelous, and her heart swelled with adoration.

Robert, shocked at her actions, put his glass down next to hers and took advantage of the moment. He pulled Suzette into his arms and kissed her deeply in return. As she moaned, responding to his hands that slid down her back, it aroused his need. He released her lips quickly, knowing if they continued it would end in the consummation of his purchase.

"Please, let me thank you. This is the only way I know how. I can give you what you paid for now," she said, lowering her eyes. "I'm not afraid."

Robert's heart pounded in his chest. "No," he said, pulling away from her body. "Not like this." He picked up his drink and walked back to the decanter to refill his glass. Suzette followed and put her hand upon his shoulder.

"Don't you want me?"

He turned and looked at her beautiful face. "Want? I burn for it, Suzette, but I did not rescue you to be repaid in this way." He shoved his fingers through his blond hair with frustration, as he tried to decide what to do next. He looked at her petite form, acutely torturing him each passing second.

"I must go. You need to sleep, so get some rest. I will be back in the morning, and we'll talk."

"Must you leave?" Suzette asked sorrowfully.

"Yes, I'm afraid so." He gave her a glancing kiss upon her cheek and cupped the side of her face in his hand. "Get some rest, Suzette. You'll think clearer in the morning, and you'll understand then."

"You said that when I wanted you as much as you wanted me that you would take me."

Suzette looked at him with such longing, he knew she had arrived at that point.

"I want you," she pleaded.

Robert's resolve weakened—he not only wanted Suzette, he needed her. He pulled her into his heaving chest and gently encircled his lips with hers and kissed her passionately. Her arms reached up around his neck in response, and a soft whimper escaped her throat. The two lovers released their yearning.

When a flurry of kisses had subsided, Robert pulled back again and looked into her pleading eyes once more.

"Make love to me," Suzette whispered.

"You don't need to do this," he protested.

"I want you, Robert. It is the only way that I can express to you my love for what you have done for me."

Robert stood speechless, looking into the pool of her amber liquid eyes that flickered from the moisture of tears. Her longing was sincere, and his desire intense.

A moment later, he began working the row of worn buttons encasing her petite form in the old dress. Robert's slender fingers moved from top to bottom until each button freed itself through the tiny frayed eyelets releasing the prize underneath. Slipping his hands around her shoulders, he pulled the dress down, revealing her porcelain skin. Drawn to her beauty, Robert trailed kisses across her exposed flesh, as his fingers enjoyed the smooth touch of her skin that still held the fragrance of perfume.

When he finished, he pulled the garment down to her waist and released it to fall in a heap at her feet. Underneath, her breasts spilled forth, and Robert lost all senses. He scooped her up in his arms and carried her body to the bed and laid her down on the satin coverlet with her head upon a pillow. Robert put his waistcoat upon a nearby chair and then unbuttoned his white linen shirt until it fell open in the front. He slipped his arms out and flung the garment to the floor.

As he drew near her with his bare chest, Suzette reached out to receive him. He closed the distance until he found her lips. As the moments of desire intensified, each stripped the other of their remaining clothing. At last, Robert found himself naked upon the innocence he had protected only an hour before.

"Do not be afraid," he assured her between kisses. "I will be gentle." His hands framed her face, and he kissed her multiple times, sweetly and softly, on her cheeks, neck, and lips. His tongue moved down toward her breasts until his lips suckled her nipples. He hands caressed them, and Suzette arched at the pleasure of his touch. Her response fueled Robert, and he placed one hand between her inner thighs. Suzette stiffened for a slight moment, and Robert assured her it would be all right.

"Please, relax . . . you will enjoy."

His lips pressed over hers, and his hand slid slowly upward until he touched her moisture. Suzette moaned with pleasure. When he aroused her until she seemed as if she could bear no more, he positioned himself to enter her body.

He stopped and looked into her anxious eyes and placed his mouth over hers, kissing her deeply while sliding himself into her innocence. As he broke the barrier of her virginity, she flinched and tightened her grip around his neck and moaned.

With each stroke of gentle lovemaking, Robert made Suzette his own. He had taken that which he had paid for, and Suzette had offered herself willingly in return. He felt no remorse over his actions. In a second, innocence was lost, and both their lives changed for eternity.

* * *

Suzette woke the next morning, surprised to find an empty bed. She rose and anxiously glanced around the room. Her eyes caught sight of a note propped up against a lamp on the nightstand, which she snatched and flipped open.

Suzette,

I hope you had a pleasant night's sleep. Since you are in need of a wardrobe, I have departed this morning to buy you clothes. I thought you might be hungry upon waking, so I arranged for breakfast. It should be sitting on a tray table outside your door.

Bon appetite, my dear. I shall return later this morning.

Robert

Suzette breathed a sigh of relief. He hadn't abandoned her, and she smiled at his endearing note. She grabbed her old dress and slipped it over her head before heading to the door. After unlocking it, she peeked around the corner and saw a tray on a small table. A silver lid covered the plate, and Suzette smelled the aroma of warm food.

She held the door open with one foot, while she grabbed the tray and carried it inside. The door closed behind her, and she set the tray down on a table. She lifted the lid and saw Eggs Benedict with fresh fruit. Famished from not having eaten anything the day before, she sat down and began devouring the food.

A pot of warm water was in a teapot on the side, and she poured the brew into a cup. The warmth of the liquid and food in her stomach brought comfort. When she finished, she read Robert's note again and smiled.

"A man shopping for a woman. This should be interesting," she mumbled aloud. Suzette chuckled as she thought of what he might bring back, but she promised herself not to tease him should his taste in clothing be atrocious.

She laid the note down, ran her fingers through her unruly hair, and contemplated all that had transpired. Unsure what would happen next, Suzette clung to Robert's words that he would take care of her, though she wasn't certain what that meant. Afraid of being alone and destitute again, she knew in her heart that things were about to drastically change.

Her thoughts drifted back to the evening before. She had heard Robert scream at Madame Laurent through the door just after arriving downstairs. *"How much?"* Unable to hear Madame Laurent's response, she wondered how much he had paid for her freedom. Robert must have settled her indebtedness and paid a hefty fee to liberate her from the Chabanais.

As she took her last bite of food, Suzette thought about the prior evening. As Nadine had warned, she was experiencing a bit of discomfort, but strangely felt no shame over what occurred. Something had come over her, and though she knew it was morally wrong to have sex out of wedlock, she needed Robert. In the heat of their passion, consequences were not in her thoughts.

She felt bound to him at present and somehow more secure that she had given Robert her virginity. Certainly, he wouldn't abandon her after last night. He had been tender and wonderful, and Suzette believed he cared for her deeply. Though he hadn't expressed it in so many words, she wanted to believe he was falling in love. There was no other reason, in her mind, to rationalize his kindness in saving her life or the amount of money he had spent for her rescue.

Her first time had not been as painful as she feared. He elicited from her body such unabashed cravings that Suzette blushed over the thought of being with him again. A moment later a knock came at the door.

"Open up, Suzette. It's me . . . Robert."

A smile crossed her face. She quickly rose and swung the door wide open. Robert stood in the hallway with a silly grin upon his face and his arms full of boxes. He looked like a juggler about to lose everything.

"Here, let me help you." Suzette walked over grabbed a few from underneath his arm, and then closed the door. He walked straight to the bed, flashing a big smile along the way.

"Here, babe . . . undergarments!" He opened one box and revealed a chemise, corset, and bloomers, along with a bottle of perfume. Suzette couldn't help but laugh at the boyish look on his face. He opened the next box, pulled away the tissue paper, and revealed a beautiful dark blue day gown. He took it out, held it in front of her, and smiled approvingly.

"The color is just perfect."

Suzette smiled when she held the garment and examined the delicate lace trim and satin. "Thank you, Robert. It's beautiful."

"You are quite welcome, Suzette. I just hope it fits, but I have a pretty good sense for size."

The smile on his face faded, and it caught Suzette by surprise.

"I need to speak with you. Come here and sit with me on the divan."

She followed him and sat down, inquisitively looking into his blue eyes. A fear of abandonment rose, and she braced herself for what was to come next.

"I'm afraid, Suzette, I'm in a bit of pickle, like the English would say." Robert lowered his gaze to the floor in avoidance.

"What do you mean?" she asked in a worried tone.

He picked up her hand and rubbed it softly. "I'm scheduled to leave for Calais today at noon by carriage, and then I board a ship for England."

Suzette's eyes grew wide, and she grasped Robert's hand tightly.

"I spirited you out of the clutches of the Marquis and paid for your freedom, but I did so without thinking ahead." He appeared sorrowful, but he wanted her to understand. "I assure you, I am not sorry for my deed. I am not sorry at all, especially after our time together last evening."

"What will I do, Robert? If you leave, I . . ." Suzette began to cry.

He embraced her and pulled her close. His heart pounded in his chest, while he carefully considered his next words. The responsibility for her life was overwhelming, and there was no other way around the dilemma.

"You'll just have to come with me, that's all."

Suzette pulled away from him. "With you?" she asked, confused.

"Yes, with me." Nervous agitation caused him to jump to his feet. He walked over to the window for a moment to collect his thoughts. It wouldn't be impossible, just difficult. There would be things that would need to be taken care of, but he could manage them in secret. Convinced it was his only course of action, he turned around. Suzette's distraught face met his.

"You see, Suzette, I only come here to Paris on holiday. I have a townhouse in London and an estate in Surrey, where my parents reside. There are duties that I must attend to, and my father has written and called me home. I must go."

He heaved a frustrated sigh, and walked back to sit down next to her again. Robert held her hand for reassurance. "If I leave you here, I cannot care for you. I do not know when I shall return to Paris. My only recourse is to take you with me back to England. There, I can provide for you a proper residence and help you get back on your feet so that you are self-sufficient."

Suzette slid her hand away. "But you are asking me to leave my home and all I've known my entire life. How can I do such a thing?"

"How can you not?" He needed her to see the wisdom of his offer. "You must see that it makes the most sense."

The clock chimed on the mantel, and he lifted his eyes and saw it was now ten o'clock. "Suzette, I have two hours—just two hours and that is all. You either come with me so that I can care for you, or I must leave you on your own. I could perhaps give you some money, but I'm afraid I just wrote a rather large sum to Madame Laurent for your freedom. My funds are limited at the moment, until I return to England for additional monies." She needed to make a decision and trust him. That was all there was to it.

As she sat motionless on the divan, Suzette's distraught face pained him. She needed time to think it over alone, so he decided it would be best to leave her now rather than pressure her to make the difficult decision. He wanted her to come of her own free will, not because he gave her ultimatums, as Madame Laurent had no doubt done.

"I have matters to attend to, Suzette. I must finish my arrangements for departure." Lifting her chin with his hand, he forced her to look in his eyes. "I'll leave you to think it over. I will return at eleven thirty to hear your answer."

He did not wish to seem cold, but time was of the essence. He would take full responsibility for his actions of the evening before and would care for her the best way he could. "I assure you, Suzette, if you come with me, I will not abandon your side. You can trust me to care for you as long as you need me. I just cannot do so here in Paris, as my life is elsewhere." He wished for some acknowledgement from her silent lips. "Do you understand?"

Suzette looked at him. She nodded but said nothing.

"Good then." Robert's heart pounded from tense emotion. He was taking on a brave task to care for a woman he barely knew. Should she decide to come, he would stand by his promise, as he was a man of his word.

"I'll be back at eleven thirty." He walked to the door and quietly left, slowly closing it behind, leaving Suzette to ponder her decision.

The *click* of the latch echoed in the room, and Suzette's body weighed heavily upon the divan. The dress she held in her hand was beautiful. New undergarments lay upon the bed, as well as a hatbox and shoes. His kindness in providing for her was overwhelming.

Suzette put down the dress down, walked over to the window, and surveyed the street below. The avenue was bustling with morning carriage traffic, and in the distance was the Arc de Triomphe. Paris was the only world she had ever known.

Her father had taught her to speak English, but her thick French accent revealed her true origin. She had never been to England and had no idea what to expect. It was a foreign world, one she had only read about in literature or history books. The thought of leaving with a man she barely knew was frightful.

Suzette turned and walked over to the fireplace and stared into the ashes thinking of the night before. She would have died at the brothel. Suzette was sure of it. Either physically or emotionally, every ounce of life would have left her being. Robert was right. She was not a prostitute, nor did she have the makings of one. The alternatives presented to her by Madame Laurent bred fright in her heart, and it pushed her to a choice she did not wish to make.

If I do not go with him, what will I do? Suzette feared the uncertainty and hell on the streets that awaited her return after his gift of money ran out. There were no guarantees she would find work again. Even if she did, it would most likely be in another sweatshop where she would end her days in poverty and squalor, or even worse in another brothel.

She walked back over to the bed, picked up the dress once more, and began to unfasten the buttons. Afraid to stay and afraid to go, Suzette made her decision. She had to trust Robert. She owed him her life, and she adored him for it.

Resolute in her choice, she bathed, dressed, and readied herself for Robert's return. There was nothing to keep her in Paris. It was time to bury the past as her father had been buried months ago.

CHAPTER 16

Robert returned to his townhouse convinced he had made a rational decision. As a gentleman, he was a man of honor, and would do just as he promised. He would take care of her to the best of his ability by bringing Suzette to England. It was the only way to keep his pledge, especially now that his duties demanded attention.

His personal attendant, Giles, who often traveled with Robert, greeted him upon his return. He reported that everything was packed and they were ready to leave. As he entered his bedchamber, the maidservants were just closing the lids on multiple trunks, while footmen waited to load them onto the waiting carriage outside.

Giles noted the forlorn look on his employer's face. "Is everything all right, my lord?" He assured Lord Holland that he had performed his duties to the letter. "As you requested, your trunks have been packed, and we shall be ready to leave when you are ready."

Robert shook his head. "Yes, I see that, Giles. Well done, as usual."

The housekeepers had draped white sheets to protect the furniture from dust during his absence from Paris. Everything had been removed, even his decanter of brandy. "Do you think you can find me a drink somewhere, old man?"

"Of course, my lord. I'm sure there's still a bottle in the kitchen. Will that be brandy or Irish whiskey?"

"Whiskey will do just fine. I need something to relax me before this trip."

"Very well," he said, turning on his heels.

Robert knew that, in a few moments, his assistant would return with the alcohol. He needed to explain to Giles that they may not be traveling alone. While waiting, he walked over to the window and glanced out at the gardens. Soon, the curtains would be drawn shut, and his townhouse would be sealed until his return. He was unsure whether he would even return to Paris in the near future. When he did, he had a strong suspicion that things would be much different.

"Here you are, my lord." Robert turned around and took the crystal glass from Giles.

"We need to talk," he said pensively. He took a sip and let the liquid course down his parched throat. The instant warmth soothed his tension. He glanced at Giles, knowing he could trust his him with his secrets, as well as his life.

"You've been with me for many years."

"Yes, my lord. I've been most pleased to serve you since you were a young lad."

"Well, I might as well come to the point." He took a swig for fortitude. Giles looked at him with an inquisitive gaze. "We may not be traveling alone to England. There's a good possibility a young lady will accompany us, but I've yet to hear her decision."

"A young lady?" Giles replied with a tone of curiosity. "I don't quite understand."

"Well, you know how I am, Giles, always picking up the strays and rescuing the needy. I'm afraid I came across a rather nice young woman who has fallen upon hard times."

Not wishing to go into the details of the brothel and his whereabouts, he left the rest unspoken. "I've offered to help her settle in England. We will be dropping by the Louvre du Hotel on our way to Calais. She is to give me her answer at eleven thirty."

He took his pocket watch out of his vest and flipped the golden lid open to look at the time. "It's eleven," he sighed deeply. "We haven't much time." He downed the rest the whiskey and handed the glass to Giles. "Let's finish closing up the place and leave. Frankly, I'm a bit anxious to leave Paris and return to England. It's been a trying holiday, to say the least."

"Very well, Lord Holland. I'll see to it."

Giles took his glass and walked out of the room to attend to the rest of his duties. Within a few minutes, everything was in order. The footmen carried out the numerous trunks and strapped them to the top and back of the carriage. Robert stood outside on the stoop and watched the last leather binding pulled tightly down. After insuring the doors were locked and secured, he climbed inside. Giles sat next to the driver and gave instructions.

"Lord Holland has a stop he needs to make at the Hotel du Louvre. Proceed there first."

With a flip of the reins in his hands, the driver urged the horses onward. Robert sat back in his seat, mulling over Suzette's anticipated answer to his offer. He was sure that he had done the right thing in rescuing her from the brothel. Through no fault of her own, she had fallen on hard times.

Relocation to England was the only way he could help her. He planned to find a modest place for her to live and pay the rent. In the meantime, he would personally recommend her for employment, which would surely increase her chances of finding work. However, what worried him the most were the demands his family would make at the same time, all of which would vastly complicate the situation.

As the carriage drew closer to the hotel, his stomach drew into a tight knot. He felt bound to Suzette after taking her virginity the evening before. He hadn't planned to do so, but the game he played at the brothel had pent up his desire. When she freely offered, he felt helpless to control the passion. After it was all done, he held no remorse. However, now he struggled with affection for Suzette, which made the situation even more complicated.

The carriage slowed and came to a stop in front of the hotel, and Giles opened the door. "Hotel du Louvre, as requested, my lord."

"This should only take a few minutes. I'll—we'll return shortly."

Upon entering, he climbed the stairs to the third floor and quickened his step to the suite. He decided that if she declined, he would open his wallet and leave with her a sum of money to help her through the next few weeks. He feared she would eventually be back in dire straits, though, if she decided not to accept his offer.

He hesitated in front of the door for a moment and then rapped on the wooden surface with his knuckles. A few seconds later, it opened to reveal Suzette wearing her new dress and hat, along with a pleased grin upon her face.

"Hello, Robert."

He smiled and bowed. His excited voice spilled forth. "My God, you look absolutely stunning. Does everything fit?"

Suzette laughed. "Yes, except for the shoes. They were a little big, but I stuffed the toes with tissue. They are fine now." As hard as things had been, she had learned some helpful tricks along the way.

They both stood silent. Robert's eyes searched hers, and within them, he saw the answer. "Have you decided?"

"I'm terribly afraid, Robert. I won't deny my fears."

Robert reached out and grabbed her hand. It was cold and clammy.

"I shall come with you, but you must promise me that you will not abandon me, Robert. Please promise me that I can trust you. I shall die if I'm back on the streets again, even if it's on English soil."

Robert watched the tears well in her eyes and spill over her cheeks.

"Oh, my dear, I shall not abandon you. I am a gentleman and a man of my word. I assure you." With his thumb, he gently wiped the moisture from her cheeks and then gathered her into his arms, embracing her with warmth and reassurance. "Be comforted, Suzette. You've been through enough these past months. It is not my intent to bring you further harm."

Eventually, he felt the tension ease from her body, and she became limp in his arms. He released her and stepped back, holding her hands. "It's time, sweetheart. Say your last goodbyes to France and come to a new life."

Suzette nodded and tried to say something but could not. Robert knew that her voice had choked from emotion, so he smiled in reassurance. He led her through the door, closed it behind them, and then escorted her downstairs.

"Wait here, just for a minute, while I settle the bill." She stood in the foyer, and he smiled at how beautiful she looked in her new dress. He walked to the desk and spoke with the clerk. Moments later, after business had completed, he returned to her side and held out his arm for her to take. As soon as she did, he felt the tremor of her body. Giles stood by the carriage door holding it open for their arrival.

"Thank you, Giles. The young lady has decided to accompany us to England."

Robert assisted Suzette to her seat, climbed in, and sat across from her unsure of how she would react. Giles closed the door, and a minute later the carriage headed for Calais.

Suzette's eyes widened with fear, and she wrung her hands together in her lap. It was apparent that she needed comfort. He slipped across the seat and drew her close, giving her a hug, and then leaned down and kissed her on the cheek.

"Be of good cheer, Suzette. Enjoy the trip."

His presence appeared to calm her body, and eventually her trembling subsided, though she often sighed. Within a few minutes, they had reached the outskirts of the city, which gave way to a plush green countryside and tree-lined lanes. With the gentle, consistent rocking of the carriage, he encouraged her to rest upon his shoulder.

"We will arrive in Calais late afternoon, Suzette, and then board the ship for England. Why don't you take a nap? You'll need your strength for the remainder of the trip."

The fear and anxiety had taken its toll upon Suzette, and she succumbed to the gentle rocking and warmth of the man who held her in his arms. A faint whisper left her lips before she closed her eyelids and finally drifted off to sleep.

"Thank you, Robert. Thank you for everything."

He stroked her hair and kissed her once more gently on the side of her head. "You're welcome, Suzette. You're more than welcome."

* * *

The carriage jerked to a halt, and Suzette, startled over the movement, opened her eyelids. It took a few moments to make sense of her surroundings, but she still felt the warmth of Robert's arm around her. He removed it from her shoulders and stretched.

"We've arrived at Calais," he said, obviously pleased.

Suzette yawned and then glanced out the window. Curious about the ships in port, she told Robert nonchalantly, "I've never been on a ship. I'm afraid I've never been to England either."

Giles opened the door, and Robert jumped out to assist her from the carriage. Her foot stepped on the pavement, and Suzette inhaled the fresh ocean air laced with a fishy smell from a boat nearby. It was late afternoon, and the warmth of the sun felt glorious upon her face. Her vision captured the seagulls screeching overhead, and she smiled enjoying the sights, sounds, and smells.

Robert grabbed her hand and patted it.

"It will not take long to cross the channel from here. We'll be in Dover within a few hours. It's only thirty-five miles."

He led her down the dock a few yards, while Giles gave orders to the footmen to unload the trunks and carry them to the ship. As soon as they were finished, he would board with Suzette.

"Do you need something to drink, perhaps, or a moment to freshen up?"

"Yes, that would be nice," she replied, needing a few moments of privacy.

"There's a small café on the right a few doorways down. We'll stop in there for a minute while they load my things."

Suzette held Robert's arm tightly and followed him to the café. Upon entering, she inquired for the location of the ladies' parlor and disappeared from Robert's side for a few minutes. He ordered tea and pastries. Upon her return, he escorted her to a nearby table where they sat together.

"I thought you might like something to eat."

"Thank you."

Suzette settled into the chair with Robert's help and began sipping her tea.

"I hope I don't get seasick," she said with a chuckle. "I have no idea what to expect."

"Just a gentle rock," he responded, "no more than being on a carriage—even a little smoother in its motions." He sipped his tea and decided to share a private thought. "Frankly, I love the sea. I find great comfort in its beauty and its ever-changing nature. One moment it can be peaceful as heaven, and the next stormy as hell itself." He looked at Suzette with a playful gleam in his eyes. "Just like a woman."

"Oh, you think women are changeable from one extreme to the other?" she queried, with a sly grin upon her face.

"At times," he said, chuckling.

"Well, I find your comparison quite interesting." Suzette enjoyed the moment of levity between the two of them. It had been a long time since she laughed and it felt odd. A burden lifted from her heart.

"I wonder what father would think, if he knew that I was leaving Paris," she mused aloud. Suzette thought of the pictures in her purse and wondered if she dare share with Robert a part of her past.

"Would you like to see a picture of him?" she timidly asked.

"Of course, I'd like that."

Suzette opened her purse and pulled out a small photo that was one of the few she had left of his memory. She glanced at it first with love and then handed it across the table to Robert.

"Papa was an intelligent and kind man, Robert."

Robert took the photo in hand and immediately saw the resemblance of the father and daughter. "You have your father's eyes, he noted, as he studied the picture." He handed it back to Suzette. "Thank goodness you still have something tangible to remember him by, Suzette, after all you have lost."

She took the picture and put it carefully back in her purse. "Yes, I know. When I left home after the sale of his estate, my only possessions were a few pictures, my rosary, and . . ." Suzette stopped not wanting to mention the letter. "Well, I had little, and what I did have by way of clothes were stolen at the charity house."

They finished their tea and pastry, and Robert pulled out his pocket watch from his vest and noted the time. "We should go now, Suzette. It's near time for departure."

Suzette sipped the last of her tea, and then allowed Robert to pull her chair back. As she stood up, he held out his arm for her once again and led her to the door, where they proceeded outside and down the boardwalk. He helped her up to the gangplank, and Suzette's heart beat wildly in her chest. For a moment, her fear returned, and she felt slightly dizzy. She held tighter to Robert's arm for support, and he responded by a firmer grip in return. Once on board, her eyes darted about taking in all the interesting scenes.

"It will be all right, Suzette," he assured her again.

Suzette forced a smile.

"Would you like to stay on deck and watch the ship leave port? If you prefer, I can take you down to one of the cabins below."

"Oh, no. I would love to watch," she blurted out in excitement.

"Good then. Come with me, and we'll walk toward the bow out of the way of the men as they rig the sails."

Reaching out, he took her hand and gently led her to the front of the ship on the starboard side. Suzette watched as the men untied the lines, and the sails dropped overhead. The captain called out orders. Fascinated with all that was occurring around her, Suzette's eyes darted back and forth. A smile spread across her face as anticipation grew. The wind caught the sails, and the ship pulled slowly away from the dock. As the distance increased from the shoreline, Suzette looked upon France for what she believed was the last time.

"Goodbye, Papa," she muttered under her breath. Robert came up behind her and placed his arm around her waist, pulling her closer to his body.

He heard her farewell and spoke tenderly. "I think, Suzette, that your father would understand your choice. He would want you to have a good life, not what you chose at the brothel."

Suzette swallowed the lump in her throat. She grabbed the railing tightly with both hands and inhaled the ocean air, while saying a silent prayer of goodbye to France and pleading for strength to face the future.

Robert held her tightly until eventually she let go of the railing and turned around to face him. "What is it like?"

"What is what like?"

"England, I mean."

"A grand place," he said enthusiastically. A broad smile spread across his face. "It's my home, Suzette—my heritage, my life, my family." He sighed in embarrassment as he admitted his weakness. "I only come to Paris when I wish to be rebellious." A mischievous twinkle in his eyes spoke honesty. "My dear mother, the Duchess, would absolutely die if she knew I frequented the brothels. Father, on the other hand, turns a blind eye."

Suzette looked out over the channel as the ship headed for England. "You're right; it's like the gentle rocking of a carriage, only smoother. I think I will be all right," she replied relieved.

"I'm glad to hear that." Robert kept his arm around her waist. "In a few hours we'll board a train at Dover Priory and arrive in London late tonight."

Suzette tried to enjoy the moment. As the sun lowered in the late afternoon sky, the shards of silvery rays over the water were breathtaking. The skies above were clear, but a slight chill of the ocean air sent a shiver down her spine. Sensing her discomfort, Robert took his coat off and placed it around her shoulders.

Suzette looked up at him with thankful gaze. Her life was changing again in the arms of a man she adored.

* * *

Robert was thankful the trip proved uneventful and the sailing smooth. He had often been stranded between France and England because of high seas and stormy weather, but the gods were on his side today. He could think of no reason why, except that maybe they were blessing him for rescuing the latest throwaway.

Suzette seemed to enjoy herself immensely. He observed her face that appeared like a child's, displaying wonderment as she watched the ship traverse the waters. She was also fascinated by the seagulls overhead, which added to her enjoyment. Robert acquired some bread from the cook below deck, so she could feed the gulls. In no time, the boat was surrounded by gulls, but after a disapproving gaze from the captain, he decided to forgo the sport.

Throughout the voyage, Robert watched Suzette closely. It was obvious by her demeanor that her virtue, which he had taken the night before, had changed her into a young woman. She appeared mature, though apprehensive over her future. He tried hard not to encourage the adoring gazes she would throw his way. Instead, he inhaled the fresh air and watched the scenery.

During the journey, they strolled on the deck, sharing and laughing about superficial subjects. Suzette's countenance was joyful, but Robert occasionally felt her trembling hand betray her nerves.

Upon their arrival in Dover, the sun had set, and night was upon them. The ship docked, and Giles stayed behind to ensure the trunks were unloaded and placed on board the train for the next leg of the journey. They proceeded to the Priory Train Station and boarded a private rail car for the remainder of the seventy-five-mile trip to London. In a few hours, they would arrive, and Robert was thankful to be home.

The train pulled from the station, and Robert offered to take her to the dining car for something to eat. Tired and weary already from the trip, he wondered how Suzette was holding up. He could have stayed the evening in Dover, but decided to forgo the delayed return due to pressures from his family.

The waiter greeted them as they entered the car and escorted them to a table for two. After sitting, Robert took it upon himself to order dinner for both, as well as a bottle of Chardonnay. He handed the menus back to the waiter and paused until he left them alone before speaking to Suzette.

"I hope you'll forgive me for taking the liberty of ordering for you." Suzette's eyes were forming dark circles underneath. "You looked tired, my dear. I apologize for the long day of travel."

"I am tired," she said, fiddling with her linen napkin next to her the silverware. "It has been a very long day." She confessed further, "And a stressful one, I'm afraid."

"Understandable," he replied.

The waiter arrived and poured two glasses of wine. Robert picked up the crystal glass and lifted it to Suzette. "Here's to your new life. May it be one of happiness and safety, Suzette. If I have anything to say about it, I assure you that it will be just that."

A smile spread across her face. They touched their glasses together and drank to his toast. Neither took their gaze off the other.

"This wine will certainly put me to sleep. I'm half there already," she chuckled.

It brought an endearing smile to Robert's face. "After dinner, we'll return to my compartment, and you can take a nap." As he took another sip of wine, his mind wandered to all that needed to be done upon his return. "When we arrive in London, I'll take you to a hotel. I have my own townhouse, but I don't wish to bring you there alone. It's not proper behavior, I'm afraid, in London society, to bring an unmarried woman under a bachelor's roof."

Robert was not worried about Suzette's reputation; he was more concerned about his own. There was no need for his household staff to raise their brows, as he had always acted as a gentleman in his private aristocratic life. What he did while in Paris, however, was another matter entirely.

"That sounds fine, Robert. I just feel terrible how much money you have spent on me already." She bit her lower lip. "After all, you paid for my freedom, purchased clothes for me, and now this. How shall I ever repay you?"

Robert reached across the table and touched her hand. "No, don't worry about it. It's my pleasure to help you, Suzette. From the moment I met you, my heart was moved and touched by your beautiful spirit. Think nothing more of it. Promise me," he implored.

Robert wished to speak further, but the waiter arrived. He pulled his hand from hers and took his napkin and flipped it open to drape it upon his lap.

"It looks as if our food has arrived. Eat and then we'll rest."

* * *

Suzette opened her eyelids after hearing the squealing of the metal wheels on the track. She felt Robert's hand upon her own, and she examined her position of having fallen asleep on his lap. A bit embarrassed, she sat up quickly.

"Sleep well?"

"Apparently," she said, yawning. "I told you the wine would do me in, and I see it has." She looked out the window and realized that they had pulled into the London rail station.

"It's close to midnight. I hope that I can get you to a room quickly and make sure you are safe. Then you'll have the remainder of the evening to rest."

He stood up and slipped his arms through the sleeve of his waistcoat and picked up his hat and cane. After putting on his gloves, he helped Suzette to her feet and put his topcoat around her shoulders. "Here, wear this. The London night air can be a bit chilly."

Robert opened the compartment door and escorted Suzette until they reached the end of the railcar and descended the stairs. Giles greeted them.

"The carriage is waiting, my lord."

"Very well. See to it my trunks are returned to my townhouse. I will return later this evening after I take the Mademoiselle to a hotel."

"As you wish."

Giles retreated from their side, and Robert led Suzette to the waiting carriage. He gave instructions to the driver to take them to the Midland Grand Hotel. Suzette sat in the carriage looking out the window at the beautiful London streets lit with gas lamps. In spite of her inward jitters about the move, it felt exciting to be somewhere other than Paris.

The carriage pulled up to the hotel, and the footmen opened the door for Robert and Suzette. Robert led her over to a chair by the window.

"Wait for me here while I procure a room. It should only take me a minute."

Discreetly, he arranged for a small suite of rooms under his name, paying for seven days in advance. When he had procured the keys, he returned to Suzette and escorted her to the suite.

"I've booked a small suite for your use for a week, Suzette, until I can find you more permanent housing."

After entering the suite, Robert felt the need to leave. He was tired from the trip and overwhelmed at the thought of the days that lay ahead. After making sure that everything in the room was in order, Robert opened his wallet and pulled out a few pounds and handed them to Suzette.

"I'm sorry, but I need to leave and return to my townhouse. Take this money, and when you get hungry, feel free to get something to eat or call room service to bring food to the suite."

He wrapped his arms around her body, pulled her close, and then bent down and kissed her lips. She responded softly, and Robert quickly pulled back, not wishing for it to go any further.

"Get some sleep, and I will return in the morning, I promise," he said in sincerity. "I will return."

"I trust you, Robert. I know you haven't brought me this far to leave me now," she confessed. One more time, Suzette wrapped her own arms around his neck and kissed him on the cheek.

"Tomorrow then," he said, exhausted.

Robert handed her money and the key to the suite and then headed out the door, closing it quietly behind him. He walked back to his carriage and instructed the driver to take him home. Tired and worried, he headed back for a much-needed rest, hoping for a clear head in the morning to sort out his muddled life.

CHAPTER 17

After the door closed, Suzette stood in the middle of the room motionless for a few minutes, fighting the fear of abandonment. She tried desperately to trust the man, who had just taken her to his country and walked out the door. She looked at the bills in her hand, folded them neatly, and tucked them into her purse.

The trip had taken its toll upon her, as well. In fact, the entire day had drained her of every ounce of energy. She swung her legs onto the bed and grabbed a nearby pillow, clinging to it between her arms. A slight chill caused her to reach for the corner of the blanket, and she pulled it over her shoulders. The last thing she remembered was closing her eyelids, until the next morning when she heard the sound of a soft knock at her door.

Momentary confusion finally gave way to the awareness of her surroundings. Again, the knock came, more persistent this time, and Suzette flung off the covers and rose to answer it. Concerned about who might be on the other side, she inquired first before unlocking the door.

"Who is it, please?"

"I am Madame Renard, a seamstress from a local shop."

Suzette slowly opened the door and saw a short, stout woman with a sewing basket in hand and an outrageous hat upon her head.

"Good morning, Mademoiselle. Lord Holland has requested that I measure you for a wardrobe."

"Oh, dear," Suzette said, feeling a bit unkempt from having slept in her clothes. "Please, come in."

She ran her fingers through her hair and pushed back strands behind her ears. Quickly, she attempted to smooth the wrinkles in her skirt, but it proved futile. After sleeping in her dress, it had left deep creases that only an iron could remove. Suzette walked to the middle of the sitting room and stood watching her visitor. The seamstress placed her basket down on a side table, grabbed a tape measure, and approached Suzette with a determined look upon her face.

"I wish to take your measurements, and then we can discuss styles and fabrics."

Suzette was surprised to hear her accent. "You're French?"

"Oui, Mademoiselle. I'm from a local haute couture. We do business here in London, as well as in Paris."

She eyed Suzette up and down, looking over her form, size, and coloring. "You are quite petite, but I am sure we can provide you with fine gowns very quickly."

The door swung open, and Robert stood in the entranceway alongside a young man holding bolts of fabric. "Not without my input, I'm afraid!"

"Robert!" Suzette squealed in relief when she saw his face. He gave her a wink and directed that the fabrics be placed on the settee. After giving the man and tip, he waited until he had left the room and closed the door behind him. He placed both his hands on his hips and smiled broadly at Suzette.

"Well, Madame Renard, measure her petite figure, and let's get the young lady some clothes."

The seamstress raised her eyebrows. "Oui, Monsieur, I would be more than happy to. However, I need the young lady to remove her dress, as I will be taking her measurements in her undergarments." She glared at Robert and continued with a huff. "I hardly think your observance of such a task would be the respectable thing to do!"

Suzette looked at Robert's astonished face over being scolded by the seamstress.

"I'm sure Lord Holland has no intentions, Madame, of watching me disrobe in his presence." Suzette pointed to the dressing screen and made a suggestion.

"Would you mind, Robert, taking a walk out on the balcony while Madame Renard and I proceed behind the screen for measurements?"

"Yes, yes, of course," he said, reluctantly. He opened the white French doors and walked out on the balcony. "I shall look at the scenery outside instead of inside, Madame Renard. Will that do?"

"Very well. I shall let you know when the Mademoiselle is decent and able to be in your presence."

She grabbed Suzette by the arm, like a protective mother hen, and led her behind the dressing screen. Her eyes shot a disapproving look at the wrinkled gown. "Remove your dress, please."

Suzette complied, and the next few minutes were spent with a tape measure around her waist, chest, and arms. This was the first time Suzette had been measured for dresses, as her father could not afford custom clothing from any dressmaking shop.

"There. I have all of your measurements written down. You may get dressed."

Robert overheard they were through and immediately returned inside the room before Suzette completed dressing. The seamstress threw him a disapproving glare.

"Now, let's get down to business," he said, ignoring her scorn. "Suzette, hurry and come here. Give me your opinion, will you?"

Madame Renard opened her portfolio showing sketches of designer dresses. Suzette stood flabbergasted, not knowing which to choose. Robert, however, was not shy in the matter as certain styles caught his fancy. Suzette raised her eyebrows over the low necklines, but she decided not to interject her opinion over fashion. After all, he was presenting her with gifts she could never afford, and it would be rude to complain.

"Mademoiselle, tell me which fabrics and colors you like," asked Madame Renard, hovering over the bolts.

Suzette gladly obliged and let her hand roam over the material while Robert chimed in on the colors he thought highlighted Suzette's complexion and hair. Suzette felt like a pampered queen, only this time it wasn't inside a brothel.

After what seemed like an eternity, the seamstress finished taking the order, and Robert inquired about delivery. "So, when can you have the dresses delivered?"

"Within a few days."

"A few days are not good enough, I'm afraid."

"I'm fine, Robert," Suzette interjected, not wishing to cause problems. She could wait in the dress she wore; it just needed to be pressed. Robert returned a displeasing look in her direction, which gave her a start.

"Nonsense," he spoke quickly. "See to it the dresses are made immediately, and I shall pay you a premium."

"As you wish, Lord Holland." Madame Renard curtsied before leaving the room. "I'll send my messenger to pick up the fabric samples later today."

After the door closed, Robert turned to Suzette and brought her into his arms. "Don't second-guess me, my dear. We are in England now. This is my country, and I'm well known in London. People do as I request with no argument."

"All right," she meekly answered. He exuded an air of power in his homeland, and she began to wonder if his dealings with her would change now that he had returned.

"Besides, I only wish you the best. You're too pretty to waste away."

"And you are too kind to me, Robert. I cannot repay you for such benevolence."

"Don't worry about it, please." He picked up her hand and kissed it. "Now go freshen up. I'll take you to breakfast, and then we'll go shopping." He looked at her feet and grimaced. "Let's purchase some shoes that fit, a few more undergarments, purses, hats, a parasol, and any other accessories every lady in London requires!"

Suzette giggled.

* * *

Dresses, shoes, hats, gloves, nightgowns, cloaks, jewelry, perfumes, and anything that Suzette could possibly need, Robert purchased that afternoon. He treated her like a queen, and Suzette basked in the attention and his gifts.

Robert had made a promise to care for her, so showering her with presents was easy to justify. He purchased everything out of his heart to rescue a woman who had nothing and made sure she had everything.

Suzette, however, found words inadequate to express her gratitude, and she gave to him that evening out of the only tangible way she knew how. He did not protest when she initiated another heated moment between the two of them. They spent the night in her hotel bed wrapped in each other's arms. Robert and Suzette slipped into a familiar intimacy that each immensely enjoyed.

By the end of the week, her shyness in lending him her body had entirely vanished. As an ardent and tender lover, Robert taught her the intimate ways of a man and woman. To his delight, Suzette was an attentive pupil. If their relationship continued as such, Robert knew he'd never set foot in a brothel again as long as Suzette shared his bed.

Each day when he visited her at the hotel, he would arrive with a small bouquet of lilies in hand that always made her smile. He would remind her, "You will find happiness." It seemed as if now, she truly believed his words.

As far as Robert was concerned, he had difficult decisions ahead regarding any permanent future with Suzette. He recognized her growing affection, but felt cautious not to express too much of his fondness in words. There were times she took his breath away, and her presence in his life brought him immense joy.

Robert spent time away from Suzette to speak with area landlords, as he looked for a modest, but safe place for her to live. To keep her indefinitely at the hotel was out of the question. The situation already looked questionable to the hotel staff, and he did not wish to breed seeds of gossip in London about an affair. He succeeded already in building a bit of a reputation abroad, and the local news needed nothing to print to make its way back to Surrey and into his father's hands.

Finally, toward the end of the week, Robert came across an adequate, fully-furnished country cottage located on the outskirts of London. He made arrangements and hired a live-in housekeeper to act as a cook and maid for Suzette. She would need no other staff to care for her, and he was satisfied that he had adequately provided for her needs in every possible way. He had successfully delivered her from destitution and placed her in a comfortable lifestyle.

When it was time to move her to her new quarters, he arrived early in the morning with two footmen and trunks.

"They are here to pack up your things, my dear," he announced.

Suzette looked surprised over the unannounced move, and he offered his hand. "Come with me. Your clothes and accessories will be delivered this afternoon. I have a carriage waiting."

"Is it time to leave the hotel, Robert?"

"Yes! I'm happy to say that I've found you a permanent dwelling."

He held out his arm to her, and Suzette wrapped hers around his, as he escorted her from the hotel. Robert decided to sit across from Suzette, so that he could observe the expression upon her face when they arrived. As the carriage traveled down the London streets, he enjoyed watching her face aglow with anticipation.

"I do like London," she interjected, as she looked out the window eyeing the city she had not yet become acquainted with.

"Well," he replied with a sigh, "you've only seen the good parts, I'm afraid. We do have some problem areas of poverty and crime, much like Paris, I'm afraid."

Eventually, the carriage left the cobblestone streets and traveled down a lane lined with large oak trees. A few minutes later, it slowed and arrived at its destination.

"I'm sure you will be quite comfortable here, Suzette, until we can talk more of your future. In the meantime, this will be your home."

The driver jumped down and opened the door. Robert exited and offered Suzette his hand. When he led her up the small stoop to the front door, the housekeeper opened the door, as she had been waiting for their arrival.

"Lord Holland," she said with a curtsy, eyeing Suzette as she entered alongside him.

"I trust everything has been prepared as instructed?"

"Yes, Lord Holland, just as instructed."

"Good then. Suzette, this is Madame LeBlanc."

The maid greeted Suzette. "Bienvenue à votre nouvelle maison."

Robert smiled at the surprised look that came across Suzette's face. "I thought having the company of another French lady in your presence would be a warm welcome."

"Oh, indeed!" Suzette spoke, her eyes shining. "Merci, de votre accueil chaleureux!"

Robert felt the clutch of Suzette's arm around his own, sensing her pleasure. Proud that he had made the correct choice for a housekeeper and companion for Suzette, he began to lead her through her new home room by room.

The two-story country cottage contained a parlor, dining area, and kitchen downstairs, as well as a modest room that would be used for the maid's quarters. He escorted her up the stairs to the second level and showed her the main bedroom and small guest room.

Upon entering her bedchamber, Suzette looked at the surroundings that were somewhat reminiscent of her former life with her father. This was the first permanent dwelling she could call her own since the day she left the apartment. It was too much to bear.

As the tears trickled down her cheeks, Robert took notice and gathered her in his arms, tenderly holding her against his chest. "Don't cry, Suzette. You'll be safe here. I'll see to it."

As she lifted her head from his chest, he spotted a few moist curls and brushed them away. The light in her eyes touched his soul. They kissed, and when their lips met, he could no longer control the urge to take her. He reached for the door, closed it, and set the lock to inaugurate their new bed of lovemaking.

* * *

Suzette opened her eyes and sat up, discovering herself draped in a sheet on an unfamiliar bed. She glanced around the room and realized she had fallen asleep. Robert wasn't there. The clock on the fireplace mantel showed 6 o'clock. She looked out the window and saw it neared dusk.

She threw the sheet from her naked body, swung her legs around, and sat on the edge of the bed. The memory of their intimate moments earlier brought a smile to her face. Robert had worn her out, and she remembered Nadine's statement, *"There's something about hours of pleasure that relaxes you like a drug. I come back, and I'm out like a light."* Indeed there was, Suzette admitted.

Suzette knew she was quickly falling in love with the handsome lord. His constant care and generous outpourings of gifts were more than enough evidence for her to draw such a naïve conclusion that he too felt the same. Though he never spoke the words, Suzette felt it with every fiber of her being, especially when he made love to her with such tender attentiveness.

She rose from the edge of the bed and retrieved her corset and bloomers off the floor, then went into the washroom to freshen up. A few minutes later, she emerged dressed.

Suzette wondered where Robert had disappeared to and made her way downstairs to the parlor looking for him. Instead, she ran into Madame LeBlanc. Immediately, she lowered her eyes in embarrassment that the housekeeper knew what had transpired upstairs. Her maid smiled and spoke in French.

"Lord Holland departed, Mademoiselle, but left you this note."

Her hand stretched forward, and Suzette took from her a folded piece of paper. Quickly, she opened the note and read his penned words.

Suzette,

I hope that you are comfortable in your new surroundings. You were sleeping so peaceful; I had not the heart to wake you. I will be gone for a few days, as family matters and responsibilities are demanding my attention. As soon as I return from Surrey the end of this week, I will call upon you and see how you are faring.

Fondly,
Robert

Suzette's face turned sullen.

"He also asked me to give you this." Suzette took an envelope from her hand and opened it, finding a large sum of bills. Madame LeBlanc's eyes grew wide as Suzette gazed inside the envelope.

"A generous benefactor, oui?"

Understanding the inference in her statement, Suzette immediately closed the envelope and corrected the housekeeper's misconception. "He is not my benefactor."

"I apologize, Mademoiselle," she said. "Your trunks arrived. I will see that they are emptied and your clothes are put away."

"Yes, thank you," Suzette replied tersely, irked over her maid's belief she was Robert's mistress. "Is there anything to eat?" she asked. "I'm famished."

"Yes. I have a small dinner ready. I will serve it shortly in the dining room."

She scurried off to the kitchen area, and Suzette stood silently in the hallway glancing at the trunks that had arrived. An overwhelming desire for Robert's caring arms tugged at her heart, and she wished he hadn't disappeared so abruptly without saying goodbye. She wanted to be in his arms, safe and secure. Now, the entire week lay ahead. She was alone in a new home and in a new country with nothing to do.

She folded the note and envelope and shoved them both in the pocket of her skirt before making her way to the dining room. Suzette worried whether his return to England would draw them closer or push them apart.

CHAPTER 18

As soon as the carriage lurched forward toward its destination, Robert leaned back in the leather seat and heaved a sigh. He wondered whether he had made the right decision regarding Suzette. Even though he adored her, he feared she would expect more from him than he was able to give due to his station in life.

Right now he had to turn all of his attention upon family matters. He was due in Surrey—in fact overdue. His father had sent numerous communications to him at his townhouse after his return. Though he was not deliberately ignoring his father's request for a visit, he was procrastinating due to his situation with Suzette.

As much as he respected his father, the Duke expected him to assume his duties. Each time Robert returned home, the pressures to act his age came from everyone. Even the household butler seemed to raise his brow upon his return, as if he knew what bed he had just visited.

His frequent jaunts to Paris were for the sole purpose of escaping his pestering family and choking responsibilities. He much more preferred to frequent brothels, casinos, and horse tracks than the stuffy estate in Surrey that housed his family. After his arrival, the lectures would ensue about his need to settle down, assume his role in society, and marry. Robert took bets in his mind as to which one would lay into him first.

The twenty-mile carriage ride to his family estate took enough time to allow Robert the opportunity to gather his thoughts on what lay ahead. When the carriage finally pulled down the long tree-lined lane to the residence, Robert's demeanor turned pensive. The Holland estate looked regally placed in the midst of manicured green lawns, steeped in centuries of history. As beautiful as the land and residence appeared, the estate walls loomed above him like a prison. Upon his father's death, the lands, and title of Duke would be his to assume.

As the carriage stopped before the doorway, Robert inhaled a deep breath, preparing for the inevitable onslaught. He waited until the uniformed footman opened the door, then he gathered his hat and cane and stepped out resolutely to face his fate. As his boots landed on the small round pebble stones of the drive, he dug his heels in with resistance. Merely a symbolic act, it somehow brought a strange comfort and delight to show an ounce of rebellion upon his return.

With lips pursed and hands clenched, he strode toward the door. It opened by the hand of their faithful butler, Nelson, who greeted him with the anticipated raised brow.

"Lord Holland, welcome home. It is indeed a pleasure to see you again." Instantly, Nelson reached for his hat and cane and assisted Robert in removing his cloak.

"Where is my father?"

"In the study, your lordship." Nelson bowed once at the waist and then left.

Robert pulled his jacket downward to straighten the creases from the trip and stomped down the hallway toward the study to his waiting father. The sound of his heels clicked across the marble foyer, until he reached two double doors, with one slightly ajar. The smell of cigar smoke filtered into the hall. Robert clenched his fist until his knuckles turned white and then tapped on the thick wooden entry.

"Enter," his father replied, in his deep stoic voice. Robert walked inside and found the Duke sitting behind his desk, cigar in one hand, quill in the other, penning a document. Silence filled the distance between the two, except for the scratching noise of the feather's tip meeting the paper. His father flicked the cigar ashes into a nearby container without looking up at his son to acknowledge his arrival.

"Gracing us with your presence, I see." His voice, terse and cold, continued. "I suppose that I should thank you for responding to my request for a visit. I have some matters of estate that we need to discuss once you are settled."

As the quill penned its last stroke, he lifted his eyes to his son. The Duke's face was tired and drawn, and Robert thought he looked pale.

"How long will you be with us this time, Robert?"

"For a few days, and then I must return to London for an engagement."

"Huh, engagement! Interesting terminology for your next departure to pleasure."

The Duke returned his eyes back to the parchment underneath his quill, waving his other hand to dismiss his son until later in the evening.

"You may go." Instantly, he picked up his cigar, taking a long puff and blowing the smoke into the air. "We'll speak after dinner this evening."

"Yes, sir."

Robert turned around, leaving his father in silence, wondering why the change in demeanor. He was cold and distant, unlike other greetings upon his arrival home. His father's usual tolerant patience had disappeared. It confirmed Robert's suspicions that his summons involved something far beyond a friendly visit.

Not bothering to close the door, he strode toward the grand staircase and took two steps at a time until reaching the landing above. With his hand racing through his blond hair, he let out a sigh of respite, quickly proceeding to his personal suite.

"Robert!" He stopped at the sound of her voice and turned to face his mother.

"Finally, I get to see my darling son."

Duchess Mary Holland, still quite strikingly beautiful for a middle-aged woman, flew into her son's arms.

He tolerated her hug. "Mother," he replied, as he bent down and gave her a kiss on the forehead. The strong scent of her doused perfume gagged him.

"Your sister shall be quite pleased to see you, my dear," she said, patting him on the side of his cheek with the palm of her hand. "Are you staying long or returning quickly to your playground?"

"I will be here for a few days," he said, showing no emotion. "If you don't mind, mother, I need to unpack and relax. I'm a bit tired."

The Duchess frowned in disappointment. "Always in a hurry to scurry off from your mother."

Robert merely smiled, taking the palm of his hand and patting his mother's cheek in return. He despised her show of affection by a pat on the cheek. He turned away and left her standing in the hallway.

He entered his suite of rooms and closed the door behind him. On the side table, he spied a decanter of brandy. He picked up an empty glass and poured the liquid. With a quick swirl around in the crystal container, he brought the glass to his lips and took a sip.

He strolled over to the window and looked out over the estate grounds. At least the weather was decent. His eyes drifted toward the Holland stables, and his familiar yearning for his favorite pastime called his name like an enticing adulteress. The other woman in his life needed attention, which was a black Arabian mare. An enjoyable ride sounded like a momentary diversion.

He flung off his waistcoat and walked over to his wardrobe looking for his riding jacket. Quickly, he downed the last ounce of brandy before leaving his quarters.

As luck would have it, no one lay in his path between his suite and the front door. Once outside, he headed for the stables. Upon entering, he walked down the row of stalls to the one that held his prized possession. Adara turned her head and whinnied upon seeing his approach, stomping her foot a few times. Robert smiled.

He instructed the groom to saddle her, while Robert stood nearby, stroking her muscular neck. When the saddle was on, Adara told him with a flare of her nostrils that she was ready.

Robert reached into his jacket pocket, took out a pair of soft leather gloves, and pulled them onto his hands. He grabbed the reins and placed his booted foot into the stirrup and mounted the horse in a quick gliding motion. With a slight kick of his heels, he sped out of the stables and across the estate grounds, leaving a swirl of dust in his wake.

The sound of the Adara's hooves beat on the ground like thunder. It was music to Robert's ears. She left in her path clods of dirt and grass flying into the air, while she ran like the wind. Rider and horse joined as one, and finally Robert found a moment of peace through another passion in his life—horses.

Adara possessed a heart much like his own. She was unbridled, spirited, and full of life when out on a run. When stabled, she became docile and quiet, but when released from the confines of her stall, she transformed into a horse whose speed no one in the county could match.

For the first time in hours, as he sped across the estate grounds and beyond, a broad smiled brightened his sullen face. As he watched Adara's mane flow in the wind, his thoughts turned to the flowing auburn tresses of Suzette. He adored his petite French doll from Paris and realized that he truly missed having her by his side.

After enjoying his fast gallop across the countryside, Robert returned to the stables refreshed. A sense of determination and strength replaced his depression, and with confidence, he strode back indoors. His boots echoed across the marble foyer floor and brought notice to another family member that he had successfully dodged until that moment.

"Robert, where have you been hiding? Mother told me that you were here." His sister, Marguerite, quickly approached him, wrapped her arms around his neck and planted a peck upon his cheek.

"God, Robert, you need a bath," she moaned, wrinkling her nose from his sweaty body. "Were you out riding again?" She stepped back and looked at him from top to bottom. "Still as handsome as ever, even when you smell like a horse."

"Hello, Marguerite, and you are still as lovely and irritating as the last time I saw you," he replied, while pulling off his riding gloves.

"Get ready for dinner, dear. I have a surprise for you!"

"Pray tell, *who* now, might I ask?"

"No, you may not! You'll just have to see the lovely young lady I've chosen this time when you sit next to her at the dinner table," she announced with a giggle.

Her news irritated the hell out of him. Every time he came home, his sister played the role of matchmaker, determined to see him married. No doubt, she had found another lady to entice his interest.

"Fine," Robert relented as he headed for the stairs. "God, will you never stop trying to marry me off to one of your friends?" He gave her a wink to soften the comment.

He returned to his suite, bathed, and dressed for dinner. When seven o'clock arrived, he joined his family in the formal dining room. His father, mother, and sister were already at the table waiting for his arrival, along with a stunningly beautiful woman that immediately caught his attention.

He glanced at Marguerite, who smiled from ear to ear. Robert tried his hardest not to show his interest, but his facial expression had already betrayed his thoughts.

"Robert, I would like you to meet Lady Jacquelyn Spencer," she said glowing.

Robert walked over to her side at the table. Lady Spencer raised her hand for the usual complimentary kiss.

"Lord Holland, I am so pleased to meet you. Your sister talks about you constantly."

He took her hand and kissed it, and then turned his eyes toward his sister in response. "I'm sure she does, Lady Spencer. She's always talking about me." As he glanced back into her beautiful face, his eyes sparkled. "It's a pleasure to meet you."

He took his seat by her side and relaxed for dinner. It was difficult not to take a keen interest in their dinner guest. To his surprise, this one actually piqued his curiosity. Robert decided to pay particular attention to her every movement and hear every word that fell from her pink lips.

She was unquestionably attractive. Her fair complexion gave way to a rosy blush, betraying her shyness as she made small talk during dinner. She was gorgeously adorned in a powder blue, low-cut gown, with a sapphire necklace that encircled her swan-like neck. The color of her hair resembled pure gold, and Robert could barely take his eyes off the cascading curls that fell from her upswept hairdo.

While they ate, he noticed a slight shaking of her hand when lifting her fork. It was obvious Lady Spencer was taking her introduction to him as one of considerable importance. When he glanced at his father and mother, he recognized their clever smiles of approval. There was no need to ascertain Marguerite's opinion, which radiated over her entire face.

After dinner, Robert excused himself, when his father invited him for a drink and cigar. Before obliging his request, he turned to Jacquelyn and lifted her hand once more to place a kiss.

"Excuse me, Lady Spencer. It was a pleasure meeting you. Perhaps I will have the pleasure of calling upon you in the near future."

He left the dining room and tried to ignore the grinning faces of his mother and sister, who were pleased by his acceptance of their latest offering. Robert had a distinct feeling they were privy to information regarding Lady Spencer that he was not. No doubt, they deemed her a perfect match, possessing all the qualities of societal acceptance as a future Duchess.

He followed closely behind his father, apprehensive about the conversation ahead. Once inside his study, the Duke headed for the side table and began pouring two glasses of cognac.

"Close the door, will you, son?"

After doing so, Robert approached his father's side. He knew from experience when the man called him *son*, their conversation would be a serious one. His father handed him a glass and proceeded to his cigar box on the corner of his desk.

"Cigar?" Without hesitation, Robert accepted the offer. After snipping the tip, he lit the end on a nearby candle. His father did the same.

"Have a seat, Robert."

He sat in a nearby chair, and Robert took a puff from his cigar and a sip of cognac, bracing himself for a lecture.

"I will get straight to the point. Our family physician tells me that I don't have long to live."

Surprised at the brash announcement, Robert's eyes widened, and he sat straight up. "Father, I don't know what to say." For a moment, Robert was stunned, and then offered the only words he could think of. "I am sorry."

"Don't start with the bullshit, Robert," his father retorted in irritation. "It's life. Apparently, my heart is on the verge of giving out. It's not beating correctly, and I often have chest pains. What can I say?" He drew in a large puff on the cigar, which caused the tip to burn bright red, then released the smoke from his lungs into the air above his head. "This probably doesn't help," he said, with a hearty and congested laugh.

The Duke walked over to his son's side and expressed his wishes. "It's time, Robert. I can no longer afford you to sow your wild oats. When I pass, the estate will need managing." He paused for a moment and took another puff on his cigar. "I have been quite patient with your activities, but you must come to a point in your life when you assume the responsibilities into which you were born."

Robert could not deny his father's words, nor could he rebel against his calling after hearing of his father's physical condition. He somewhat expected this conversation months ago, when he announced his last trip to Paris. He now understood what was behind the Duke's disapproving look upon his departure.

"As I see it, Lady Spencer would be a fine match for you. She comes from a well-bred family, a good bloodline. She has an acceptable dowry, as well." He paused for a moment before emphasizing the most important matter. "You are my only son, and the Holland legacy will not continue unless you marry and bear children."

Robert knew what his father was going to say next, and he resigned himself to the inevitable announcement that he was about to make.

"I've already been in discussions with Lady Spencer's parents regarding an arranged marriage between the two of you. It will be a good match, and she's not unpleasant to the eyes, as you can well see."

The Duke took a few puffs upon the cigar. The air grew thick in the room, while Robert dealt with the blow and struggled with the seriousness of the situation.

"So tell me, how were your weeks in Paris?" his father asked, changing the subject. "Enjoy your trysts at the brothel?" The old man chuckled, flashing an inquisitive look in his son's direction.

Robert was aware that his father knew of his frequent visits to the Chabanais. They were part of his Parisian entertainment while away, and they had discussed it before. What he did not know was the recent development about his last visit. The hasty rescue of Suzette began to bear its consequences, and Robert needed to clear the air with his father regarding the matter.

"My visits were pleasurable, as usual. Except, I must confess that I believe I've done something rather rash."

His father's brow rose over his son's confession. "Rash? And what might that be?"

Robert gulped, took a drink, and then spoke. "I've brought a Parisian woman back to England with me."

"You what?" his father bellowed. He leaned into Robert's face demanding an answer. "Why in hell's name would you do such a thing?"

"Her name is Suzette, and I met her at the Chabanais," Robert responded.

"So you decided to bring your own private whore back to England?" His eyes glared in disapproval.

"No, father, it's nothing like that," he said, shaking his head in disagreement. "She was a victim of circumstance, a homeless woman after the death of her father. I believe she was forced into prostitution. I was to *break* her in, so to speak, at Madame Laurent's price, and I had not the heart to do so." Robert felt embarrassed, though he continued to justify his actions.

"Well, be honest with me Robert. Is she your whore or not? What do you intend to do with her?"

"She's not my whore, father. She's not like that, but I have taken her as my own," he said, confessing his actions.

"For God's sakes, Robert! You are just like you were as a young boy, rescuing every stray dog in the county, because you couldn't stand to see the flea-bearing animals suffer." The Duke paced across the room and shook his head in disbelief. "Bad choice, son. Bad choice."

"Yes, I know," Robert reluctantly admitted.

Silence filled the room, and both pondered the situation until Robert's father insisted on knowing his intentions with the woman.

"Well, do you intend to keep her as your mistress or what?"

Robert sighed, admitting his own weakness. His first intentions were merely to provide Suzette a safe place to live, find her work, and get her back on her feet. However, as the week progressed, their intimacy grew, and he enjoyed her immensely. He took a moment to assess his motives in the matter and knew in his heart that he was not ready to release her to another life. He wanted to keep her, even though he couldn't marry her. His adoration for her ran deep, and letting her go was out of the question. "I believe I will."

"Well then, keep it as quiet as possible. You can have your mistress. God knows, I've had a few of my own."

Robert lifted his eyes at his father's frank admission. Though he knew it to be true, it was something they never discussed between the two of them.

"Keep her if you wish. Enjoy your sexual trysts. But I am afraid, my son, it will soon be time for you to seriously consider taking a wife, and I believe Lady Spencer is that woman."

Robert stood and moved to his father's side.

"I understand, sir, and will comply with your requests in these matters. Will you pursue the match with Lady Spencer's parents?"

"Yes, of course. It's almost a done deal as we speak. Her father is Lord Spencer of Yorkshire. She comes from a fine family with a strong background."

"Very well." Robert's words half-heartedly fell from his lips, and he doused the last bit of alcohol in his glass.

"Good. I think it might be appropriate to start courting Lady Spencer when you are here. And for God's sake, Robert, try to keep the other matter under wraps until after the wedding at least. Wives eventually understand the needs of men go beyond a marriage bed. They are to produce heirs and run households, while our mistresses are to satisfy our sexual fantasies." His father shot his son an understanding wicked grin.

Robert reached toward his father an offered a gentleman's handshake. "As always, father, I shall obey your wishes." He clasped his hand tightly, sorrowful to see his father's body wasting away. He could tell by the cold touch of his flesh and weak grip that his beating heart failed to pump the needed blood through his veins. His facial features were dull and gray in complexion. Robert felt an alarming urgency to comply with his father's demands.

After releasing their handshake, he walked toward the door and glanced over his shoulder before leaving the study. The Duke had turned toward the window, and unbeknown to Robert, his father's eyes welled with tears.

Robert returned to his suite and thought of his future and the days ahead. It would have been better to marry for love had he been given the chance to find a wife on his own. However, he had squandered his youth and played the wrong card. Fate had sealed his future, and now he was paying for years of selfish living.

He needed a wife, a Duchess, to carry on his father's legacy. Robert wanted his father to die in peace knowing that his wayward son had finally become responsible. He felt indebted but remorseful, because what could have been his to choose had fallen into the hands of his parents. Arranged marriages were for alliances, money, convenience, and heirs. Old ways were hard to break.

Now that he was bound to court the young lady he had met at dinner, he wondered what she was like. She appeared alluring, but Robert could only hope her personality would be just as pleasant. In order to get to know her better, he would need to travel between Surrey and London often in the next few months. They would need a respectable time to court before an announced engagement and subsequent marriage.

His life had turned into a complicated mess, with Suzette back in London and wholly dependent upon him for her livelihood. He was not willing to release her from his care. In fact, the only question he faced was her willingness to continue their relationship as his mistress. Only time would tell, but in the interim, he would treat her as the only love in his life in order to win her completely. There was no need to share with Suzette his personal affairs. That part of his life would remain private, as well as his impending marriage to another woman. Jacquelyn Spencer would obtain his title and name, but Suzette would retain his deepest affections.

CHAPTER 19

Months passed, and Robert and Suzette's life fell into a routine. Each time Robert visited Suzette, he lavished more gifts, expressing his adoration. When he needed to return to Lady Spencer's side, he used the excuse of being called back to the estate by his father to attend to business affairs. He lit the candle at both ends, courting one woman for an impending marriage and romancing the other as his naïve mistress. His prideful ego grew over his successful pursuits, with neither woman the wiser to his escapades.

Suzette, who was now spoiled and dependent upon the rich lord, had fallen head-over-heels in love with her benefactor. Robert continued to provide for her every need, visiting her bed whenever possible. She blindly believed his feigned excuses when he needed to leave. He merely spoke of his father's illness and matters that required attention. Suzette felt sorry for him and encouraged him to go home.

When Robert was in London, the two were inseparable. Practically living at her small cottage on the outskirts of town, Robert discreetly took her to the horse track and casinos, knowing that most men frequented them with their mistresses on their arms. However, he purposely refrained from expensive restaurants and the theatre, circumventing places where those in society knew him personally—the places he took Lady Spencer when she visited London.

Suzette, during his absence, busied herself with handcrafts, embroidery being her favorite, as well as tending a garden of flowers that included a wide assortment of lilies.

She had no need to look for employment or even consider such a change in lifestyle, for Robert took care of everything. The matter was never discussed.

She conversed very little with Madame LeBlanc, resenting the fact the woman accused her of being Robert's mistress. Each time he arrived at the cottage, her face would smirk and her brow rise knowing his intentions. Suzette, on the other hand, refused to see their relationship as anything other than lovers, hoping one day for a proposal. She willingly allowed Robert to frequent her bed as security to seal her future.

In the process, the innocence of Suzette melted away. She had quickly become an artful lover, who failed to get her fill of Robert. In the heat of their passion, she would whisper words of love. He would respond lovingly in return, albeit never speaking the exact forbidden phrase. Suzette did not mind, for she had truly grown to love the handsome lord who saved her from the Chabanais and gave her a life of luxury and care.

Robert, on the other hand, adored and cared for her deeply. Their moments of lovemaking kept his former wayward side satisfied, although he never could consider any commitment beyond her bed chamber. It was impossible to do so, for a wedding date had been set to take Lady Spencer as his wife.

Bred to be a nobleman's wife, he found Jacquelyn Spencer intelligent, well read, talented in the art of playing the piano, socially acceptable, and polite. Though Robert found her beautiful and her company agreeable, he felt no passion toward the woman whatsoever. His innate passions belonged to Suzette, and he truly believed he could keep her as his mistress forever.

Fate, on the other hand, had a different plan. Out of Suzette's past, inscribed in a letter she had carefully burned at the Chabanais, another part of her life resurrected when she least expected it to happen.

* * *

The day began like any other. Robert had spent the week with Suzette but inconveniently found he was out of cigars. He decided to take her with him on a quick shopping trip into the center of London. Robert favored a particular tobacco shop, tucked down a side street that carried imported cigars to his liking.

After their arrival, he invited her to come inside, but Suzette protested. "Oh, Robert, don't make me inhale that infernal smell," she pleaded.

Robert laughed, frankly looking forward to a few moments alone, sniffing the various imports before he decided on a purchase. With his finger, he gently touched the tip of Suzette's nose. "I wouldn't think of ruining that pretty little nose of yours!"

With a quick peck on the cheek, he opened the door, and Suzette heard the ringing of the bell announcing to the proprietor a customer's arrival. She stood outside on the sidewalk, her face tilted toward the bright noonday sun. The warmth felt heavenly as she enjoyed the last few days of summer. The leaves were just beginning to change color and autumn would soon arrive.

Suzette turned and glanced through the plate-glass window, watching Robert sniff cigars. It was a strange male art of twirling a rolled paper filled with tobacco under one's nostrils that she would never understand. As she watched him adoringly go about smelling one after another, her attention was interrupted by a voice calling her name.

"Suzette!"

A startled gaze into the reflection of the window caused her heart to skip a beat. Her knees buckled beneath her, and she hastily reached out for the ledge of the windowpane for support.

"Suzette, is that you?"

Her throat closed, rendering her unable to make an audible sound, as she slowly turned around to face the uniformed man who stood only a few feet in front of her. At the sight of his face, the pounding in her chest increased tenfold, and her eyes widened, displaying both fear and pleasure.

"Suzette, it is you!"

The relief upon his face was evident. Suzette let out the breath she held in her lungs, and spoke softly, acknowledging his discovery.

"Hello, Philippe."

"My God, Suzette!"

He stepped forward and embraced her, pulling her close. Suzette stumbled as the strength of his arms caught her off balance. She wanted to turn and see if Robert was watching the scene unfolding, but was helpless to do so.

Philippe immediately sensed her reluctance in returning his ardent embrace. Instead, her arms were cold and unresponsive, and the chance meeting suddenly turned awkward. He released her and stepped back, confused.

"I thought you dead," he said, searching her eyes for emotion. "When our ship pulled into Calais for furlough, I immediately set off to Paris. I went to your father's apartment and found another living there. You were gone."

Suzette could only imagine what surprise and grief filled his heart.

"What happened to you?" His voice pleaded for an answer from his fiancée.

Suzette glanced away, unable to keep her eyes upon his questioning gaze.

"Many things, Philippe," she mumbled, inhaling deeply to regain her composure. She looked at him once more, and his deep brown gaze melted her soul, as they radiated his undying love.

"Father died in his sleep. They think it was his heart or a stroke," she conveyed, with a shaking voice.

"My God, Suzette, no," he gasped, letting the sorrow escape his lips. "I'm so sorry."

"I didn't know, but he was deeply in debt and his entire estate was sold, and I was left destitute."

"But you look well now, Suzette. What are you doing in London? Why aren't you in Paris?" Philippe's puzzled expression revealed his confusion.

"I might ask the same of you," Suzette retorted, a bit irritated at his questions. "What are you doing in London?"

"Our ship docked on the Thames, and I have been given a leave of absence. I searched Paris high and low for you."

Suzette watched his facial expression change. Suddenly, he looked at her from top to bottom, surveying her clothing, expensive jewelry, and maturity about her face that he had never known before. He understood, and Suzette confirmed his suspicions.

"I waited, Philippe, but you were at sea." Her own voice filled with desperation and excuses. "I had no means to contact you. I was left alone."

Philippe listened to her strained explanation, and fear gripped his heart, waiting for her to say she had married another.

"I was homeless, Philippe—pitiful, alone, and homeless. The Daughters of Charity could only care for me for a few weeks, and then I was faced with life on the streets."

Philippe abruptly interjected. "Have you found another and married? Let me see," he said, grabbing her left hand to look for a wedding ring. He felt her bare finger underneath the glove. His eyes darted back at her dress, and his expression changed.

"You don't need to tell me the rest, Suzette. No single woman of your means is adorned in such an expensive gown and jewels, unless you've become someone's mistress." The words cut deep, and for a brief moment, he regretted his accusation. "Tell me that I'm wrong," he pleaded.

"Don't judge me, Philippe. I have a wonderful man who cares for me and gives me a home. He saved me from the most horrid of lives—from a brothel!"

Philippe's mouth opened in disbelief. "A brothel?" He stumbled over his words. "We were engaged, Suzette," his voice pained with disappointment. "Could you not have tried to contact me?"

His disgust was evident, and Suzette's heart sank at his judgmental tone. She turned around quickly and looked into the cigar shop. Robert was completing his purchase with the clerk.

"You must go now, Philippe. He'll be here soon."

"At least tell me where you live, Suzette, so I can talk to you again. Please," his voice implored. His hand reached out and touched her arm.

"Philippe, you must leave," she insisted. "Robert will be coming out of the store any moment!" Suzette's face turned to panic as she did not wish the two of them to encounter one another.

"Suzette, I beg you . . . please, for our sake—for our past, your father."

She blurted out her address. "It's 72 Crown Lane, on the outskirts of London. For God's sake, do not come without making arrangements first!"

As soon as the words left her lips, the door opened. Philippe released her hand from his tight grip. Robert noticed the action, bringing a displeased frown to his face.

"Is he troubling you, my dear?" Robert flung a look of agitation at the unnamed gentleman.

Suzette leaned into his body, trying to gain strength from his protection. Instinctively, he slipped his arm around her waist, claiming her as his own.

"No, Robert. It's just a former acquaintance from my youth. We are both quite surprised to have bumped into each other, aren't we, Philippe?"

"I see," he said, raising his eyebrows, suspicious of her answer. "I'm Lord Robert Holland, and who might you be, sir?"

"Philippe Moreau," he answered curtly. He felt no pleasure over the introduction, only a need to remove himself from the uncomfortable situation. "I shall take my leave," he announced. He bowed at the waist before Suzette, saying his departing words. "I am glad to see that you are well, Mademoiselle." Philippe turned and then quickly strode down the street and out of sight.

"Are you all right? You look pale." Robert leaned over and kissed her cheek, waiting for her response.

"Yes, I'm quite fine. It was just a shock seeing him. I thought that he was dead."

"Dead, you say? He looks quite alive to me—especially the way he was looking at you."

"He's been away at sea. He's a Naval Lieutenant, an old friend of my father, and he was saddened to hear of his passing. He was just expressing his condolence, that's all." Suzette feared that Robert suspected more and lightheartedly changed the subject.

"What takes a man so long to choose a box of cigars? I'd really like to know. Don't they all smell the alike?" She burst forth with an insincere laughter, which seemed to satisfy and allay Robert's curiosity for the moment.

He walked her across the street to the jeweler and gazed in the showcase window, spotting an emerald broach that caught his fancy. "I say the one on the right—the broach. Do you like it?"

"Yes, it's beautiful, but you don't have to keep buying me things. You know how I feel about you without all your gifts."

Robert looked into Suzette's eyes saddened by her refusal. He brushed his thumb tenderly across her cheekbone to assure her of his intent. "I need to do these things for you, my love. Don't deny me the joy of what I can give you."

Suzette knew in her heart Robert gained immense satisfaction in caring for her needs. At times, she felt guilty but would never spurn his display of affection. After all, she owed him her life.

"No, of course, not. I would never deny your show of love."

Robert smiled. "Well then, let's go look at that broach." He opened the door to the jeweler and led her inside to purchase the most outrageous emerald broach in all of London.

* * *

Weeks passed, and no word came from Philippe, which greatly relieved Suzette's anxiety. Robert did not pressure her about the subject, and everything returned to normal.

Feeling lucky one Saturday afternoon, Robert wished to spend the day at the horse track. Suzette agreed to accompany him for the entertainment, having learned that horses were another one of his passions in life, though not her forte.

Upon their arrival at the track, Robert escorted her to his private box and sat discreetly by her side, showing no outward affection.

"I hope you don't mind, Suzette, if we don't act extremely affectionate in public today. There are those who know me here, and I don't wish to start gossip."

Suzette felt the word *gossip* cut like a knife, and she wondered about his inference. Not wishing to start an argument, she conceded.

"Of course, Robert. I wouldn't think of embarrassing you."

Robert appeared distracted as the hour passed and race by race occurred. He moaned his losses and cheered at his winnings over his bets. As the fourth race was about to begin, a woman's voice came up behind them, which startled them both.

"Brother? What are you doing here?"

Robert's face contorted as he felt the kiss of his sister on the side of his cheek. Her hot breath whispered in his ear, "Who is this?" she said, pinching him on the shoulder. After hearing her demand for an answer, he stood and greeted her.

"Marguerite, what are you doing here?" he asked, his eyes conveying his disapproval.

"Oh, Lord Chambers brought me here for a boring afternoon of horse racing," she said. "I just happened to arrive in London for the weekend and had intended on dropping by your townhouse."

She looked at Suzette for a moment and then returned her eyes to her brother. "Now look, I've bumped into you and found you with a woman. Don't be rude, big brother! Introduce your sister to your lady friend."

Robert glared back at his sister with narrow eyes, expressing his displeasure. "Marguerite Holland, this is Suzette Rousseau."

Marguerite's brow rose. "Oh my goodness, a French Mademoiselle!" she exclaimed, eyeing her from head to toe. "Do tell, Robert, where did you two meet?"

"She's an acquaintance," he insisted. "A friend."

Suzette's heart pounded as she watched the nightmare of deception spill from Robert's lips. Her only conclusion was that he was embarrassed to be seen in public with her, and extremely horrified to introduce her to a family member. Hurt, she inhaled a deep breath, and exclaimed, "Lord Holland, you didn't tell me you had a sister." She looked at Marguerite and curtsied. "It's a pleasure to meet you."

Marguerite eyed her with disdain. "Robert, why don't you be a dear and go get us a drink, will you? I'm parched."

"You don't need a drink," Robert complained, knowing she had intended to corner Suzette alone for a few moments. "Find your Lord Chambers to wait on you."

Marguerite sensed her brother was not about to budge and give her the pleasure of talking to the woman alone, so she relented. "Oh, very well then. I'll leave you alone with your lady friend," she sighed, disappointed. She looked at Suzette and sneered. "It was nice meeting you."

Marguerite reached out, straightened her brother's ascot with her hand, and then patted him on the chest. "Don't be a stranger, dear. Come home soon. Daddy misses you."

Marguerite departed, and Robert sat back down sickened over the unexpected exposure of his private life to Suzette. "Sorry about that." What else could he say? He didn't wish to discuss the matter of his family with her, so he returned his attention to the next race hoping to God she would let the matter pass.

The races ended, and the carriage ride home was one of tense silence between its passengers. Suzette said little, and Robert seethed with anger. The chance encounter with his sister had been poor timing. He felt cornered. Suddenly, a part of his life had been uncovered, which he wished to remain hidden from Suzette. Her displeasure with him was obvious, when her demeanor remained less than attentive.

When they arrived at the cottage, Madame LeBlanc met them at the door and took Suzette's parasol and hat. Suzette immediately begged to leave.

"I'm extremely tired, Robert, and I'd like to retire . . . alone."

She turned to go upstairs, but he stopped her and pulled her into his arms. "I'm sorry. You have every right to be upset with me."

Suzette wished to resist his touch, but she found herself laying her head on his shoulder instead, sighing over his apology.

"There are things about my life I have not shared with you, Suzette, and you have been gracious enough not to pry. My life is very complicated when I am away from London. I have duties and a family that you know very little about."

Suzette raised her head. "Am I also a duty that you attend to, as well, Robert? Just another matter you take care of when you're here in London?"

"You are not a duty," he protested. "I adore you. You know that."

"Perhaps," Suzette said, pulling away from him. "But for how long will you adore me, and do I have any kind of future with you? You treat me like your mistress and not like the woman you love."

Robert's countenance fell, and his silence answered her question.

"I must go, Suzette. I'm sorry, but as my sister mentioned, I'm due back at our estate in Surrey again." He lowered his eyes, unable to look at her directly. "Unfortunately, I will be gone much longer this time, but I'll contact you as soon as I return."

"How long?" Suzette demanded.

"A few weeks."

He pulled her back into his arms and kissed her pouting lips. At first, he felt a resistance that bruised his heart. Then, as he persisted in his passion, Suzette melted into his arms and returned his kiss with the same ardor as his own. When he finished, he glared at Madame LeBlanc, who had been standing off to the side watching the entire encounter.

"Next time, I'd prefer privacy," he said, clearly irritated at the woman's intrusion into their personal moment.

Robert left, and Suzette began to cry after the door closed. She turned around and looked at Madame LeBlanc, who displayed the usual smug expression.

"Don't you dare say another word," Suzette hissed. She stormed up the stairs, slammed the door, and hid in her room for the remainder of the day.

CHAPTER 20

The weeks passed painfully slow, and Suzette received no word from Robert. Daily, she tortured herself about the incident at the racetrack, questioning whether she was simply his mistress and nothing more. She loved him, but seeds of doubt had burrowed into her heart. Anguished over the thought she was merely a sexual rendezvous for his pleasure when in London, bred recurring fears he would one day leave.

When he was away, Suzette spent the days idly trying to entertain herself with her empty hobbies, which had become painfully tiresome. She carefully tended her garden of lilies that were the symbol of hope she would find ultimate happiness. Up until that moment, Suzette thought she had. It seemed the weeds recently discovered in her flowerbeds were trying to tell her something. They were like dreadful omens threatening her contentment. She forcibly pulled them out, digging at their roots tenaciously until she was sure their invasion had been fully eradicated.

When her gardening did nothing more than to upset her, she retreated to her parlor for a cup of tea and thought about grabbing a book. Mindless reading often helped to take her mind off of Robert. It was obvious that today she desperately needed a reprieve.

She snuggled into her favorite chair and opened to the chapter where she had left off. Since her arrival in England, she had become acquainted with female English authors that wrote sublime love stories. They all seemed to have happy endings where women married the men they loved, in spite of obstacles or class differences. If it could happen in a storybook, Suzette believed it could come to pass for her, too.

Madame LeBlanc entered the room interrupting her at an interesting scene, and Suzette snapped at her intrusion.

"Yes? What is it?" The startled look upon her maid's face made her feel awful, and she immediately apologized. "I'm sorry." She despised the woman, but it wasn't an excuse to treat her poorly. Madame LeBlanc handed Suzette a note.

"A courier just delivered this for you, Mademoiselle. That is all."

Suzette reached for the envelope, her heart racing, thinking it was a letter from Robert. Her countenance fell as she recognized the all too familiar penmanship.

"Thank you. Leave me now."

Suzette broke the seal and pulled out the letter. Slowly opening it, she braced herself for Philippe's words. She hoped he had forgotten her, but it was apparent he had not.

My Dearest Suzette,

I have these long weeks, since I found you on the London streets, kept my distance. After we parted, I returned from furlough and have resigned my commission with the French Navy. It was well overdue. Afterward, I took residence in a small flat in London, purely with the hope that you would allow me to see you again.

May I have the honor of your presence over lunch and perhaps a subsequent stroll in the gardens along the Thames? I assure you that I will respect your privacy and treat you, as I have since the day we met, with the utmost respect and love.

I will procure a table for two at the Beauberry House at noon tomorrow. For your convenience, I have hired a carriage to arrive at your residence at eleven thirty. If you do not arrive by the noon hour, I will know you refused the transportation and decided not to attend. In that case, I will have a leisurely lunch by myself and understand that you do not wish to see me at this time. I cannot promise you, however, that I will not try again to entice you to lunch in the future.

I do hope you will find it in your heart to give me a few moments to enjoy your presence and catch up on old times.

Fondest regards,

Philippe Victor Moreau

Suzette folded the paper, her hands shaking from emotion. A few moments later, she reopened it and read it again, trying to decide what to do. His penmanship was so reminiscent of the letter written years before, which he posted from some exotic land during his voyage with the French Navy. Suzette had missed him terribly.

Each night, she had carefully opened the letter and read its contents before returning it back to her hiding place for safekeeping. When she burned it at the Chabanais, she did so because her hopes and dreams of one day being his wife died—only ashes of the past remained. Then, as fate dealt its hand, Robert arrived and filled the void in her life, and she gave her heart to another.

Suzette sat motionless for a while, pondering his request. She rationalized that if she did not agree to see him, he would relentlessly pursue her until she gave in. Philippe loved Paris, and to take a flat and remain in London was quite unlike him. No doubt, he was scheming to win her back, and Suzette wanted to dissuade him as soon as possible. Surely, one lunch and a walk in the park would be a harmless activity, so she decided to dine with her former fiancé to put an end to his fanciful dreams.

* * *

Philippe arrived at the historic Beauberry House and requested a secluded table away from the bustle of patrons.

Led to a table for two that met his requirements, he ordered a glass of Chardonnay to calm his nerves.

For weeks, he toyed with the idea of leaving Suzette alone. However, when he read the announcement in the news the day before, a glimmer of hope returned to his broken heart. His adoration for Suzette had not waned. They grew up as childhood sweethearts, and Philippe's love was as strong as the cords that bound the anchors of the ships he sailed.

He joined the French Navy on a whim in his youth, hoping to make his fortune, so that he could one day return and marry his beloved Suzette. For years, he sailed the seas, writing letters as often as possible and posting them at various ports throughout the world.

He had done well and been promoted to Lieutenant, which gained him a modest income that was enough to start a life with the woman he loved. Upon his furlough and return to Paris, to his heartbreak, the only thing that greeted him was an abandoned apartment and a woman who disappeared off the face of the earth.

Philippe painstakingly attempted to trace the trail of Suzette, only to find spotty information from her landlord. Fortunately, he was able to tell him the name of her neighbors who helped her shortly after her father's death. They left a forwarding address in Rouen, and Philippe contacted them by mail, but only received sketchy details in return.

His first clue was the Daughters of Charity, who referred him to a washhouse that led to a dead-end trail. No one spoke a word, except to say that Suzette had been fired and was never seen or heard from again. Called back to duty, they had docked ship in England, when by the grace of God, he found Suzette on the streets of London.

To Philippe, it was nothing short of a miracle to find his beloved, and he considered it an answer to prayer. The only thing standing in his way to regaining what he lost was her obvious benefactor, Lord Robert Holland. He tried not to despise the man but found it difficult. For the past weeks, he had done his own investigation into this mysterious lord who held Suzette in his clutches. It was obvious Holland did not intend to marry Suzette and only kept her for sexual favors, which sickened Philippe to no end.

Philippe wanted Suzette back in his life, and he was determined to forgive her for whatever transgressions she had committed out of desperation. His burning desire to rekindle the love in her heart and woo her back to his side drove him each day to wait for the right moment. It seemed as if it had arrived.

He took a sip of Chardonnay, and when he glanced up at the entrance he saw her arrival. He put the glass down and stood to his feet. She was breathtakingly beautiful. The girl he had loved since childhood was now a woman. Adorned in a burgundy satin gown that swirled as she walked, she looked like an angel from heaven. When she reached his side, she smiled warmly, and his heart melted at the sound of her voice.

"Hello, Philippe."

"You came."

"Of course, I came, silly."

He grinned when he remembered her childish phrase of calling him *silly* whenever she teased him.

"I couldn't very well ignore your invitation, now could I?" she spoke sweetly.

Philippe helped her to the chair and then sat across the table. His countenance glowed at the sight of Suzette sitting only a few feet away. He felt tongue-tied and didn't know where to begin. He picked up the menu and glanced at the cuisine while he regained his thoughts.

"Have you been here before?" Suzette asked.

He peeked over the top of the menu and answered. "No."

"The food is quite good, actually. I've been here once with—" Suzette abruptly stopped her words, and Philippe finished her thought.

"With Lord Holland, I assume," he said, quietly trying not to sound irritated.

"I think I'm ready to order," she said abruptly.

The air became tense between them, and Philippe regretted his last comment. He placed his order after Suzette, and they handed their menus to the waiter. He took a sip of Chardonnay and was surprised that Suzette only ordered tea, silently congratulating her on the composure that he obviously lacked.

"Please," Suzette pleaded, "tell me about your tour of duty on the Pacific during the campaign. I read articles in the news and thought of you and often prayed for your safety."

His face grimaced. "We were fortunate. Our voyages were mostly fair-weather. The China Coast and the seas around Formosa are quite beautiful but different from anything I've ever seen. The Sino-French conflict is not something I wish to share with a lady," he added reluctantly. "I still struggle with my own nightmares from the atrocities my eyes beheld."

"Oh, I am sorry, Philippe. I don't think I'd care to hear about the horrors of war myself," she confessed.

The waiter interrupted, placing a pot of tea and a cup and saucer in front of Suzette. Watching her delicate hands pour the steaming liquid into her cup, he couldn't help but express his thoughts.

"You look wonderful, Suzette—even more beautiful than I remember when we last met."

"You are too kind," she answered embarrassed. "Beautiful in some ways, perhaps. In others, I'm afraid not." She lowered her eyes to the teacup, dropped two cubes of sugar, and then mindlessly swirled it around in circles, waiting for it to dissolve.

"Tell me what happened." Philippe needed to know.

She sipped her tea to bide a few moments before answering, and then put the cup down on the saucer. Her eyes filled with pain, and Philippe reached across the table and touched her hand. He sensed her flesh next to his own, and a rush of emotion and love flowed through his body, bringing warmth to his heart.

"Simple, really. My father went to bed one night and never woke up again."

"I'm sorry, Suzette, truly." Philippe paused, watching the painful memories flash across her face. "I loved your father and will miss him. He was a wonderful man."

"I miss him as well, Philippe." She took another sip of tea and sighed. "Father was deeply in debt and owed many creditors. I had no idea. His entire estate—all our belongings, everything—were sold by court order to pay his debts. I had no money to give him a proper burial, so I stood and watch as they hurled his body into a common grave."

Philippe saw the lingering grief in her heart as she spoke and attempted to halt the conversation. "You don't need to tell me anything further, Suzette. I don't wish to cause you distress."

She inhaled a deep breath to contain the threat of tears. "No, that's all right. You have the right to know, Philippe." She took a sip of tea and then continued. "The Daughters of Charity sheltered me while I looked for work. I found a job as a laundress, but the hours and conditions were terrible."

Philippe's brow furrowed at the thought of the hard labor Suzette no doubt endured. Surely, she had suffered at the hands of the managers or employees, but what he heard next was even more shocking.

"One of my first assignments was to haul the laundry back and forth to one of their customers. It was a brothel, of all places, the Chabanais."

"The Chabanais?" Philippe sat up in his seat.

Suzette smiled and raised one brow in his direction, almost surprised at his response. "You've heard of it, I see."

The food arrived and conversation ceased. Philippe sat silently in thought.

"Why don't we eat first?" she suggested. "I'll continue my story later." She lifted her pleading eyes in his direction, and Philippe agreed.

"Of course, whatever makes you comfortable, Suzette."

The meal continued, and the two exchanged small talk. Philippe wished to hear the remainder of her story and purposely ate his lunch quickly. Suzette, to his dismay, toyed with her food and ate small bites, stretching out the time in an obvious attempt to avoid continuing the discussion. After seeing her procrastination, he changed his plans about finishing their conversation in a public setting. Instead, he directed their chat elsewhere.

"I've done well in the Navy," he said nonchalantly. "I resigned my commission and took my earnings."

"That is good news—very good news," she said finally after a lull between the two.

"With the money I've gained during my tour of duty, I've invested in a shipping company and purchased half interest with a gentleman by the name of Jacques Duval. I will be advising and working on procurement and delivery of goods for merchants. My seafaring days have ended, and frankly, I have had enough."

Philippe hoped that the news would please Suzette. He had made something of his life. He was more than able to care for a woman and provide a comfortable home. Unfortunately, he found her strangely silent and non-responsive.

Lunch ended, and at Philippe's suggestion, they strolled to a nearby park for a leisurely walk through the fragrant gardens. Up until that point, Philippe refrained from touching Suzette too often, but he could do so no longer. He picked up her hand from her side and slipped it around his arm.

"Beautiful ladies cannot walk unescorted through gardens, Suzette. You'll be on my arm, and I refuse to take no for an answer."

Suzette smiled in return, allowing him this pleasure as a gift rather than a necessity. After a few yards of strolling, he asked her to continue. "Tell me the rest, please."

"The rest? You wish to know, no doubt, about my stay at the Chabanais and how I ended up with Robert."

Philippe nodded.

"How can I tell you the rest, Philippe, without you thinking horrid things of me?"

"I will not judge you, Suzette, I promise," he said, calming her fears.

Suzette appeared hesitant but answered his questions. "Each day, I delivered laundry to the Chabanais. Late at evening, I was fired by the manager at the washhouse. I suddenly found myself back on the streets, in the dead of the night, with nowhere to go or sleep, so I returned to the only place I knew—the Chabanais."

Philippe slowed their walk and tightened his arm around Suzette's to encourage her to continue the discourse.

"Madame Laurent, the mistress of the brothel, pretty much blackmailed me into staying. I relented, because I saw no other recourse but to become a prostitute. I was afraid of dying on the streets. The former choice, to say the least, was much more picturesque, though it would cost me a hefty price."

Philippe motioned to a nearby park bench, wishing to sit while Suzette continued her story. "Would you mind?" he asked. They sat down, and she smoothed her skirt as she continued.

"I will be honest. I was petrified and ashamed that I had stooped to such low standards in order to survive. It was not my first choice, I assure you, but I was frightened."

"If anything, Suzette," Philippe interjected, "I do believe that to be truth. It was desperation, no doubt, that drove you there. I know you too well to think otherwise." He patted her arm, hoping to convey some sense of comfort and understanding.

"Madame Laurent procured Lord Holland to break me in my first night, but to my surprise, he would not take my virginity at the brothel. After our first meeting, he took an interest in me, though I think some of it was purely pity for my situation. I was thankful he did. He returned three nights in a row, and we carefully hid the fact from Madame Laurent until . . ." Suzette physically shuddered.

"Until what, Suzette?"

"Until Madame Laurent discovered our deception. She gave me another patron who cruelly attempted to rape me. Lord Holland found me in peril and pulled the man from my body, before he had a chance to do me harm. Then, he purchased my way out of the brothel."

Abhorred over the scene Suzette had described, Philippe now understood his rival. She felt indebted to him for saving her life.

"Do you love him?"

Without hesitation, she replied. "Robert saved me, Philippe, from a life of degradation. He paid Madame Laurent a huge amount of money to buy my freedom and then brought me here to England with him. He's provided a wonderful home and showers me with love and gifts." Suzette hesitated. "I love him, even though I feel indebted to him."

"Indebtedness and love are two different matters," Philippe breathed with a sigh. "You need to separate the two, Suzette. They are not the same."

"Of course, it's love," Suzette emphatically retorted, pulling from the grasp of his arm. "I owe him much, but I love him for other reasons too."

"Not without a price." Philippe's voice carried a sarcastic tone, which he immediately regretted upon hearing the words fall from his lips.

"I gave it to him willingly, Philippe. Willingly! Perhaps a price to you, but it was because of my affection for him that I allowed him to take my virginity. He loves me. I believe he does."

The silence between the two encircled them while the early autumn leaves rustled and swirled around their feet. Both turned cold toward the other. Suzette's justification of her actions was strong and evident in her words. Philippe knew there was no convincing her otherwise, and he removed his arm from around her shoulder and stood to his feet.

He knew the truth of Robert's love and feared telling Suzette what she apparently did not know. The man wanted to keep her as his mistress and nothing more, but his naïve Suzette refused to see the truth.

Offering her his hand, he spoke. "May I see you again, Suzette?"

"Again?"

"Yes, if it is convenient. I mean, is he around?"

"He is away for a few weeks with business to attend to. I believe his father is ill."

"Then you have time to spend with me," Philippe concluded. He carefully watched Suzette's pondering face, seeing she was torn over what answer to give.

"You may call, but we must meet elsewhere. Should my servant see you at the cottage, I'm afraid word may get back to Robert. I don't want to . . ."

"What lose him? Upset him? Make him jealous that you're seeing the man you were engaged to marry?"

"It's a matter of privacy, that's all." Suzette turned and began to walk away.

"I'm sorry. I find this entire situation difficult," he said, exasperated. "I'm not ready to let you drift back into obscurity." He followed Suzette and grabbed her arm, turning her around. "Do you understand how hard this is for me? I still love you, Suzette. When I returned to France, all I thought about was our impending marriage." His eyes spoke volumes of longing and pain. He wanted to snatch her away from him—from this life of use and shame.

"All right, you may see me again. I only ask that you do not pressure me. I am happy with Robert, and though that may hurt you, it is my life now."

She pulled harshly away from his grasp and walked down the path away from Philippe. After a few steps, she abruptly stopped, turned, and looked at him with resolve.

"I am not the same person you were once engaged to marry. I've changed, and you must accept that fact."

"You'll always be Suzette," he spoke, objecting to her statement.

With exasperation in her voice, she reiterated her conditions. "Send me notes when and where you'd like to meet for lunch or dinner or strolls again in the park, but I shall not be seen elsewhere with you or receive you at my home. Do you understand?"

"Absolutely, and I'll respect your wishes."

"Thank you." Her voice turned soft, and she begged to leave. "I must go now. Will you hire me a carriage?"

"Yes, of course." Philippe escorted her to the entrance of the gardens where a line of cabs stood waiting for hire.

"Thank you for lunch, and most of all, for your understanding." Suzette lifted her hand to Philippe, and he offered a gentle kiss that lingered.

He opened the door, helped her inside, and then gave the driver a few pounds to take her back home. As he watched the carriage depart down the street, his chest tightened with yearning. Unable to let her live a useless life as one man's mistress, he vowed to win her heart and hand in marriage. After reading the recent news, he knew he had a chance. He would pursue her relentlessly until she accepted his proposal.

It was apparent from their meeting today that Suzette had not read the announcement in the social section of the

London Gazette. The infamous Lord Robert Holland had married Lady Jacquelyn Spencer the day before. He was convinced that Lord Holland would no doubt maintain his deception and keep it from Suzette as long as he could. It was all too obvious to Philippe now why Lord Holland had procured a small cottage in the countryside for his mistress. He fully intended to keep her tucked away and ignorant of his whereabouts and social news. With Suzette being out of sight and away from the mainstream of London, he could come and go as he pleased, leading a double life.

When the time was right, Philippe fully intended on revealing the rogue's true colors. Perhaps then, she would be willing to turn away from the futility of their relationship and return to where she belonged—in his arms alone.

CHAPTER 21

Philippe did not wait long. Within a week, another note arrived at Suzette's home by courier with a request to meet him for a walk in the gardens along the Thames. If she agreed, he would arrange to send a carriage to pick her up at her cottage home.

The young boy who delivered the letter was instructed to wait for an answer, and Suzette felt pressured to make an immediate decision. She knew if she continued to see Philippe, she was playing a dangerous game with his affections, as well as with her own. Her loneliness outweighed wisdom, while she rationalized it was merely rekindling an old friendship and nothing more. She agreed to the rendezvous and wrote a quick response, which she handed back to the courier, tipping him a few coins.

Robert's absence proved harder to handle this time. Suzette struggled over their relationship, his family, and the event at the racetrack with his sister. In addition, her emotions were on edge, making her irritable, sullen, and depressed. The lack of company and entertainment was taking its toll.

The idea of a stroll through the gardens appealed to Suzette. She had already told Philippe everything, so perhaps this meeting would be less stressful. He understood her decisions, and he knew how she felt about Robert. There was no way, in her own mind, that he would dare entertain a future with her again. Eventually, he would give up. She decided to remind him upon arrival it was only a friendly meeting and nothing more.

As soon as she stepped from the carriage, the fragrance of the garden flowers and the sun on her face felt glorious. She spotted Philippe waiting patiently at the iron gate entrance. His face looked apprehensive. Suzette stood still for a moment, looking at Philippe's stance. She had forgotten the handsomeness of his countenance, his tall slender body, and dark brown hair and eyes. He was a stunning man, and part of her soul sparked with pleasure as she gazed upon him.

She recalled how her father had adored him, for he thought that Philippe possessed a heart of gold. He was a good and honorable man who respected and loved her deeply. Suzette's father held no hesitation in approving their marriage. Philippe, however, wanting to give Suzette the best in life, insisted he join the French Navy to find a solid career first and gain the finances to support her before they wed.

Like any young girl in love, Suzette cried a bucketful of tears the day she gave him her last embrace, wondering if she would ever see him again. He kissed her and spoke words of a promised return. Now, as she stood considering his stature, she saw in him a new manhood he had not exhibited before. Life's experiences had changed them both.

Philippe caught sight of Suzette, and she smiled and began walking in his direction. She saw his hands nervously clenching his gloves. Philippe took off his hat, tipped it, and spoke in French his words of greeting.

"Suzette, I am so glad you accepted my invitation."

"I am, too, Philippe. It is a beautiful day, and the fresh air will do us both good."

She spoke in her native tongue with Philippe as they strolled through the park. She missed France, but never revealed her homesick feelings to Robert.

Philippe returned his hat to his head and held out his arm for Suzette. She hesitated for a moment at the thought of touching him, but then relented and wrapped her arm around his. She glanced up at his strong, tall figure and smiled at the pleasure etched across his face.

Philippe drew her close to his side as they strolled along the path lined with oak trees. Large branches hung overhead, creating a canopy. The air was crisp, and the trees had begun to turn their leaves to a golden hue.

"How have you been, Suzette, since we last met?"

Suzette hesitated as she formulated a response that wouldn't hurt her escort. When she took too long to answer, Philippe did for her.

"You miss him, I see." His voice was tender, without an accusatory or angry tone.

"Yes, I do."

"Has he written to you?"

"Not yet, but I surmise he is busy with matters." *Matters.* Suzette could only wonder what matters. Again, the silence came between them. She felt a slight tug of Philippe's arm, bringing her closer to his side as if to support her in sadness.

"You know, Suzette, I miss your dear father. When I think of his sudden death during my absence, it breaks my heart. I should have been there to comfort and care for you." His voice shook with emotion. "After what you told me, I feel partially responsible for being absent. I could have saved you such heartache had I just returned."

"You couldn't have known this would happen, no more than I. You were where you should have been, Philippe. Please, don't blame yourself. Besides, even if I had written to you, it would have been months before you would have received my letter, let alone return. Matters would have continued to play out even as they had during your absence."

In a moment of silence, they each reminisced over years past. Suzette remembered the laughs over dinner when the three of them dined and her father's odd sense of humor that always threw Philippe into a roar. With each step, Suzette felt more at ease along his side, as if they were old friends remembering fond times together. She turned and looked up at his pensive face but dared not ask for his thoughts.

As they passed an obliging empty bench under a shaded tree, Philippe directed their steps toward the waiting seat. "Come, let's sit a while." He released her arm and let her sit first. Suzette caught a glimpse of the longing in his eyes.

"Can we talk, Suzette?" he asked reluctantly. "About your life, I mean."

"What do you mean, about my life?" She knew what he meant. Suzette suddenly wished to jump from the bench and run down the pathway away from the words she did not want to hear.

"You don't need to live this way any longer, Suzette. I'm back now. I can take care of you. We can marry like we planned, and you don't have to . . . well, you don't have to give yourself to a man to support yourself."

Suzette swallowed the lump in her throat. Her gaze avoided his and fixated upon a nearly small boxwood hedge.

"Talk to me, Suzette, please."

She looked into his pleading eyes to defend her actions and tell him what she truly felt. In one breath, she flung her answer.

"I do not stay with Robert just because he provides for me. I stay with him because I love him." The words were a welcome relief as she spun her head to the side, flipping an annoying lock of hair tickling her cheek.

"He's married now Suzette. He cannot marry you, so why do you stay? Do you want to be his mistress for the rest of your life? Is that enough for you? That is all that will ever come of it—until he grows tired of you or finds someone else to play the part."

"What do you mean, he's married?" The color drained from Suzette's face as her heart stopped for a brief moment.

Philippe reached over and grabbed her hand. "You haven't heard then, have you?"

"Heard what?" The pounding in her chest increased.

He pulled the news clipping from his pocket and handed her the *London Gazette* article. She grasped the paper and read the heartbreaking words.

Marriage Announcements — On October 22, 1878, Lord Robert Holland, married Lady Jacquelyn Marie Spencer in a lavish ceremony held at St. John's Cathedral . . .

Suzette dropped the news clipping unable to read the remainder. A gust of wind grabbed the paper and twirled it among circling leaves sending it down the pathway out of sight. Philippe's hand tightened his grasp. Suzette couldn't breathe. She felt numb as if life had drained from her body.

"I'm sorry, Suzette. I wanted to tell you last week but didn't have the heart. It's obvious you are in love with the man, but he's deceived and used you. He only intends to keep you as his mistress. Don't you see that now?"

Suzette sat silent.

"If he loved you, he would release you to a life of decency instead of using you as his kept woman for sexual pleasure."

Suzette knew he was right, but she couldn't acknowledge the painful truth, even to herself. "I'm afraid I'm suddenly tired, Philippe. I need to leave." She thrust her hand from his and stood to her feet. Her mind swirled like the wind around her body, and inwardly her soul screamed in pain.

"Suzette, please."

She ignored his plea and began walking down the pathway toward the waiting carriage. Suzette heard the sound of his boots behind her on the paved walkway as he tried to catch up. Philippe's hand grabbed her shoulder, and Suzette wiggled from his grasp in exasperation.

"Let me go!" she demanded. In anger, she spun around with the intent of slapping his face, but the world around her began to spin. Everything shifted in her vision, and her knees buckled from weakness. As she stumbled backwards into a fall, Philippe caught her in his arms before she hit the ground.

"Dear Lord, Suzette, are you all right?" He held her strongly, yet tenderly.

"I'm dizzy," she gasped, surprised.

Philippe lifted her up in his arms and carried her back to the bench, slowly lowering her down upon the seat.

"Sit down for a moment. I insist," he ordered, his voice filled with concern. He sat next to her and wrapped his arm around her shoulder for support. Suzette instinctively laid her head against his chest, waiting for the twirling sensation to leave.

He touched the side of her face, stroking her tenderly. "I'm so sorry," he whispered apologetically. "It wasn't my intention to upset you. Forgive me. I only wanted you to know the truth."

"Forgive me," Suzette responded with shallow breathing. "I haven't been well lately. I overreacted."

"What do you mean, you haven't been well, Suzette? Have you seen a physician?"

She shook her head no, suppressing the suspicion she now held for weeks. Her menses were late, and she feared pregnancy.

"I will be all right, I promise." Suzette refused to mention the possibility. Within a few minutes, her head cleared, and the world around her stabilized. "I'm feeling better now. I really should go home."

"Well, I insist on walking you to the carriage."

Suzette didn't argue. He stood up and held out his hand for her to take. Finally, looking up into his concerned and loving face, she felt peace in the reflection of his warm brown eyes. He tenderly grasped her hand, and she clutched his tightly as they walked to the waiting carriage. As she felt his strength, a part of her longed to tell him what she feared but could not. It would be devastating to reveal to Philippe that she could possibly be pregnant with Robert's child. No, it had to be kept a secret until she was sure of it.

* * *

A week later, Suzette was convinced she carried a child in her womb. The nausea was unbearable and the fatigue difficult to manage. In addition, her emotions ran wild, from the fear and apprehension of being pregnant to overwhelming joy at the possibility. At times, she would place her hand upon her stomach and laugh at what awaited her, and then at other times she felt tearful and terribly alone. There had been no word from Robert, nor did Philippe contact her after their last walk in the park.

Madame LeBlanc quickly noticed Suzette's physical distress and appearance, but said nothing until one particular morning of upheaval when she vomited uncontrollably over the side of her bed. After hearing her moans, her servant knocked on the door only to be greeted by Suzette's denial.

"I'm fine. Go away and leave me alone!"

"Ridiculous," she blurted out, as she flung open the door and went to her side with a basin in hand. She held Suzette until she heaved again and emptied the contents of her stomach. After she finished, she rose and grabbed a towel from the washroom, moistened it, and brought it back to her mistress, wiping away the residue from her lips.

"How far?" she asked, dabbing her mouth.

"What?"

"How far along are you?"

"I don't know what you're talking about," Suzette breathed in anger, denying the accusations that she knew to be true.

"You're pregnant. I can tell a pregnant woman when I see one, Mademoiselle." Madame LeBlanc placed both hands on her hips and defiantly glared at Suzette.

Suzette relented. "About six weeks, I think." Tears streamed down her face. Up until this time, she had kept a wary distance from Madame LeBlanc, but now she felt an overwhelming need for a woman's help and guidance.

"What happens to women like me when they become pregnant?" Her voice shook, afraid of the answer.

"We can talk about that later," Madame LeBlanc said with a tone of sympathy in her voice. "Go wash, put on a robe, and I'll make some peppermint tea to settle your stomach."

Suzette wandered off to the bath chamber. She stood in front of the mirror looking pale and sickly. After a few splashes of cold water on her face from the basin, she patted herself dry with a towel, and then ran a brush through her tangled hair. A quick swish of water in her mouth helped rid the putrid taste of vomit.

Wrapped in a warm bathrobe, she climbed downstairs. Upon entering, she sat down at a small table in the kitchen. Madame LeBlanc handed her the steaming cup of brewed tea. The smell of peppermint brought a fresh wave of nausea, but Suzette knew its contents would ease her ills once she drank it.

"I don't know what to do." The words fell from Suzette's lips.

"You will have to tell Lord Holland, of course," Madame LeBlanc counseled. "How he will handle the news is another matter."

She lifted her eyes toward her maid. Suzette felt very ignorant. "What do men do when their mistresses become pregnant?"

"Well, as a rule, if we were on French soil, most courtesans who serve aristocratic men would not keep the child. When the baby is born, it would be given up for adoption or provided for by the benefactor to grow up in someone else's care. Men in high positions cannot have illegitimate children claiming title to their money or name, so as a rule, they are spirited away."

Suzette gasped. "You cannot be serious!"

"Oh, quite." She hesitated to mention the other alternative. "He might refer you to an unscrupulous physician, who would attempt to abort the child. I would not recommend such a course of action, though, because your life could be in danger from the procedure."

"I would never do such a thing!" Suzette protested vehemently.

"Of course, you could keep your child by relinquishing your position as mistress with Lord Holland and raise the baby yourself. I dare say there will be no means for you to take care of it, though, will there? Not unless he cares for the bastard child by giving you money."

Suzette put down the teacup as tears spilled down her cheeks. The thought of giving away the child that she and Robert created together was out of the question. *Surely, he wouldn't insist on such an arrangement or dare suggest the other alternative. He can't possibly be so cruel,* she thought to herself.

"I see the distress upon your face, Mademoiselle, but it is the way of things." Madame LeBlanc stood silently for a few moments, pondering Suzette. "When is Lord Holland due back?" she asked inquisitively. "He'll need to be told immediately upon his return."

"Soon, I think." Suzette paused before continuing, "He's probably on his honeymoon." The confession that he had recently married was difficult for Suzette to admit, even now.

Madame LeBlanc showed no surprise over the announcement of Lord Holland's marriage. "Well, you'll need to tell him. Before you know it, your belly will start looking like a melon, and there'll be no hiding it, now will there?"

Suzette knew she was right. There would be no hiding it from anyone, including Philippe. What would he think? Certainly, he would abandon any thought of reconciliation now that she carried Robert's child. They had tried to be careful, and Robert wore some type of new sheath that was supposed to protect her from pregnancy.

After finishing her tea, Suzette retreated to her room to ponder her quandary. She was trapped, and it was her own fault. Afraid neither would want her, she retreated into her fears of homelessness once again. She could never give up her child. She buried her head in her pillow and sobbed until she fell asleep from exhaustion.

* * *

Another week passed, and Suzette was now used to the morning nausea and prepared with a bucket by her bedside to catch its morning contents.

Notes and invitations from Philippe arrived almost daily, but Suzette turned each one down, sending excuse after excuse. She hoped her continual refusal would discourage him from his relentless pursuit. It was the right thing to do. She knew if he found out about her pregnancy, he would abandon her immediately, which would break her heart. She could never tell him about the child or bear to see the horror on his face after hearing the news.

Her focus turned to Robert. She wished things had been different. Surely, had he not married Lady Spencer, he would have married her instead upon hearing news of her pregnancy, but now it was too late. She trusted his kind heart to do the right thing, and Suzette convinced herself that he would not make her give up the baby but would allow her to raise their child in secret with his provision. She told Madame LeBlanc of her plan, but she was quick to dash her hopes to pieces.

"The man is going to be Duke! He has a reputation to protect, and he will not acknowledge a bastard child in his lineage."

Suzette didn't want to believe her tirade.

* * *

Robert returned to London a week later with his new wife in tow. Their lengthy honeymoon had ended. He soon learned, however, that Lady Spencer preferred to cling to him like a leech. At the first thought of separation, she begged him to bring her to London. He insisted he needed to take care of business, but it made no difference. Unable to discard her pleading tears, he relented. After a week's time, he finally found a moment to slip away on his own to visit Suzette.

His arrival to her small cottage came unannounced, and Madame LeBlanc gasped in surprise when he appeared at the door.

"Lord Holland, you've returned!" Her face flushed at the thought of her mistress, who lay upstairs in her bed sick and pale.

Robert became immediately irritated. "Do you intend on leaving me on the doorstep?"

"No. Forgive me, Monsieur." She stepped out of the way and took his hat and cane. With a quick curtsy, she went to fetch Suzette. "I'll let the Mademoiselle know you've arrived."

Robert sensed something was wrong. He watched her run upstairs, and then he wandered into the parlor surprised to see it unkempt. Reading material lay strewn about, an empty teapot and teacup sat upon a table, and partially eaten biscuits on a plate. Perturbed at the maid's lack of housekeeping skills, he flopped on the settee, tossed a pillow out of the way, and impatiently waited.

Madame LeBlanc fled up the stairs and knocked in panic upon Suzette's bedroom door. After bidding her entrance, she ran to Suzette's bedside.

"You must get up now, Mademoiselle. Lord Holland is waiting for you in the parlor downstairs."

Suzette shot up and flung her legs around the edge of the bed. The room spun, and she looked up at Madame LeBlanc pleading for help.

"My God! Why didn't he tell me beforehand so I could have prepared?"

She ran over to the vanity, sat down, and pulled a brush through her tangled hair. "Find me another dress! I look a fright."

Madame LeBlanc filtered through the wardrobe, begging for direction. "Which one?"

"The pink satin. Perhaps it will give me some color. Hurry!"

She took the dress off the hanger and carefully laid it on the edge of the bed. Suzette struggled with her hair, and Madame LeBlanc walked over and grabbed the brush from her hand.

"Here, let me do that," she insisted. Her skillful hand pulled through the last tangle, and then in one sweep, she wrapped Suzette's hair into a neat bun and pinned it upon her head. "Now, powder your nose, and for heaven's sake, dab your cheeks with rouge. You look like a ghost."

Suzette, who had slept in her corset and bloomers, easily slipped into the dress. Madame LeBlanc buttoned the back and then turned her around, making a quick inspection.

"Find a piece of jewelry, and I'll find your shoes."

Finally, the frantic women had finished their task, and Madame LeBlanc looked at her approvingly. "I wonder how long he'll let you leave the dress on," she said sarcastically.

Angry at the remark, Suzette snapped back. "Keep your mouth shut, do you hear me?"

Nothing further was spoken between the two, and Suzette nervously descended the stairs, pinching her cheeks once more to add a bit of color to her ashen pallor.

Robert stood to his feet as she entered the room, struck by the change in her appearance. Her face appeared drawn, and he could tell she had squeezed her cheeks by the red marks on her face.

"Darling," he said, walking toward her and gathering her into his arms. "You don't look well. Are you all right?"

"Yes, of course, Robert," she answered, her voice laced with feigned sincerity. "Silly me. I was taking a nap, and you woke me up. That's why I look so frightful, I'm afraid."

Robert released his embrace and stepped back, examining her again. "Taking a nap?"

Suzette laughed nervously. "Yes, I'm afraid I stayed up way too long last evening."

Robert hesitated but then lowered his head until his lips met hers. He kissed her deeply, and a rush of relief flooded his soul. He had missed the taste of Suzette's warm mouth. In spite of his newfound status of being a married man, he discovered his new bride cold and unyielding in bed, like most English women. The thought of Suzette's lovemaking aroused his senses. As his kisses became more intense, he noted her response wasn't the same, so he released her lips and demanded an answer.

"Something is wrong. I can sense it."

"Nothing is wrong, Robert," she insisted. "I'm just surprised that you're here now. You've been away for so long." Suzette smiled and then broke out in a nervous laughter, expressing her own loneliness.

"I've missed you terribly," she confessed, nuzzling her head on his chest. "Oh, Robert, don't be gone so long next time, please." She claimed his lips with intensity to show her deep affection.

Robert waited no longer. He scooped her up in his arms and climbed the stairs to her bedroom. As they passed Madame LeBlanc on the way up, Suzette glanced at her and saw her housekeeper mouth the words, "I told you so."

Suzette glared at her in return and then buried her head in the corner of her lover's shoulder, giggling the entire way up the staircase. Once behind closed doors, they rekindled the weeks of separation with passionate lovemaking.

* * *

Robert left Suzette asleep in her bed. The hours had quickly passed, and he needed to return to his waiting wife. He descended the staircase and found Madame LeBlanc in the parlor straightening up the room. He stood in the doorway and watched her for a minute, then cleared his throat to gain her attention. Something was amiss, and he wanted answers.

"What's going on here?"

Madame LeBlanc swung around at the sound of his voice.

"Oh, Monsieur, you startled me," she exclaimed, out of breath. She brought her hand to her chest in fright and then answered his inquiry. "Nothing is going on. I'm merely cleaning, as you can see."

Robert stepped inside the parlor, unwilling to take her word. "There's something going on in this household. I can tell by Suzette's demeanor and your own. You are both hiding something." A few steps closer brought him face to face with the maid, and he raised his voice to make at point.

"I want to know now, or else you can pack your bags and I'll find another woman from France to wait upon my mistress."

He made his threat palatable, and Madame LeBlanc began to shake. The teacup rattled in the saucer she held in her hand, and she took a step back from the English lord's threatening demeanor.

"You've married," she blurted out without further thought. "Your mistress found out about your wife!"

Robert froze. The blood drained from his face, and Madame LeBlanc couldn't help but chuckle aloud. She wanted to tell him the other news but was afraid Suzette would kill her for sure.

"Now you look as pale as her, Monsieur. You wished to know," she said, shrugging her shoulders in relief. She picked up teapot and remaining dishes and then exited the room for the kitchen without saying another word.

Robert left the parlor, picked up his hat and cane, and let himself out of the cottage, slamming the door behind him with a *bang*. As he strode out the door to his waiting carriage, he climbed inside and gave orders to return to his wife. The lit candle had just been extinguished at one end, and he wasn't quite sure how he was going to handle the matter with Suzette.

CHAPTER 22

Suzette's confusion increased as the week passed with no further word from Robert. Their time together had been a physical reunion, but the many questions that nagged Suzette remained unanswered about his marriage.

He offered her no explanation about his absence; it was clear to her now that he intended to keep her in the dark as long as possible. No doubt, he was concerned about her reaction and had every right to be.

As the days slipped by, his avoidance was obvious. The growth of their child in her womb intensified her panic until it became unbearable. Finally, at the end of the week, a note arrived from Robert, which Suzette immediately tore open and read.

Dear Suzette,

I have been called back to my father's estate on business. I am aware that you have discovered my marriage to Lady Jacquelyn Spencer. You have every right to be upset over my deception. We will speak about the matter upon my return.

I am forever yours,

Robert Holland

Suzette dropped the letter to the floor as hot tears streamed down her face. Madame LeBlanc stood in the doorway, watching her reaction, and Suzette instinctively knew she was the traitor. In a rage, Suzette raced toward her, and with an open hand violently slapped her across the face.

"You bitch! You told him that I found out about the marriage, didn't you?" As she tried to slap her again, Madame LeBlanc grabbed her wrist to prevent any further hits upon her already reddened cheek.

"He threatened to fire me if I didn't tell him what was going on! You should be thankful I didn't tell him about the bastard baby in your womb, Mademoiselle."

Suzette could tolerate her insolence no longer and started pushing Madame LeBlanc from the parlor. "Get out! Get out!" She sneered at her vehemently. "Get out now and don't come back."

She pushed her out of the parlor, and Suzette followed her to the maid's quarters. Madame LeBlanc quickly stuffed her belongings into her suitcase.

"Gladly! I'll leave gladly," she muttered in haste.

Suzette thought that she could kill the woman and tried desperately to calm her beating heart, afraid for her physical wellbeing. Finally, with her last dress crammed into her bag, she escorted Madame LeBlanc out the door, slamming it shut behind her.

She fell to her knees and wailed uncontrollably, broken and abandoned by everyone until she passed out from exhaustion on the floor. Hours later, she opened her eyes to find herself curled up in a ball upon the rug near the door. Her head pounded, and her swollen eyelids hurt as she opened them. It was night, and the house was dark and quiet.

Suzette grabbed the hall table and pulled herself to her feet and made her way down the dark hallway to the kitchen. After finding the matches by the stove, she lit an oil lamp on the table.

A quick glance around the kitchen revealed a mess, and she cursed Madame LeBlanc for her laziness. Dirty dishes were stacked high and spoiled food lay upon china plates. She found the kettle to boil water for tea, and then rummaged around the breadbox until she found a piece of fresh pastry to stuff in her mouth.

The quietness of her small cottage was deafening. She knew when Robert returned, he had to be told about the baby, but she feared the outcome. He might insist the child be put up for adoption or demand she see a doctor to do the unthinkable.

She needed help, and there was only one place to turn, though she hesitated to do so. Suzette wandered into the parlor with her brewed cup of tea and sat at her writing desk. She rifled through the letters looking for Philippe's address and then penned a letter of desperation.

* * *

Robert entered the restaurant and recognized the gentleman seated at a table near the window. He halted for a moment and pulled the gloves off his hands. He wondered if his suggested dining location was a bit too expensive for the man's wallet. Nevertheless, if he wanted to meet, he certainly wasn't about to lower his standards for a decent meal, while having an unpleasant conversation.

He strolled up to the table and closely examined the Frenchman. Philippe stood to his feet and greeted him.

"Lord Holland," he said, bowing his head and looking up at his rival. "Thank you for agreeing to meet with me."

Robert looked at him with a contemptuous sigh and responded, "Yes, of course." He made no deference in return or offers to shake the Frenchman's hand. Robert merely pulled back a chair and sat down. The waiter arrived at the table, and he gave his order without looking at the menu.

"I'll have the roast duck and a cup of black tea." He handed the menu back to the waiter.

"Just coffee for me, I'm afraid. I don't have much of an appetite."

Robert raised his brow at his refusal to eat. "Are you sure, man?" he asked curiously.

"Yes, very sure," he responded. "Just black coffee."

Robert shrugged his shoulders and leaned comfortably back in the chair. "So, you are Lieutenant Philippe Moreau, correct?"

"Just Philippe Moreau," he answered coldly. "I've resigned my commission."

"Ah, I see," he replied. "And what is it that you wish to speak with me about?" After receiving a dark glare in return, he wasn't surprised to hear the next words.

"I wish to know your intentions with regard to Suzette Camille Rousseau."

Robert chuckled. "Camille," he said with a smile. "I didn't know that was her middle name. Yes, a virgin when I met her." A look of possession filled Robert's eyes as he dared the man across the table to lay any claim to what was rightfully his. "And what do you mean by intentions, pray tell?"

The waiter arrived and placed the ordered tea and coffee before the guests. Robert immediately took a sip of the steaming brew.

"Well, it's quite obvious that you have no intentions of marrying her now that you've married Lady Spencer." Philippe glanced at the wedding ring on his finger. "By the way, have you seen Suzette since your return from your honeymoon?"

Robert shifted in the chair, irritated at the man's brazenness. "And what is that to you?" he retorted. "That is a private matter." He put the teacup back on the saucer, and then began his own interrogation.

"I was under the impression that you and the Mademoiselle were merely old acquaintances, or at least that was what I was led to believe."

"Hardly," Philippe spoke, leaning forward in his chair. "Suzette Camille Rousseau is my fiancée." He paused, taking a deep breath before continuing. "At least she was before meeting you."

Robert's brow rose, and he looked at the man seated across the table with an increased interest of disdain. "Fiancée? Well, that's interesting."

"I want her back," Philippe demanded. "You cannot make her an honorable woman through matrimony. You only wish to keep her as your mistress."

Robert recognized the look of disgust in his eyes, thinking the man a hypocrite himself. "You Frenchmen have your mistresses and brothels. Why are you so appalled that an Englishman wishes to keep one?" Robert took a breath before continuing to assert his rights. "Well, whatever claim you think you have on her, I'm afraid it's too late, Monsieur. Suzette loves me and intends to stay with me." His voice turned almost nonchalant in nature.

"You seem sure of yourself, Lord Holland."

"She's aware of my marriage, if that's what you are wondering."

"Really?" Philippe doubted his response. "And have you discussed your future together?"

"Her future is my future."

"Suzette merely feels indebted to you for saving her from the Chabanais. You seem to have failed to see the obvious, however."

"And what might that be?"

"You've made her into your own private whore!" Philippe's glare bore into his soul. "Let her go."

Robert felt as if a knife had been thrust into his heart. His adoration for Suzette was sincere, and he did love her in his own way. Perhaps in her foolishness, she wished for more, but he thought she understood the ways of entitlement. He spoke of it often enough—his family duties and even his father's wishes for an heir.

He sat pondering Philippe's accusatory words. It was true that in his overzealousness to protect and care for her, he justified his actions. He was using her as his personal mistress, and it was abhorrently selfish indeed. He may have taken her virginity, but he had played upon her innocence in many other ways. She was a naïve young woman who trusted him implicitly and without question.

He turned to Philippe to ask his intentions. "And if I part ways with Suzette, will you assure me as a man who keeps his word that you will not abandon her?"

"I have no intentions of abandoning her, as I have every intention of marrying her."

Robert studied the sincerity of the man's face, but there was still another matter to consider. "And what if I let her go and she still doesn't marry you?"

"I can assure you that will not be the case."

Surprised over his confident response, Robert wondered how often the two had been seeing each other during his absence. It was obvious that more was transpiring between them, and he felt slightly betrayed over Suzette not telling him of Philippe's true identity and connection to her past. It seemed they both were playing a game of deception in order to keep one another. Robert hesitated, struggling over his strong affections for Suzette.

"I am willing to fight for her honor, Lord Holland, if need be." Philippe postured himself across the table.

Robert raised a brow at the Frenchman's audacity. "There's no need to load your pistol," he said, picking up his cup of tea and taking a sip. "I'm a man of honor, whether you believe it or not. We need not kill each other to bring about the right course of action."

Robert slowly relented when he witnessed the look of determination and love in the Philippe's eyes. The next few words ripped his heart in two.

"I give you my word, Monsieur, upon my next visit to the Mademoiselle, I will do the honorable thing."

"Very well then. I'll hold you to your word." Philippe stood from the table, no longer wishing to spend any further time with Lord Holland.

"I love her, you know." Robert tenderly spoke the truth he needed to admit to himself. "I've grown to love her very much."

"Then you have done the right thing by laying down your wishes to give her the kind of life she deserves to live— one as an honorable woman."

Philippe turned and left Robert to survey the platter of duck that had arrived at his table. He picked up his fork, cut a small portion of the breast, and lifted the moist meat to his mouth savoring the taste.

Robert enjoyed the duck, but found it difficult to swallow. His throat had closed from the painful realization over his impending loss of Suzette. Unsure what he would do without her, he shoved the morsel down his throat with a hard gulp. He poked his fork into another piece of meat, but he realized that he had suddenly lost his appetite.

CHAPTER 23

A few days after his luncheon with Lord Holland, Philippe received a post from Suzette requesting that he come and visit her at the cottage. His immediate thought was that Robert had severed their relationship, so he gladly responded and arrived at her home just before noon the following day.

Upon his arrival, Philippe knocked on the door but received no answer. After repeated knocks, he stepped away from the cottage and examined the windows. The curtains were drawn on the second floor, which Philippe assumed were bedrooms. He walked around the side of the house and noticed a window leading into what appeared to be a parlor. Lace paneled curtains covered the glass, but at least it afforded him partial view into the interior.

He awkwardly squeezed behind a hedge against the cottage and placed his hands on the window, shading the sun from his vision, while he peered through the lace eyelets. It took a few moments before his vision adjusted to the filtering light. He glanced about the furniture but saw no one in a chair or standing nearby. Then, as he was about to pull away, he spotted Suzette on the floor. She was not moving and looked unconscious.

He knocked frantically on the window calling out her name. The sound of his hand slapping the glass and his loud voice did nothing to arouse her dormant body. Frantic with fear, he pulled away and ran to the front door and tried the doorknob, but it was locked.

Philippe glanced about the yard and found a sizeable stone from the walkway and threw it through the side panel window that ran the length of the doorframe. The glass shattered at the first blow, and Philippe carefully pulled the sharp pieces away until he could reach inside and unlatch the door handle.

As soon as it unlocked, he flung the door open and ran into the parlor. To his shock, Suzette lay pale and lifeless. He turned her over and spotted blood on her skirt. He gathered her into his arms frantically trying to revive her back to life.

"Suzette! Please . . . Suzette, wake up!"

No response came. Philippe was beside himself. Her breathing was shallow. He picked up her limp body and carried her to his waiting carriage outside giving orders to the driver to speed into London and the nearest hospital.

After an hour of pacing back and forth since his arrival, he grew sick with worry. Finally, a physician approached him in the waiting area to give him news of her condition. His face was laced with concerned, but Philippe saw a glimmer of hope in his eyes.

"Your wife, I'm afraid, has spotted," he stated solemnly.

Philippe, unwilling to correct the doctor's misconception that he was her husband, let him continue.

"However, I'm happy to report there is no indication she has aborted the baby. I would recommend, however, that she be given extended bed rest until birth. Otherwise, I'm afraid she may lose the child."

"Pardon me?"

Philippe's stunned reaction drew a raised brow from the physician. "The baby," the doctor repeated, not understanding Philippe's surprise. "You didn't know she was with child?"

"No," he answered, astonished. Philippe was beside himself. Suzette was carrying Lord Holland's child! Relieved over her wellbeing, he attempted to deal with the shocking news.

The doctor seemed a bit confused over the situation but continued with his report. "It appears she hasn't eaten well or been drinking enough liquids. She's dehydrated, and that is why she fainted."

"May I see her?"

"Of course," the doctor replied. "Follow me."

The physician led Philippe down a long tile corridor leading into a small patient ward. Upon seeing Suzette, he quickly stepped toward her bedside and took her hand into his, kissing it with his lips. It was stone cold.

The physician gave further instructions. "I suggest that you allow her to rest as much as possible. When we are assured the bleeding has subsided, you may take her home. Make sure she eats and drinks plenty of liquids."

He nodded in compliance. Philippe watched the doctor leave the room and then turned to Suzette. "My God, Suzette, I thought I lost you."

Suzette turned away from Philippe and faced the wall. Her weak voice replied, "You should have let me die."

"Nonsense," he protested. "Why, because you carry Robert's child?"

Suzette's tears rolled profusely down her pale cheeks, and Philippe's heart broke over her expression of shame.

"I'm sorry, Suzette," he said, stroking her hand gently. "Please don't worry."

Suzette sobbed.

"I'll take care of you. Just get better . . . that's all I ask."

"I'm afraid to tell him," Suzette admitted. "He'll want to send the baby away, won't he, Philippe?"

"I don't know," he answered truthfully. "He can't marry you, Suzette."

"I'm well aware," she said. "I had no idea I was pregnant when he married. If I had known, I would have told him. Perhaps things would be different."

Philippe doubted it, but didn't wish to express his negative thoughts. "Rest now," he said, stroking her hand.

"Rest. Close your eyes and sleep, and when you awaken, we'll talk. I'll be here, Suzette. I won't leave you or forsake you. I promise."

He bent near her cheek and dared to kiss her pale skin. Philippe received no complaint from Suzette and was thankful she allowed his lips to linger for a few moments without resistance. He let go of her hand, and then walked into the hallway. After finding a side door that led outdoors to the alleyway, he retreated into seclusion and wept.

* * *

Suzette regained her strength quickly and was sent home under the watchful care of her pseudo-husband. Philippe quickly procured a new housekeeper to watch and care for Suzette during his absence. Suzette approved of the middle-aged English woman, and they seemed to like each other far better than her former arrangement.

On the third day after her return from the hospital, Robert made his final visit. Suzette had spent the past days mentally preparing for their meeting, as she had something to tell him that he needed to know.

Upon his arrival, her housekeeper brought him into the parlor. Her eyes lifted to his tall stature standing in the doorway, and her heart broke at the sight of him.

"Hello, Robert," she said, greeting him warmly. "I've missed you."

Her words seemed to soften his stoic countenance, and he smiled in return. Surprised over the new housekeeper, he inquired. "What happened to Madame LeBlanc?"

Suzette hesitated but told him the truth. "I fired her. The woman was incorrigible."

Robert didn't argue the point. "You look well, Suzette," he said, drawing close to her. He stood for a moment looking fondly into her eyes. Then nearly choking over his words, he spoke. "We need to talk."

Suzette immediately interrupted him while he drew a breath. There was something to talk about, but it wasn't his marriage, because that deed had already been done.

"It's fine, Robert. I'm happy that you are married, and I wish you all the happiness in the world. I'm sure that Lady Spencer is a fine match for you."

Robert was stunned at her admission. He found the words hard to believe.

"Now, there is something I need to tell you." Her eyes looked into the blue pools that she loved so dearly, and with a smile, she informed him of her recent decision. "You see, I have a confession to make. I've been a bit naughty while you were away for so long. I spent quite a bit of time with Philippe Moreau, and I . . . well, I have discovered that I still love him." Suzette blushed at the boldface lie.

"I'm leaving with Philippe for France at the end of the week." Her voice resonated with certainty. "Philippe has asked me to marry him, and I've consented." Suzette boldly kept her gaze upon Robert's face, searching for any remorse over the news.

"Oh? Is he going to marry you?" he said, acting surprised over her announcement.

"Yes, he is." Suzette inhaled deeply, attempting to sound convincing. "You see, Robert, I didn't realize how much I still loved him until our paths crossed again. I was engaged to him, you know, before we met. When my father died, I had no way of telling him about my misfortune because he was away."

"I see."

"He relentlessly pursued me during your absence, and I couldn't resist his charms."

Robert had surmised as much, and he felt his heart bleed within his chest. He had wanted to give Suzette the respectability she deserved now that he was married, but it was harder than he imagined. Her desire to leave him sliced him to the core. He inhaled a deep breath suppressing every ounce of emotion, trying to keep the proverbial English stiff upper lip mentality.

"Well then, I wish you happiness, as well. Perhaps it is for the best."

He couldn't leave without touching her one more time, so he took his hand and slid it across her cheek tenderly. Suzette closed her eyes at his touch, and he whispered, "I shall miss you, my petite and innocent Mademoiselle." With a longing gaze, he kissed her cheek and spoke in French to his dear Suzette. "Never forget I was your first, oui?"

He pulled abruptly away, winked, and saw tears well in her eyes. Had she lied to him about her love for Philippe Moreau? Perhaps it was all a ruse, so she didn't have to hear his words that he wished to let her go. As he stood looking at her, he knew it mattered not. It was over.

"I'll take my leave now."

Robert turned and strode from the room and out of Suzette's life. Duty and honor were now his mistress, and he despised the thought of life without Suzette.

When Suzette heard the door close behind him, she thought she felt movement in her womb, though she knew it was far too early. Perhaps it was her imagination, but she couldn't help but wonder if the baby inside grieved that its father had walked out of his or her life.

Suzette sat down on the settee, buried her head in her hands, and sobbed. Philippe entered the room and came to her side. He gathered her in his arms to comfort his soon-to-be wife.

"He was going to let you go out of love, Suzette. He's an honorable man who realized you deserved more than he could give." He stroked her hair and reassured her decision. "And you, my love, have done right thing by keeping his child as your own and providing the baby a family it deserves."

Perhaps she had done the right thing—perhaps not. Suzette only knew that the love of her life had left, and all that remained was an empty gaping hole of remorse in her heart. Without the hope of holding one day in her arms a part of Robert himself, she would have gladly joined her father in death to escape the morbid pain of loss.

CHAPTER 24

The week that followed was undoubtedly the worst of Robert's life. He had in essence lost the woman he truly loved. For the first time in his life, he learned what it meant to sacrifice himself for another human being to give them dignity and happiness.

It was true that he had rescued Suzette, which in itself he considered a noble deed. However, it was to his shame, that his good deed had been sullied by his selfish desire to keep her as his mistress without having an ounce of remorse for his actions.

Robert returned to Surrey and his wife, and put away for the moment his wayward conduct to pursue his marriage and obligation to family. Jacquelyn, he discovered, was the most dreadful woman he could have ever married. He found her high strung, moody, needy, and, most of all, frigid in bed. They had copulated often enough that she should have conceived by now, but instead her womb remained empty.

He had only tried to produce an heir for the sake of his father, whose health had turned worse as the months passed. By the beginning of winter, he finally succumbed to a failing heart and died with his family around his bedside. His dream of holding a grandson had never arrived. Instead, the Duke's last glance into his son's eyes begged Robert to claim his rightful place as head of the family.

The funeral was held on a cold winter's morning. His body was laid to rest in the family plot on their vast estate. Thankfully, the ground had not yet frozen, and the hole was easily dug by the land caretakers. His mother, sister, and

Jacquelyn all stood by on a windy day wrapped in black hats, scarves, and coats, listening to the vicar recite the burial rites.

When it was all said and done, Robert leaned down and took a handful of dirt in his gloved hand and let the earth slip through his fingers on top of the coffin. His wife, mother, and sister did the same, and they walked back to the estate to mourn their loss.

Robert knew upon the burial of his father that his old life had died too. The revelry of his youth no longer lived. Only responsibilities to the title of Duke, which he now bore, remained. He was saddled with a wife he did not love, and his emptiness of heart was difficult to bear. His mother, now the Dowager Duchess Holland, needed to be cared for in her elder years, and his sister Marguerite would soon marry the unlikeable Lord Chambers.

The only comfort he gleaned were the fond memories of Suzette and their carefree loveable times together whether in or out of bed. Though the loss was painful to recall, it was the only thing Robert had that he could call his own when it came to an ounce of contentment.

As he looked back upon the woman he lost, he realized without a doubt that he would have been happily married to her the rest of his life. However, he had not the strength to do as he willed. Rather, he succumbed to duty, the way things had always been done, and obeyed what he was told to do, in order to honor his dying father.

It was far too late now. Suzette had returned to France and married another. Both of their lives had charted a different course, and he would never see her again. However, in all of his grief, he felt consolation that perhaps Suzette had finally found the happiness she deserved.

* * *

Six Months Later

"Madame, you must push!" the physician sighed in desperation.

"I am pushing!" Suzette's voice echoed off the walls of the bedchamber as she grunted to push out the life that so pained her at that moment. She flopped back upon the bed, and the nursemaid dabbed her sweating forehead with a cold towel.

"Next contraction, Madame, you must push harder."

Suzette glared at the doctor, taking deep breaths anticipating the next stabbing pain that would throw her into oblivion.

It had been six months since she left London and returned to Paris. She wed Philippe as soon as they found suitable housing, and then she spent the majority of her long pregnancy in bed by order of her physician.

As the months passed, Suzette's belly grew, along with a returning affection that had been buried in the corner of her broken heart. Philippe's unconditional love and acceptance of a child that was not his profoundly touched her soul. As a result, they rekindled affections, which she believed pleased her deceased father. Philippe, without judgment or condemnation, freely forgave her for the past, though Suzette struggled with forgiving herself and with the lingering, strong love for her English lord.

Time healed her hurt but memories persisted as Robert's child grew in her womb. She agreed with Philippe that it was best not to tell Robert about the baby. It would serve no purpose and open wounds that could create problems. If they returned to France, he would never know.

Though Suzette felt great affection for Philippe, her love for Robert never waned. He was, after all, her knight in shining armor that had rescued her from a life of prostitution. Robert would always retain a special place in her heart. How could he not? He had been her first to take her virginity, and now she was about to bear their child.

Philippe, on the other hand, had no qualms about accepting the baby as his own, as long as his beloved Suzette was his wife and by his side. He impatiently paced the floor outside of her bedchamber, distraught over her cries, and waiting for the moment of birth that would change their lives.

The next contraction, more severe than the last, took hold of Suzette. A loud, deep moan escaped Suzette's lungs, and the doctor crouched between her legs, waiting for the arrival of a newborn babe.

"Madame, push! The head is crowning . . . now push!"

Suzette grunted and screamed, and then a sudden release of life slipped into the hands of the waiting physician and the cry of a baby was heard.

"You have a son, Madame—a fine son."

Suzette broke out in laughter and tears. "Let me see!"

The physician cut the cord and then lifted the child, cradling the newborn's head with one hand and his tiny bottom in the other. The baby cried with such ferocity that Philippe burst through the door to see the child.

"It's a boy, Philippe." Suzette's face glowed.

The nursemaid quickly cleaned the baby while the doctor finished with the birth matter and Suzette. She watched Philippe's kind eyes as he walked to the table. A smile spread across his face.

"He looks like you, Suzette."

When Suzette was ready, she sat up in bed with her arms outstretched toward her husband. Philippe took the child, swaddled in a blanket, and brought it to his wife.

At first glance, she saw in his face the resemblance of his father. She looked at Philippe, but all he saw was the resemblance of his mother. Suzette smiled and lifted her eyes toward her husband.

"Are you sure, Philippe? It is a boy. Are you sure you wish to do this?"

"I promised, and I shall keep it, if that is what you wish, darling."

Suzette looked down upon the baby, now quietly resting in her arms, trying to focus his young eyes upon his mother's glowing face.

"Hello, Robert Philippe Moreau," she said. Suzette kissed his red cheek. "Welcome to your new home."

The End

AUTHOR'S NOTES

The brothel depicted in this fictional work resembles the Chabanais, located at 12 Rue Chabanais, in Paris, France. It opened its doors to patrons in 1878 and closed in 1946. Additional information regarding the brothel, its real mistress, unique rooms, and clientele can be obtained by visiting the author's website at: http://vickihopkins.com

The Bureau des Mouers (Bureau of Public Morals) was established by the French government in 1802 to regulate prostitution in France and closed its doors in 1903. It was responsible for registering prostitutes, including physical examinations of workers, and routine inspections of brothels. Legalized brothels in France closed in 1946.

THE LEGACY SERIES - BOOK TWO

Book one, *The Price of Innocence*, was an enjoyable story to write, but it's far from over. Book Two, *The Price of Deception*, continues the tale of your favorite characters five years after the birth of little Robert. It's a thrilling continuation, in the second of a series of three books.

Book two begins with Duke Holland's chance encounter with Philippe and a young five-year old boy while on holiday in Paris. Still nursing regrets from the past, he is further devastated after being told that Suzette has died. Philippe plays a dangerous game to keep his rival from knowing the truth about his wife and the young boy who bears the resemblance of his father.

The story unfolds as a tangled web of deceit ensnares all the characters, when they strive to hold onto what they love or strive to regain what they've lost. Robert searches for truth. Philippe struggles to keep his livelihood. Suzette worries about her son being discovered. Duchess Jacquelyn Spencer-Holland evolves into a troubled woman.

Of course, it wouldn't be romance, unless Suzette and Robert came together. What remains between the petite French Mademoiselle and her handsome English lover? Will they reunite and resurrect their lost love? Will it be enough to bring them back together in spite of the insurmountable obstacles that have kept them apart?

Find out in *The Price of Deception*, now available in eBook and paperback.

www.ingramcontent.com/pod-product-compliance
Lightning Source LLC
Chambersburg PA
CBHW061600100726
47898CB00002B/453